A KNIGHT'S TALE

A KNIGHT'S TALE

EDWARD JOHN CROCKETT

PEGASUS BOOKS
NEW YORK

A Knight's Tale

Pegasus Books LLC
45 Wall Street, Suite 1021
New York, NY 10005

First Pegasus Books edition 2007

Library of Congress Cataloging-in-Publication Data is available.

ISBN: 978-1-933648-49-1

Printed in the United States of America

For Sheila – *per sempre*

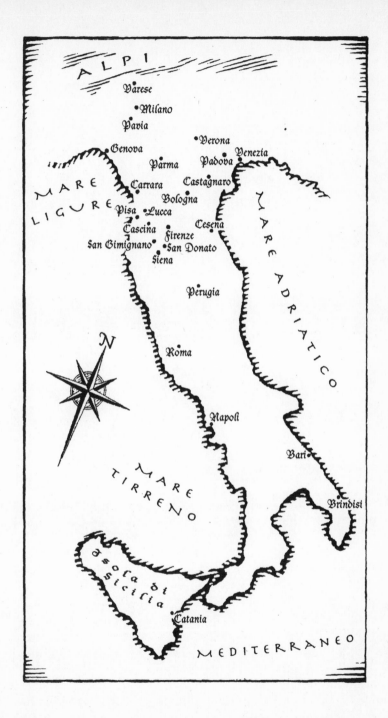

'Tis no matter what lord one serves,
only that one serve him well and with honestie . . .

John Theodore McDonald,
Free Company of Mercenaries,
Florence, 1376

I

Prologue at Poitiers

Maupertius-Nouaillé Field, south of Poitiers
Monday, 19 September 1356

The day dawned dank and overcast. Skeins of low-lying fog drifted up from the reeds and grasses of the marshland on the army's left flank near Saint-Pierre Wood and, to the right, below the hamlet of Beauvoir. The first rays of a gangrenous sun gradually warmed away the last wisps of morning mist.

The Black Prince knelt and crossed himself, intoning a prayer of thanks that the French king had called a truce the previous day. It was not fitting to do battle on the Lord's Day. Yet nothing in the rules of engagement precluded making preparations for battle.

The prince and his officers had used their Sunday well. On the advice of Sir John Chandos, he had deployed his forces to higher ground. His heavy cavalry of knights were arrayed with their backs to Nouaillé Wood; in the vanguard and to his right were ranged the troops of the Earl of Salisbury, and on the left flank were those under the Earl of Warwick. On the higher ground on the right and beyond Beauvoir was the small Gascon contingent commanded by Captal de Buch. The rearguard was under the command of the Earl of Suffolk. In all, there were some seven thousand men, many armed with longbows.

Towards eight that morning the fog cleared. The Black Prince looked across the undulating terrain towards the massed armies of King Jean le Bon, which stood between him and the English-held city of Bordeaux. Retreat north across the Loire river was out of the question now that the French had destroyed the bridges. There was nothing else for it. He would stand his ground and fight.

The French had formed for battle. In the van, two contingents of mixed cavalry and infantry, including a Scottish regiment and some three hundred German pikemen mercenaries. Behind, three successive ranks of infantry regiments led by the Dauphin, by the Duke of Orléans – King Jean's brother – and, to the rear, by the king himself. Twenty thousand men or even more: cavalry, footsoldiers and crossbow archers.

The Black Prince exchanged glances with Chandos. Both men knew their force was greatly outnumbered. But both were veterans of the battle of Crécy-en-Ponthieu ten years before, when a twelve-thousand-strong French army under Philippe VI had floundered to defeat in wet marshland and been slaughtered almost to a man, caught in a withering crossfire from English longbows.

The attack began.

Three hundred elite mounted knights and the German pikemen advanced uphill through the narrow funnel of firm terrain, maintaining good order until the first flights of English arrows scythed into their ranks from the secure vantage points of the marshy ground on the left flank and from behind dense hedgerows on the right. The attackers continued to drive uphill but the initial impetus was soon lost. They broke formation and died or were taken captive as they reached the English lines. The first attack had failed.

At a signal from King Jean, the Dauphin launched a second wave of two thousand footsoldiers and mounted knights. They charged the English positions, only to be cut down like those before them. Their ranks decimated by arrows and in hand-to-hand combat, they withdrew to lick their wounds and regroup. The second attack had faltered.

On the far mound, the Duke of Orléans had witnessed the carnage. Ordered to advance, he hesitated, then thought better of it. Seeing how easily the Dauphin's force had been routed, he departed the field.

The Black Prince's first instinct was to order his mounted knights to counter-attack and give chase to the fleeing duke and his men. But the French king, enraged at his brother's cowardice and desertion, immediately ordered his main force of some eight thousand to advance on the English positions. It was a brave but foolish decision: he had no cavalry or bowmen to support his attack.

The prince did not hesitate. He deployed one unit of horse to attack King Jean's flank and ordered the remainder to charge downhill directly into the ranks of the oncoming French. The Gascon cavalry squadron under Captal de Buch deployed right to attack from the rear. The French held ranks momentarily, then broke and fled. The king and the knights by his side fought on resolutely to the last, but were eventually overpowered and captured. The Black Prince had carried the day.

A count the following morning revealed that some two thousand French had fallen; several thousand more had been captured and would be held for ransom. The Black Prince sent word of the outcome to his father, King Edward III of England and claimant to the throne of France. It was time to count the spoils and costs of victory.

II

Hawkwood

He had done nobly in his sovereign's war

Poitiers, 19 September 1356

'Yield, *sire*! Damn you to Hell, yield!'

The French knight made no sign that he had heard or understood. Instead, he swung his broadsword in a laboured arc. The blow glanced off the plate-armour epaulette on Sir John Hawkwood's left shoulder, inflicting no damage but throwing him off balance. Hawkwood stumbled forward under the weight of his armour, grunted, steadied himself, then instinctively swept his own sword viciously upwards, striking at his adversary's sword arm and severing it below the elbow.

Blood spurted from the arm and the Frenchman dropped to his knees, raising his elongated kite-shaped shield above his head to ward off the *coup de grâce*.

'Yield, I say again! Yield!'

Hawkwood towered above his opponent, sword raised high over his head. He could feel the sweat coursing down his back under the quilted leather undergarment. His heart was pounding and he gulped for air through the tiny vents in his helmet. The metal codpiece chafed his genitals. His arms were leaden. It had been a long day.

The French knight pitched forward on his face. Hawkwood lowered his sword and eased open his visor. To his right, he saw the pitiful remnants of the French force clustered round their king, desperately fending off the attentions of Hawkwood's fellow knights. The dead sprawled in grotesque postures, their armour streaked with blood, their chain mail shredded, their flimsy surcoats in tatters.

Hawkwood had killed other men that day and had taken several captives. Mercifully, this final adversary was still alive, if only just. He eased the Frenchman over onto his back and removed his coif helm. The man's heavily bearded face was grey with shock, but he was alive and Hawkwood intended to do everything he could to keep him that way. In death, the French knight would be merely one corpse among many; alive, he was worth a fortune.

This was no run-of-the-mill knight. Hawkwood's reading of the man's shield told him at once that at his feet lay none other than Gauthier, the sixth Count of Brienne, Duke of Athens and Liege Lord of Lecce. The heraldic blazon was unmistakable: *d'azur semé de billettes d'or, au lion du même brochant sur le tout* – azure billetty, a lion rampant or. Two hands clutching vertical swords extended from clouds painted below the blue-gold blazon, signifying that Brienne's rank was that of a *connétable* of France, entrusted with supervision of the king's armies.

Hawkwood beckoned over two men-at-arms and ordered them to bring a litter. They appeared moments later with a sturdy wooden board with poles lashed to the corners to serve as handles. In the meantime, Hawkwood had fashioned a crude tourniquet from a short stick and a strip of cloth torn from his own surcoat. He applied the tourniquet and secured it. The bleeding slowed but did not stop.

Brienne, his breathing shallow, was lifted onto the board and the party scurried back up the hill to Hawkwood's tented quarters. Hawkwood followed as best he could, his progress impeded by the heavy plate armour he had worn since daybreak. When he reached his *pavillon*, the men-at-arms and his squire had already removed Brienne's cuirass and stripped off his *ailettes*, byrnie and protective *gambeson* undergarment.

A stubby dagger was plunged into a glowing brazier. It glinted white hot in the dim light in the tent. Hawkwood retrieved the dagger and approached Brienne, who appeared to have fainted. In one swift movement, he applied the blade to the raw stump. Then again and again, until the wound was fully cauterised. Flesh sizzled and contracted. The stench was nauseating. Brienne moaned repeatedly, but did not cry out. Hawkwood inspected his crude handiwork and found it adequate. He had done what he could.

He removed his undergarment and crouched on his haunches, exhausted. He ran a massive hand through his tousled hair and rubbed the sweat from his eyes. Every muscle ached, every joint. Welts on his shoulders and chest were already beginning to discolour. Wearily, he wiped away the trickle of blood that ran down the inside of his left arm. He flexed the fingers of his left hand. Dried sweat had congealed in his beard and his mouth was dry. It was ever thus, he thought, ever thus as the exhilaration of combat abruptly receded and the body began its silent protest.

Hawkwood reached for a skin of wine and gulped down several mouthfuls. He glanced over at his prisoner, who lay still, his face drained of all colour. *Deo volente*, Hawkwood told himself, God willing, Brienne would survive – *must* survive.

On the stroke of noon the following day – 20 September 1356 – Gauthier, Count of Brienne, Duke of Athens, Liege Lord of Lecce and *connétable* of France, lapsed into a coma. He died several hours later. Sir John de Hawkwood knew his own future now hung in the balance.

Bordeaux, 3 October 1356

Edward III of England and his retinue sailed into Bordeaux just after daybreak, and came ashore early that afternoon. The Black Prince, his distinctive ostrich-plumed helmet clasped in the crook of his left arm, stood on the quay to receive them. Behind him, close on three hundred knights of the realm formed serried ranks.

The king drew off his gauntlet and extended his hand. His son clasped it. To a man, the assembled knights had gone down on one knee as a mark of respect for their sovereign lord, but now they came to their feet, breaking into a sustained cheer as the king embraced his son. After a full minute, the two men separated.

The king spoke. 'Gentlemen, you have served me and our

country well and with much honour. It grieves me I was not at your side on the day of your signal victory. Yet I share with you a father's pride in a son who once more has acquitted himself with valour.' The cheering started up again. The king smiled indulgently, then gestured for silence. 'I salute you one and all. And I swear that, by God's grace, none shall go without his just reward.'

The banquet given at the Abbey of St Andrew later that day was worthy of a king, thought Hawkwood. Two kings, more like, for Jean le Bon was seated next to Edward at the table of honour. Hawkwood sat at a lesser table presided over by the Black Prince, who, to the manifest approval of all present, had respectfully declined to sit with his father and Jean out of deference for their kingly rank. Captive French nobles sat at the prince's board, including the Dauphin, Jacques de Bourbon, Jean d'Artois and the Seigneur de Tancarville.

That captors and captives were now seated side by side was as it should be. Although the French king had failed to carry the day, he had fought courageously to the last and, as a worthy adversary, he commanded respect. Besides, the two monarchs had much to discuss. There was a ransom to be negotiated: a king's ransom.

Servants carried in platter after platter: *civet* of wild boar, spit-roasted suckling pig, whole haunches of venison, gigots of French mutton, broiled pheasant, larks' tongues in coriander, fennel and ginger-flavoured aspic, baked swan, pheasant and blackbird, oysters from the Vendée, poached quenelles of pike from the nearby Garonne, crayfish, clams and whelks, figs, olives, grapes and assorted sweetmeats, the whole accompanied by earthenware flagons of robust red wine from the Médoc.

Hawkwood smiled ruefully at the thought of what this feast must have cost. Enough, perhaps, to equip a small army? But he and many of those around him knew only too well what King Edward intended by this lavish demonstration. It drove home a point which would not be lost on the French king and his lieutenants: that England had immense wealth and resources at its disposal, more than enough to wage a war of attrition that might last for many years.

Nothing could have been further from the truth. England had precious few resources left. Swingeing tithes and levies imposed to underwrite the war with France had bled the country almost dry. There were insufficient funds in the nation's coffers to carry the war through the next six months, let alone for years to come. Rumour had it that Edward had even pawned his crown to help pay his retainers.

England had waged sporadic war against the French for almost two decades, ever since 1337, when Edward had first asserted his claim to the throne of France. The claim was not unwarranted – Edward was a direct descendant of Philippe IV, through his mother, Isabella of France – but it was a claim England could ill afford to enforce. True, England had carried the day at Crécy, when the Black Prince had earned his spurs at the age of only sixteen, and again at Poitiers, where the French had been fool-hardy, their battle strategy flawed and their tactics woefully outdated. But they would learn – of that, Hawkwood was certain – and this war waged on foreign soil might not always go England's way.

Such thoughts were tantamount to treason, and Hawkwood shook his head to banish them. He speared a slice of venison and turned his attention to the conversation around him.

The Black Prince held the floor. Somewhat unwisely, Hawk-wood felt, he was reliving the battle, reviewing his tactics and extolling the decisive role of the English longbow. Not surpris-ingly, the French nobles proved attentive listeners. They had survived the battle and, even in defeat, each knew he would eventually be ransomed to fight another day. Any insight into how the perfidious English deployed their forces would then prove invaluable.

Hawkwood listened as the prince explained at some length how he had made the fullest use of the terrain and as the prince described how and under what conditions a superior force could be routed. He said nothing as the prince tactfully but forcefully suggested that the French might have carried the day had they not been so hesitant. And he looked on as the prince aligned walnuts, figs and olives on the trestle table to represent the disposition of his troops and to illustrate the points he was intent on making.

Hawkwood had considerable respect and affection for the Black Prince. His bravery was beyond question, and Hawkwood was mindful that it had been none other than the king's son who persuaded John de Vere, Earl of Oxford, to confer a battlefield commission on Hawkwood himself, elevating him to the rank of knight after Crécy, where the prince and Hawkwood had stood and fought side by side. The honour had been fully justified, Hawkwood felt, when, some years later, he had saved the prince's life during the siege of Narbonne. Since then, the prince had appeared to resent Hawkwood – as one often does when placed in another's debt as a result of dramatic circumstances. There was no bad blood between them, however, although the prince at times seemed to resent Hawkwood's greater experience and coolness in the field.

The prince himself was widely regarded as too impetuous and quick to anger, and was inclined to nurse a grudge. Hawkwood had once committed a grave error by chiding him about his fiery temper and impetuosity. The prince had not taken the rebuke well – he was the heir to the throne, when all was said and done – and their friendship was now tenuous at best. Since then, Hawkwood had been at pains to keep his own counsel and avoid offending the young man again.

He listened and watched until he felt the prince had gone too far. *Perhaps he has downed too much wine*, thought Hawkwood. *But this had to stop.*

'It is my belief, your Grace, that we do our French guests a disservice by reminding them why they are among us today,' he said with a wry smile.

The prince stopped in mid-sentence and glared at him across the table. 'And I would remind you, Sir John, that these guests are men of noble lineage and rank who have proved worthy adversaries.'

'All the more reason, sire, to be temperate in one's discourse.'

'You try my patience, Sir John.'

'If so, unwillingly.'

To Hawkwood's relief, Jean d'Artois spoke next. 'As for myself, I confess I have learnt little this night that I did not learn to my cost on the field of combat. I would say only this: we shall doubtless cross swords again and, God willing, the contest will be foursquare.' He chuckled and reached across the table to where the prince had deployed his walnuts, figs and olives. 'Until that day dawns, we shall comport ourselves as befits our rank.'

He scooped up two walnuts and weighed them in the palm of his right hand. Slowly, he closed his fist over them. His knuckles whitened briefly as the two walnuts came together and cracked. He opened his fist and let the fragments of shell fall on the table. 'As you see,' he said, 'what is done is done and cannot be repaired.'

Laughter broke out round the table. Hawkwood joined in. The Black Prince smiled but his eyes were obsidian. Watching him, Hawkwood realised that, although he had certainly not made an enemy, he had with equal certainty lost a friend.

Sible Hedingham, Essex, 22 March 1359

Lady Margaret de Hawkwood sat by the massive stone hearth and gazed out over the insipid Essex countryside. Her husband had sent riders ahead to alert her to his return.

She had mixed feelings about it. In one way she was glad, glad he was alive and well, glad he had come unscathed through a long and arduous campaign, glad he would be on hand to resolve all manner of outstanding issues on his estate. Yet she could not pretend that the prospect of sharing his bed and responding to his physical demands was one she relished. Margaret de Hawkwood was afraid of her husband.

Sir John was a big man in every sense. He was extremely tall, towering over those around him. Years in the field – he had fought at Crécy those many years ago – had filled out an already imposing frame. His thighs and calves were heavily muscled from many months in the saddle, his shoulders immensely powerful, his arms thick from wielding lance and broadsword in practice and in combat. His beard was full and coarse, his hair bushed over his ears and curled tight and dark against the nape of his neck. His hands were those of a woodsman. His eyes glinted slate-grey and dangerous. Lady Margaret had long since concluded there was nothing about her husband that was remotely delicate, nothing that hinted at tenderness or sensitivity.

She had been betrothed to him when only fifteen years old, and they had wed some two years later. Her mother had warned her of the ways of men and told her what to expect, but Margaret had been largely unprepared for her wedding night. She had felt demeaned by the brutality of it all – the sheer size of him, his weight pinning her down, crushing her against the hardness of the horsehair mattress, the pain as he entered her, the urgency of his coupling, the merciful release as he ejaculated, and her humiliation as his seed spilled down the inside of her thighs. Then he rolled away, his breathing laboured, sweat glistening on his matted chest hair, and within seconds he was asleep, his arms and legs spread wide.

Over time, Margaret came to understand and even accept what was expected of her. When he took her from behind – as he often did – she even felt the first stirrings of response as he plunged deep inside her, his underbelly slapping wetly against her buttocks and his huge fists clutching painfully at her breasts.

He said nothing while they copulated, merely strained and grunted and occasionally cried out as he climaxed. He said nothing then or afterwards, and in the light of day he made no mention of these frantic and feral couplings.

What saddened Margaret most was that she had no one to turn to, no one in whom to confide. Not even her own mother, whose disappointment at Margaret's failure to conceive was unspoken but ill concealed. And certainly not the self-righteous priest who dutifully presided over the daily offices in the modest chapel at Hawkwood Manor.

Lady Margaret understood where her duty lay. She was

required to produce an heir to continue the Hawkwood line. As the months and years passed and she remained childless, her husband's impatience grew and his demands intensified. She accommodated him as best she could, waiting only for the day when he would leave again to do what he did best: serve his king and country on the field of combat. Now he was coming back, and the cycle of pain and humiliation would recommence.

The question uppermost in her mind was how long he would elect to remain.

Hawkwood's brows furrowed as he and his small retinue slowly approached the manor house along the broad poplar-lined path. He noted with growing unease that some of the estate's strip farmland had been left fallow and untended. The Black Death had taken its toll, even out here in the under-populated Essex countryside.

The plague had begun in the East and moved inexorably along the caravan trade routes to the West, striking on the lower Volga, then fanning out into the Caucasus and the Crimea. By 1347 it had reached Constantinople, Alexandria and Cairo, where several thousand fatalities were recorded every day. From the eastern Mediterranean, it had swept across northern Europe, spreading – if accounts were to be believed – up through the Italian peninsula from Messina, in Sicily, when a dozen Genoese merchantmen had docked there. The pest had destroyed the population of Messina itself, then spread to Catania, where the entire population was also said to have died. Early in 1348, the Black Death had reached Marseille. By April that year it was in Paris, by September in England.

The warring armies of England and France had been so decimated by the plague that they laid down their arms and fled. Hawkwood had seen the fever take hold, seen the dreaded burn blisters appear on face, thighs, arms and neck, and small lumps knot in armpit and groin, swelling rapidly and hardening into goose-egg protrusions. Then came the vomiting of dark blood and the discoloration of the skin as victims lay shivering helplessly in gutters and ditches, crying their agony until they were mercifully released in a matter of hours rather than days. He had surveyed the massive pits of the dead, where mounds of corpses piled noble next to serf and farmyard animal next to cleric. And he had recognised not only the suffering of individuals but the social and economic devastation the Black Death had wrought.

The plague had receded now, but it was said – and Hawkwood had no reason to doubt it – that one out of every three persons in Europe had died. In some cities, as many as three-quarters of the population had been lost. Florence and Venice had been particularly ravaged, as had Avignon, where half the population perished and the exiled Pope Clement VI had seen fit to consecrate the Rhône river as a burial site for the city's dead.

Like many of his contemporaries, Hawkwood could not shake off the belief that the scourge might be a punishment from God, and he prudently thanked his God that he had been spared. As a man of some learning, and above all as a realist, he believed that, while miasmas, earthquakes, comets, cats, dogs, lepers, gypsies and Jews might have been root causes, poor sanitation and overcrowded, rat-infested towns and cities and human contagion must have contributed to the spread of the Black Death.

In 1348 alone, the English and French armies had lost substantially more men to the plague than to the enemy and Hawkwood had vowed then and there to regard proper sanitary conditions and matters of health generally as a prime factor in military strategy.

The Black Death had not reached Hawkwood Manor but its effects had been felt. In Hawkwood's absence, many of his serfs had been illegally lured away to neighbouring estates whose working population had been depleted. Others had seized the opportunity to leave for the cities – a paradoxical choice on the face of it, but understandable: fear of the plague was largely mitigated by the prospect not only of living as free men but also of earning a much better living now that wages had been inflated in the wake of a greatly reduced labour pool.

Although Hawkwood was angered by the neglect the manor

had suffered, he was not unduly troubled by it. His estate was large, running to close on seventy acres of woodland, rich arable land and meadowland to feed the draught animals. Taken together, the acreage was more than sufficient to provide for the needs of the Hawkwood household and the serfs who lived in the thatched wooden-frame, wattle-and-daub cruck houses that comprised the estate village.

Besides, he was already a comparatively wealthy man. If nothing else, he would have been wealthy by virtue of his military prowess alone. As a seasoned veteran of the wars against France, he had amassed *butin* – 'booty' – and substantial ransom income over close on ten years. But there was more – much more.

The Hawkwood lands had been gifted to his Norman ancestor, one Gilbert l'Epervier, who had come over with William the Conqueror and gone on to distinguish himself in the Norman king's service. Strictly speaking, the land had been gifted in tenancy to a Baron d'Houart de Honfleur who, in turn, had assigned a portion to Gilbert. The estate deeds had been duly recorded in the Domesday Book of 1086 and the family had enjoyed the sub-tenancy ever since. Sir John's father, another Gilbert, had anglicised the family name to 'Hawk' and added 'wood' some forty years previously. He had also founded a flourishing tannery on the outskirts of Colchester, acclaimed for its excellent grade of *cuir bouilli* – leather treated and hardened in boiling wax – which was in great demand for saddles, light armour, leather garments and even upholstery and wall-hangings.

As the most recent in a long line of minor nobility and as a knight in his own right, Sir John de Hawkwood felt that continuing to operate the tannery – albeit at arm's length – was somewhat beneath his knightly dignity and status. That said, he also recognised it as a remunerative and sustained source of income.

Annual profits from the tannery were ploughed into an activity that Sir John felt was more commensurate with his chosen profession. Throughout England and in many parts of Europe, he had forged a reputation as a breeder and trainer of destriers, the large and sturdy battle horses that were the ultimate resource of the knight in battle. They were heavy, coarse-ruffed, stubby-haired creatures of an evil disposition, bred for combat: fast but uncommonly manoeuvrable, and capable of inflicting serious wounds on opponents by trampling, biting or slashing with their leg blades. A destrier properly trained to the saddle and lance was held to be worth its own weight in gold – equivalent, it was often said, to the aggregate value of one hundred oxen, those most costly of farm animals. The coursers bred and trained by Sir John de Hawkwood were adjudged to be among the very finest.

Hawkwood and his attendants crossed the fixed bridge over the shallow moat and dismounted. The manor was built in natural stone and was arranged round a central courtyard. He strode through the entrance porch and across the Great Hall that had originally served as a communal space for eating, sleeping and transacting business. At the far end of the hall was a raised platform – the solar – which had once afforded the lord of the manor and his immediate family a modicum of privacy. Leading off it, there were now additional half-timbered rooms, including private bedchambers and reception areas.

Lady Margaret came forward to greet her husband. His embrace was perfunctory.

'You appear in good health, Sir John.'

'As do you, Lady Margaret.'

He shrugged off his loose cape and removed his leather gauntlets. 'It is as well that I have returned,' he said.

Lady Margaret smiled. 'For that we must all give thanks,' she replied.

Windsor Castle, 9 May 1359

King Edward of the House of Windsor and of England sat astride his chestnut palfrey and watched intently as the peregrine, released from her jesses and hood, soared skywards. She hovered only momentarily, her wings beating rapidly as she scanned below for suitable prey. The king's heart skipped a beat as he saw her suddenly arc into a precipitous dive, swooping down at uncommon speed to bind to the unsuspecting grey heron, carrying it to earth and sinking her outsize talons into its vital organs.

Of the countless hawks that Edward kept at Windsor, this peregrine falcon was by far his favourite. He had taken her at hack from the nest when she was fully fledged yet still flightless and had trained her on the block, carrying her on the thick leather gauntlet for hours, days and months on end, all the while whispering softly to her and caressing her magnificent plumage with an eider feather, soothing and cajoling her at one and the same time. When she was weaned off the soft leather rufter hood, he had schooled her for the hunt, first feeding her from the padded lure with its tasty morsel of pigeon, then teaching her how to select her own prey and fly aggressively towards it once it was flushed.

The king loved this graceful creature even more than he did his wife, Philippa, daughter of Count William of Hainault and Holland, to whom he had been betrothed at the age of eleven and who had since grown into a pious if at times insipid wife whose principal redeeming feature in his eyes was her ability to give birth with monotonous regularity.

In truth, the peregrine came second in the king's affections only to his first-born son, Edward of Woodstock, popularly known as the 'Black Prince' – allegedly on account of the black battle armour he wore in the field but, as some would have it, because of his consistently foul temper.

Squires retrieved the dead heron. The peregrine obediently flew to his outstretched arm and he gently hooded her and re-affixed her jesses.

Smiling, he looked across at his son. 'In all faith, this is indeed the sport of kings.'

'That it is, father, and more besides.'

Edward took his son's meaning at once. He had nurtured the lad as he had nurtured the falcon, grooming both for pre-eminence. He glanced down at the bird, admiring her spurs and thinking back to how this valiant son of his had won *his* spurs – and his now legendary ostrich plumes – at the battle of Crécy a decade before. Edward had been proved right to grant the prince field command of the English forces in 1346 and had now been rewarded with this famous victory at Poitiers. He took undiluted pride in his son and in the latter's achievements, not the least of which had been the capture of the French king, who was now quartered in the Savoy Palace in London.

The negotiations in Bordeaux had been successfully completed. Minor nobles had been ransomed back to France, while others of higher rank had been released after the battle on a solemn pledge to raise monies to indemnify the English crown. Edward knew that they would honour those pledges to a man. As for King Jean, an unprecedented ransom of three million gold crowns had already been mooted, together with territorial concessions which would go a long way towards consolidating English footholds in the Aquitaine and elsewhere. The sum was outrageously high, but France must ultimately pay if it were to retain its dignity and honour. Failing that, thought Edward, I will lead a fresh expeditionary force to France and bring that treacherous country to its knees.

Much of the ransom monies raised in Bordeaux had already been spent in order to pay Edward's conscript army. Besides, with the exception of payments made and pledges given on behalf of those of the highest rank, ransom revenues accrued properly not to the crown but to the individuals who had carried the day. Equipping and sustaining an army in the field – and in a foreign land, to boot – was a costly affair and the English exchequer was greatly depleted. Until such time as the French ransomed their king – indeed, until such time as they could *afford* to do so – the war would be at a standstill.

The thought sobered Edward and he confided it to his son.

The prince hesitated before replying; but the contretemps between himself and Sir John Hawkwood after Poitiers still rankled. 'Permit me, sire, to say that our coffers would be less depleted had certain of those who fought with us at Poitiers displayed greater loyalty to England than to their own narrow interests.'

The king's dark eyebrows arched. 'You speak in riddles, my son. If you have aught to say, speak your piece clearly.'

'I speak of Sir John de Hawkwood, a most intrepid knight I warrant, but one whose intemperate nature has done you a disservice. A knight who has now returned to England, his wealth bolstered by our deeds in France.'

'That is his good right. But, pray, in what manner did this disservice come about?'

'By the slaying of one Gauthier de Brienne, a *connétable* of France, whose capture and ransom would have greatly benefited the exchequer.'

'Think you so ill of a comrade-at-arms that you would blacken his name in this way?'

'I seek neither to blacken his name nor to gainsay his honour. I say only this: that on that day of victory he failed his king and his country.'

The king made no reply. He gathered in the reins and urged his mount to a walk. The Black Prince followed, suddenly ashamed of what he had said. His resentment had been building ever since that day in Narbonne when Hawkwood had rescued him from the jaws of death and then publicly questioned his temperament and military acumen.

His father seemed angry at his denunciation of Hawkwood but the prince did not regret it. He was confident his father would raise the matter again in due course and then he would make his case against Hawkwood even more forcefully. When all was said and done, thought the Black Prince, wars were fought for honour but also for personal advancement.

III

Points South

Fortune and her treacherous wheel
That suffers no estate on earth to feel
Secure . . .

Milan, 22 May 1359

It was common knowledge in Milan that the Visconti women were the most beautiful in all Italy. Although the proud citizens of Rome, Florence and Venice might well have taken issue with this, none who had seen Donnina Visconti in the flesh could deny her grace and radiance.

Today was her twentieth birthday, and celebrations were planned in her honour. Attendants fussed over her, combing out her shoulder-length dark chestnut hair, arranging and re-arranging the folds of her translucent slate-grey silk gown and adjusting the gold cord that encircled her slender waist and emphasised the curve of her hips and the outline of her thighs.

She waved her maidservants to one side and contemplated herself in the full-length mirror, nodding in satisfaction. The overall effect was as she had hoped: simple, striking, virginal. She smiled as she turned away.

Virginal? Scarcely. Donnina had ceded her virginity almost two years previously to a handsome and well-muscled stable lad called Ludovico, whose adulation she had nurtured for several weeks before yielding to his – and her own – unfettered lust. He had pinned her against a stable door and reached between her thighs, roughly massaging her pubis, probing her with his stubby fingers and prising her wetness apart. She remembered the sharp pain as he entered her and the disappointment when he ejaculated almost immediately. She also remembered how, as if in compensation, he had continued to caress her until he was ready to enter her again.

The second time was different. She recalled his length and hardness as he mounted her and rocked her this way and that on the mound of urine-soaked straw, how she had locked her legs round his back and arched upwards in response. The sensation had been unlike any she had ever imagined as her body flooded with wave after wave of undiluted pleasure.

Ludovico had long since been discarded in favour of Federigo di Castellante – a much older man and a close friend of the Visconti family – who had patiently instructed Donnina in the arts and techniques of intercourse, substituting subtlety for urgency and sustained pleasure for instant gratification.

She was an intelligent young woman – certainly intelligent enough to realise that her growing obsession with the pleasures of the flesh threatened irreparable harm to her value as a political commodity when her hand was ultimately offered in marriage. That said, she was also intelligent enough to realise her secret was safe – at least for the time being. She knew Ludovico must have been sorely tempted to boast of his noble conquest, but she was certain he had not, for admission of the illicit deflowering of a Visconti would have resulted in swift and fatal retribution – preceded by slow and agonising castration. By the same token, it was inconceivable that Federigo di Castellante would ever disclose their relationship: to do so would result in, at best, his banishment from the ducal court and, at worst, his sudden and mysterious disappearance on the orders of her father, the self-styled Duke of Milan.

She had turned these thoughts over and over in her mind as she lay in bed on the morning of her twentieth birthday and had resolved she must in future be more circumspect. She lived in a state of constant anxiety that her relationship with Federigo would be revealed by some unforeseen circumstance or other and that she would be discredited as 'damaged goods'. She had come to a difficult decision: she would inform Federigo that the relationship must end. He would have no choice but to agree.

One day – and she hoped that day would come soon – she would find a man to whom she could commit herself openly and without reservation.

Donnina composed herself as a peremptory knock came at the door of her bedchamber. A maid hurried to open it.

Bernabò Visconti, Duke of Milan, stood in the doorway, admiring his daughter. He extended his arms to welcome her into a gentle embrace, then stepped back a pace and took her hands in his.

'You are truly a vision, *cara*,' he said softly, 'and one day you will make some fortunate husband as happy and proud as your devoted father is today.'

He laid her hand lightly on his arm and prepared to escort her down the magnificent staircase to greet the assembled guests.

'That is my own most fervent wish, dear father,' replied Donnina Visconti, smiling her most virginal smile.

Council of Guilds, City State of Pisa, 26 May 1359

'Florentine scum!' Tommaso Gracchi's fist crashed down on the oval table. He glared at the assembled *anziani*, the city elders. These bankers, wool merchants, cloth finishers and other prominent citizens drawn from Pisa's merchant and professional guilds were the most powerful – and the wealthiest – men in the republican city state, but they cowered as Gracchi's fist pounded on the table.

'Scum, I tell you, scum!'

Gracchi was not a handsome man, least of all when he spoke in anger. Small and squat, beetle-browed, with a bulbous nose and a disconcerting cast to his left eye, he was an intimidating figure. For all that, he was held in high regard. As president of the Council of Guilds, he commanded respect if only because, although reputed to be among the richest men in Pisa, he had never sought power and had never abused it. Other Italian city states might have their *signori*, but Pisa was ruled by consensus, not by a despot. Besides, in both his private life and his business dealings, Gracchi was generally held to be fair. He was a dedicated family man, a patron of the arts and a generous giver to charity and to the *popolo minuto*.

Gracchi went on in a more measured tone. 'We have no need of Florence, it is Florence that has need of us. We need no Bardis and Peruzzis, we have our own bankers. We do not need their wool and cloth, we have our own. We do not need their meddling ways. We do not need their artists and architects. Pisa has its own.'

There were murmurs of agreement.

Encouraged, he continued. 'But we do need to defend ourselves and our way of life against the incursions of these *stranieri*, these *invadenti*, these *oltramontani*.'

Foreigners, interlopers, invaders from 'beyond the mountains'. Gracchi spat the words out with all the contempt he could muster.

There was a ripple of applause. The council needed no reminding of the dangers that threatened from fifty miles to the east. Florence was the largest city state in Tuscany and had been the most prosperous for over a century. It straddled the north–south trade routes and was a hub of economic activity and an established European banking centre. Unlike Pisa, however, it was an inland city, with no direct access to the sea. Its economic expansion, and particularly that of its burgeoning cloth industry, needed a maritime portal in order to exploit to the full the highly profitable international textile markets that had opened up in the wake of the decline of the cloth industry in Flanders.

Pisa was to be that portal.

But Florence was in economic disarray, its population decimated by the Black Death and its municipal coffers drained virtually to the point of bankruptcy by King Edward of England's repudiation of his massive debts to leading Florentine bankers – debts incurred to underwrite his costly war against France. To recoup those losses and reassert its pre-eminence as a centre of European commerce and finance, Florence needed to expand. It had already tried more than once to annex by force the neighbouring city state of Lucca, but had failed at each attempt. Pisa would be next.

Florence's military resources far outstripped Pisa's; every man in the room knew as much.

Giacomo Albertosi, Pisa's senior magistrate, raised a hand to claim the floor. 'The Florentines' intentions are plain for all to see. At issue before us is what steps we must take to frustrate those intentions. That Florence's ambitions are distasteful and contrary to the best interests of Pisa, I willingly concede. But I ask you: are we not ill placed to defend ourselves? Can no accommodation – no *financial* accommodation – be proposed?'

Gracchi responded without hesitation. 'I fear there can be no such accommodation. To buy them off buys us time, but how much time? A year? A decade, perhaps? No, my friends, there can be no accommodation with such vermin. We must stand our ground. We must ready ourselves.'

'War!' exclaimed Massimo Mastrodonato, an octogenarian whose family had prospered over three generations as bankers and money-lenders. 'War? Have you no thought of anything but war? Tell me, what has war ever accomplished? Death, destruction, butchery, civil unrest, ruin – that is what war is all about. And that is *not* what has made Pisa prosper. Are you all too young to remember Meloria? Because I, for one, am not.'

The council fell silent. Meloria was rarely invoked in Pisan circles. That day, 6 August 1284, had been the blackest in the city's history: the Pisan fleet had been destroyed almost to the last vessel in a sea battle fought off Meloria Rock, scarcely a mile beyond the Arno estuary. Some eight thousand of Pisa's most prominent citizens had been hauled away in ignominy and in chains into Genoese captivity. As a result, Pisa had been deprived of access to its valuable holdings on the islands of Corsica and Sardinia and effectively relegated to the status of a minor city state.

'You talk of Meloria as if it were yesterday,' ventured Gracchi.

'I talk of Meloria because my own grandfather died that day, as did thousands like him. I talk of Meloria because this city of ours has prospered not because of Meloria but despite it. Look around, I beg you. What do you see? You see our Duomo, you see our Campo Santo, you see the Campanile, you see our fine *casatorri*, our beautiful churches. That is what we have and that is what we stand to lose. War destroys and tears down. War despoils, peace restores. War diminishes, peace builds. What we have accomplished here comes not from war but from peace and prosperity. This fair city of ours is the work of men of greatness who despised war: Taddeo Gaddi, Giottino, Cimabue—'

Gracchi cut the old man off in full flow. 'The talk is not of war but of self-defence.'

'We do not have the means to defend ourselves,' put in Gennaro Altobardi, the youngest man in the room.

'That is true,' replied Gracchi. 'But we have the means to acquire the means.'

The councillors looked at one another, then back at Gracchi.

He was calmer now, composing himself to put forward the proposal he had been mulling over for several days. 'We must purchase our defence,' he said.

Several men spoke at once. Gracchi raised his hands to restore order. He gestured to Giacomo Albertosi, who, as a magistrate, was held to be a model of impartiality.

'It is regrettable that we have insufficient means to defend ourselves,' said Albertosi, 'and it is true we have much to defend and much to lose. It surely follows that we must pay others to ensure our defence.' He paused. 'We must engage the services of a *condottiere*.'

'That is your proposal?' This from Gracchi.

'That is my proposal,' replied Albertosi. 'It is a step I advocate with great reluctance and subject to the most stringent conditions. We must be most prudent in our choice, and we must be mindful of the consequences.'

There were immediate objections. Gracchi waited patiently. Sooner or later, one of the councillors would present him with the opening he needed. As it happened, it was Mastrodonato who obliged. Predictably, the old man was vehemently opposed to the notion of retaining a mercenary force, and he made his feelings plain.

'I have said time and again that we must learn from history and I say so once more. We must learn even from Florence itself. Does none among you recall how Florence suffered in 1342 when the city fathers hired that odious Frenchman Gauthier de Brienne to restore civil order? Let me tell you this: they would have been better advised to invite the devil himself into their midst. Brienne and his hirelings posed a greater threat to Florence than all its enemies put together. It is unthinkable—'

'You speak of Gauthier de Brienne, the self-styled Duke of Athens?' Gracchi interrupted.

'Yes, yes,' said Mastrodonato, irritated by the interruption. 'Of course I mean Brienne. Who else but Brienne and his murderous rabble?'

'Then perhaps you also recall that he fell at the battle of Poitiers in 1356?'

Mastrodonato clearly did not. 'I know only that Florence was well rid of him.'

'And that he died at the hands of an English knight, one Sir John de Hawkwood?' persisted Gracchi.

'I fail to grasp your point, sir,' said Mastrodonato.

'My point, sir, is this. The war between France and England is at a standstill; a truce has been called and may last for years. There are many in England who would be willing to put their longbows and cavalry at the service of Pisa. Among them perhaps – I cannot be certain – this Hawkwood.'

Magistrate Albertosi rapped sharply on the table. All heads turned.

'Are you seriously proposing to this council that an Englishman come to the defence of Pisa?'

'I am seriously proposing that we discuss the possibility,' said Gracchi. 'Or would you rather that our saviour be French?'

'God forbid,' said Albertosi with a smile. 'But an *Englishman*? In all faith, the English are such uncultured and unsavoury rogues.'

'Perhaps,' replied Gracchi. 'But Hawkwood would be *our* uncultured and unsavoury rogue.'

IV

Exile

What misery it cost him to depart

Sible Hedingham, 4 August 1359

John Hawkwood took stock of his life and found it wanting.

He sat on a stony outcrop on the shallow incline above the manor house and looked out over his estate. The harvest was in. The corn had been gathered, threshed and winnowed. Two granaries were full and a third three-quarters full. Hay and winter fodder for the livestock had been secured. Below, narrow strips of farmland lay fallow, waiting for the next crop to be planted. Shards of flint in the freshly turned soil glinted wet and dark in the watery sunlight. Rents had been collected, church tithes assessed and paid, dues calculated and settled. Two serf families who had deserted the estate to seek their fortune elsewhere had since returned. Two other families had not.

Hawkwood professed little knowledge of farming, but it was clear to him that better ploughs and better use of them would lead to better crops. He also knew that the value of an estate was gauged in terms of the number of ploughs and teams of oxen it owned. Hawkwood had recently acquired two new mould-board ploughs and, because they were extremely heavy and unwieldy, had purchased a further team of oxen to draw them. In addition, he had converted a portion of the estate's common land to make available to his tenants a number of additional one-acre strips of farmland. Not least, in a bid to prevent tenants from leaving the estate, he had waived a modest part of the annual rents due to him. The gesture was much appreciated.

There was little more to be done now, other than sit out the

long winter evenings in the desultory company of Lady Margaret,
and to exercise each day so as to hone his skills of war.

Twice he had sent a squire to Windsor to discover King
Edward's intentions with regard to the continuance of the French
war. Both times the squire had returned with unwelcome news.
The hostilities were in abeyance. Exchequers were empty. Enthusiasm was at a low ebb. English forces still held Calais,
Bordeaux and large tracts of Aquitaine. King Jean remained
hostage in London, unransomed. Edward had raised taxes again.
His queen had borne him yet another son. The Scots were causing
havoc in Northumberland. The Black Death had decimated the
population of London.

And so on.

Hawkwood picked up a smooth stone and weighed it in his
hand. Out of the corner of his eye he had seen a flurry of
movement to his left. A rabbit. He waited patiently. When it
moved again he took careful aim and hurled the stone viciously at
the hapless creature's head. He missed. The rabbit scampered off
down the slope, disappearing into a burrow. Seconds later, it
popped its head out again and eyed him speculatively.

Sir John de Hawkwood shook his head in disbelief. The
veteran of Crécy and Poitiers had been bested by a rabbit.

The king's messenger approached Hawkwood Manor late that
afternoon, flanked by an escort of twelve. The party entered the
courtyard and dismounted. Hawkwood went out to welcome them.

The herald-at-arms stepped forward and saluted. 'I bring news
from Windsor, Sir John.'

Hawkwood's pulse quickened and a broad smile spread across
his rugged face. This was what he had been waiting for these
three long years. Three years almost to the day since the momen-
tous battle on Poitiers Field.

'I welcome such news, Master Herald.'

The man, whom Hawkwood judged to be in his mid-twenties,
hesitated, then averted his gaze and drew a parchment scroll from
under his leather cape.

Hawkwood's eyes narrowed as the herald handed it over. There was something wrong here, he thought.

Hawkwood broke the seal and unfurled the document. It was in Latin.

Let it be known that by solemn and irrevocable decision of His Most Royal Majesty King Edward III of England and of France, it is by the present established and declared that the conduct of the Knight of the Realm Sir John de Hawkwood is deemed unbecoming and dishonourable to his rank and title; in pursuance whereof, it is by the present decreed that henceforth and in perpetuity the aforesaid knight shall be excluded from that rank and title; yet, inasmuch as John Hawkwood has long served the Crown, it is the King's most gracious pleasure and gift that John Hawkwood continue to enjoy the usufruct of all present estates and all privileges and servitudes appertaining thereto; it is further decreed that, forthwith and without further recourse, the aforesaid John Hawkwood shall be enjoined and admonished to indemnify the Crown of England in the amount of twenty thousand gold crowns and eight destriers trained to the lance. Given under my hand and seal at Windsor Castle on the ninth day of September in the Year of Our Most Glorious Lord One Thousand Three Hundred and Fifty-Nine, Eduardus III Rex, King of England and France.

Hawkwood read it through once, then a second time, slowly. He looked up at the young man and gave a curt nod. 'I thank you, Master Herald, and I bid you convey my respects to His Majesty and assure him of my continuing allegiance. You are to inform him that it shall be as he has ordered.'

The herald seemed uncertain what to do next.

Hawkwood smiled. 'Your escort will wish to water their horses.'

'I thank you, Sir John,' replied the herald, then blushed at the *faux pas*. 'Permit me only to say that—'

Hawkwood held up a hand. 'There is nothing to be said, save that I thank you for your courtesy and wish you God's speed.' With that, he turned on his heel and walked back into the house.

He strode through the Great Hall, up the two stone steps to the solar and through the metal-studded oak door into his private quarters. Lady Margaret – no, he corrected himself, plain *Margaret* Hawkwood as of this instant – sat at her needlepoint. She glanced up as he entered the bedchamber, took in the expression on his face and knew at once that his mood was even blacker than of late. She said nothing, too afraid to speak.

Hawkwood paced the floor, pausing at intervals to pound his right fist against the oak support beams at either end of the chamber. The sound reverberated in the room and his wife flinched at every blow. Suddenly, and without a word, he thrust the king's message in her face.

She looked down at it. 'But, Sir John,' she whispered, 'I read no Latin.'

'*Sir* John is no longer,' Hawkwood growled. 'No longer – by the express order of His Most Gracious Majesty King Edward III of England and of France.'

'I-I do not understand,' she stammered.

'What is there to understand, woman? What, I ask you? Only that I have been stripped of my rank and title by a king no man has served more loyally.'

Margaret offered no reply. She understood little of life beyond the walls of Hawkwood Manor and knew almost nothing about her husband, save that he was a soldier knight held in high esteem throughout the land.

Hawkwood started to pace the room again. It was unthinkable that one well-intentioned cautionary remark to the Black Prince those many months ago could have sparked a situation such as this. Unthinkable and unjust. Worse, there was little to be done about it. The Black Prince was behind this, of that he was certain. It seemed inconceivable that the prince should have been so petulant, but Hawkwood had incurred the king's displeasure and against that there was no appeal. True, he might bring his case before the Court of Nobles and Barons, but they would scarcely take issue with the king over such a trivial matter. The Court had been granted extensive powers under the provisions of the Magna Carta, but those powers were intended to be exercised only *in extremis*.

Hawkwood had to concede that the king had acted shrewdly. The financial penalty was well judged. Although extortionate, it was one which – as the king knew only too well – Hawkwood could afford. Besides, money was not the principal concern. Hawkwood had been stripped of his honour and his name had been blackened.

The conduct of the Knight of the Realm Sir John de Hawkwood is deemed unbecoming and dishonourable to his rank and title . . .

He crushed the parchment into a ball and hurled it across the room. As God is my witness, he vowed, King Edward shall have his twenty thousand crowns and his eight destriers trained to the lance. But I, John Hawkwood, shall deliver them to him in person. Edward shall have his blood money, but I shall have the satisfaction of looking him in the eye and witnessing his discomfiture at the grave injustice he has done me at the behest of a son I once called friend.

Windsor Castle, 3 October 1359

It was several years since Hawkwood had last visited Windsor Castle and he was astonished at the changes that had been made. Few traces remained of the earthwork and timber palisade structure hastily thrown up almost two centuries before by William, Duke of Normandy. The Curfew, Garter and Salisbury towers built to the west of the Lower Ward by Henry III had long been a familiar sight, but it was common knowledge that Edward had added magnificently appointed royal apartments, an inner gate with twin cylindrical towers, and a royal chapel dedicated to the Virgin, St George of Cappadocia and St Edward the Confessor. The rampart fortifications which ran along the south and east sides of the Upper Ward had been extended and heightened, and Hawkwood had heard that William Wykeham, Bishop of

Winchester, had been commissioned to build yet another great tower.

The sprawling edifice that loomed over the steep hill running down to the Thames was now a profusion of gargoyles, pinnacles, buttresses and crenellations. Roofs were clad in precious lead, immaculate courtyard gardens had been laid out, swathes of parkland had been cleared and stained glass glistened from every window.

This guardian of the western approaches was beyond question the jewel in the crown of castles and forts that ringed London, a day's march away. A jewel, certainly, but one not without imperfections. As a soldier, Hawkwood doubted Windsor's strategic value. By its very nature, the castle was static and could easily be outflanked and bypassed by a hostile invading force. As a defensive position, it had great merit but, essentially, Windsor Castle appeared to exist purely to defend Windsor Castle.

Hawkwood had been in Windsor for several days. He had delivered eight warhorses – the cream of his current stock – to the royal stables and had deposited twenty thousand gold crowns with the Keeper of the Royal Purse. Not unreasonably, Hawkwood felt, he had also sought an audience with the king. This had been refused on the grounds that His Royal Majesty was for the present preoccupied by 'affairs of the realm'. Hawkwood had been as insistent as the king's chancellor had been adamant: no audience could or would be granted for the time being. He would have to wait. He would have to be patient.

Patience, as Hawkwood would have been the first to admit, was not one of his virtues. He had spent the long days riding in the Great Park and the even longer evenings in the taverns of Windsor town, where he was instantly recognised. His reputation had preceded him but few who crossed his path seemed willing to exchange more than the essential courtesies. His fall from royal grace had been noted. He was an outsider.

At last, the audience he felt was his due was granted. To his dismay, he was ushered into the presence not of the king but of one of his sons, the Duke of Gloucester. The duke, a pale-complexioned youth with a withered left hand, was clearly unnerved by the occasion.

'My father bids you welcome to Windsor and regrets that pressing business in France prevents him from receiving you himself.'

Hawkwood nodded.

The duke cleared his throat and continued, 'I am commanded by my father to acknowledge your contribution to the exchequer and to express his wish that you live out your days in peace on your estates.'

Hawkwood nodded again.

'The king also commends your long service to the Crown of England. This has not been forgotten.'

Another nod.

Gloucester seemed at a loss for words. There was an awkward silence. Then: 'Is it your wish that I convey your respects to the king?'

'It is my wish that you inform your most noble father I had hoped to see him in person.'

'Alas, that will not be possible.'

'Then it is my wish that England may continue to prosper under his reign.'

'It shall be so.'

Hawkwood bowed almost imperceptibly, turned and walked from the chamber. The audience was over and, with it, all that had been most precious to him. As he rode out of the gates of Windsor, Hawkwood felt the salt sting of tears. Angrily, he swept a hand across his face. The day was chill, he told himself, and the wind had blown specks of dust into his eyes.

He regained his lodgings in the town and ordered his squires to ready themselves for departure. They would leave for Hawkwood Manor at dawn the following day.

That evening, as he sat in a modest tavern in Windsor town and drank his fill, he noticed a handsome young man sitting alone in the far corner of the taproom, studying him intently. As Hawkwood made to depart, the young man rose and came across to his table.

'By your leave, Sir John, I would speak with you.'

'Then speak, I pray you.'

'My name is Gennaro Altobardi. I am the envoy of the Council of Guilds of the city state of Pisa.'

'And?'

'And I am entrusted by that council to approach you on its behalf.'

'To what end?'

'To retain your services. Pisa has great need of your courage and experience.'

Hawkwood sat down on the wooden bench again and gestured to Altobardi to do likewise.

'I am flattered there are still those who hold my modest skills in some regard,' said Hawkwood. 'Pray continue. I shall listen.'

Altobardi explained his mission and Hawkwood listened intently until late into the night.

V

The Company

Banners on display and all the host beside

Calais, 4 January 1361
John Hawkwood and Gennaro Altobardi stood on the afterdeck as the flotilla of seven vessels prepared to anchor off Calais. The crossing had been short and uneventful, but Hawkwood was no seafarer and wished only to feel terra firma under his feet again.

Hawkwood could make out the six round towers, the massive keep and the wide moats constructed more than a century previously by Philippe Hurepel, Count of Burgundy, to protect Calais from English and Flemish marauders. He remembered these fortifications: they were what had enabled Calais to hold out for the better part of a year against Edward III when he besieged the town in 1346 and 1347 following his victory over France's King Philippe VI at Crécy.

Hawkwood had spent tedious months at the siege of Calais once the English armies had struck out north from Crécy-en-Artois, looting, pillaging and living off the land, desperate to secure and hold a port – any port – from which to re-embark for England. They had believed the once-modest fishing village of Calais to be easy pickings, much more vulnerable than its close neighbour Boulogne. But the citizens of Calais had mounted a resolute defence until that memorable day in early August 1347 when the town at last capitulated. King Edward had vowed to put its entire population to the sword. Hawkwood would never forget the bravery shown by those six prominent citizens of Calais who had come barefoot and with nooses round their necks to present the king with the keys of the town, offering to give up their own lives in exchange for clemency shown to their fellow citizens. Had it not been for the timely and compassionate intervention of Edward's wife, Queen Philippa, they would have died on the scaffold; instead, they were taken as prisoners to England and held for ransom. Hawkwood and many of his fellow knights had roundly applauded the bravery of those six men, and to this day he could still name them: Eustache de Saint-Pierre, Jean d'Aire, Pierre de Wissant, Jacques de Wissant, Jean de Fiennes and Andriens d'Ardée.

He had recounted this episode in tiresome detail (and more than once) to Altobardi, who seemed suitably impressed, although careful not to voice the suspicion that, in similar circumstances, the city state of Pisa might be hard pressed to find six citizens to do likewise.

To all intents and purposes, Calais was now an English town. On King Edward's orders, the majority of the French population had been banished from within the city walls, to be replaced by wool merchants, shippers of wine, chandlers, tavern-owners and brothel-keepers who were now as much at home in Calais as they had once been in Dover, Plymouth or Southampton.

Hawkwood's party came ashore early that afternoon. Supervising the vessels as they loaded in Dover, Hawkwood had proudly surveyed the command he had assembled over the previous months since he had been approached by Altobardi. Twenty mounted knights, forty squires and sergeants-at-arms, a hundred and fifty pikemen, a full company of foot and four hundred Welsh and English longbowmen, all battle-hardened veterans, all fully equipped and provisioned. On disembarking in Calais, however, he had second thoughts: his command numbered scarcely a thousand. To be sure, they were a fine body of men, but it was a paltry force compared to the reported military might of Florence. Worse, he had yet to traverse more than twelve hundred miles of potentially hostile terrain before reaching Pisa. There was no knowing what the following days and weeks would bring.

'It is of no consequence, Captain-General,' Altobardi hastened to reassure him. 'Calais teems with seasoned campaigners who seek their fortune bearing arms. They will rally to our standard at the prospect of booty.'

Hawkwood remained unconvinced.

The men billeted a full mile beyond the town walls, on a plain of intermittent marshland close to fresh water. Immediately to the south of the encampment a second 'Calais' had sprung up, a self-sufficient timbered township which housed the large English garrison left by Edward III to protect the port, together with several thousand freemen who had remained in France, persuaded the truce would soon be lifted and they would once more be retained to bear arms in pursuance of the English king's designs on the French crown.

The arrival of Hawkwood's command was a major event and there was much rumour and speculation as to its meaning. Was this the advance party of a larger army? Had King Edward – now reported to be back in France and besieging the city of Reims far to the east – called for reinforcements? Was the war about to start again? Could this be the same Sir John de Hawkwood who had recently fallen into royal disfavour?

Hawkwood knew there was no time like the present. As soon as his men had been quartered, he assembled a small party of knights and equerries and despatched them to the neighbouring camp. Their instructions were unequivocal: they were to announce the arrival of John Hawkwood, Captain-General of the Free Company of Essex, and to proclaim a tournament to which all were welcome who professed skill in the use of the lance and longbow. There were great prizes to be won by any who could best the champions of Essex.

They came in their thousands.

Hawkwood was sorely tempted to enter the lists himself, but thought better of it: if he were defeated, his standing would be eroded and his plan might fail. Instead, he selected eight knights to represent the Essex Company. They acquitted themselves beyond all expectations. Two were unseated in the early rounds of the joust, but the other six prevailed, routing their opponents with comparative ease. He had chosen his champions well.

The joust, for all its colour and excitement, was not the only attraction of the day. Wrestling and fist-fighting competitions were staged and, to Hawkwood's immense satisfaction, his men carried the day in each. Elsewhere, massive blocks of stone were lifted and carried fifty paces in a contest declared an honourable draw. Men from both camps vied for the distinction of lifting the stoutest tree trunk, leaping the farthest or highest, and outrunning their opponents over shorter and longer distances. Generous prizes were awarded for various feats: hurling stones, felling trees, saddling a horse, twirling a battle standard, even spitting the farthest.

Hawkwood savoured the competition and revelled in the comradeship that only those who have borne arms together can fully appreciate. This was the life he had relished since early adulthood, this belonging, the exultation of being a first among equals.

Beyond all doubt, the main contest of the day was the archery. Sixteen men from each camp were admitted, and thousands of wagers were taken on who would prevail. The Essex Company had their champion and favourite in Sergeant-at-Arms Geraint Llewellyn, a giant from the Vale of Glamorgan, whose prowess with the longbow was legendary. It was said that he had skewered upwards of thirty French knights at Crécy, sending volley after volley through their plate armour with such force that they were knocked off their feet to become easy prey for the footsoldiers.

English commanders in the field grudgingly conceded that Bordeaux and Toledo steels were the finest in Europe, and some even asserted that prime longbow yew staves could be had in Spain. Not so Geraint Llewellyn: he was a staunch advocate of English yew. He went into combat with several spare bowstaves, with three cords held in reserve for each. A tall man, he drew an exceptionally long bow – nearly seven feet. Over time, his already powerful shoulders had broadened even further. His massive forearms testified to the strength required to wield a 160-pound drawstring. The first three fingers of his draw hand had thickened out of all proportion to those of his left.

The thirty-two archers were arrayed in a single rank. They set aside their steel helmets and removed their surcoats. Many wore earrings; others had broad leather or chain-link bands round their necks. Some were bearded, others clean-shaven; some were leather-skinned veterans, others fresh-faced youths. All had demonstrated their skill in competition and on the field of battle.

The contest would unfold in four phases. First, a test of distance, then one of accuracy, followed by depth of penetration and rate of fire. The winner would be judged on the aggregate of his ranking in each of the four phases. A minimum of eight competitors would be eliminated after each of the first three rounds.

Hawkwood raised his right hand and let it drop by his side. Thirty-two longbows drew taut, then elevated to a sharp angle. Almost simultaneously, thirty-two swine-backed feathered shafts hissed skywards, curving gracefully together for what seemed an eternity before the first of them tilted and plunged towards the earth.

The distances were meticulously paced out. The first arrows had landed just beyond two hundred and thirty paces; many more were grouped close to the three hundred mark. Several had travelled almost three hundred and fifty, but one had far outdistanced all the others, plummeting into the ground over four hundred paces away.

There was a roar of approval from the watching throng. The black, green and purple feathers on the shaft were unmistakable: Llewellyn of Glamorgan.

Twenty-four straw targets were set out at a distance of two hundred yards and a square of white cloth was positioned in the middle of each. Twenty-four arrows sought their mark. Of these, nineteen found the straw, but only fourteen punctured the white square – Llewellyn's among them.

Those fourteen men took up position one hundred paces from an ox carcass suspended from a hook attached to a cross-pole. Each man stepped up in turn and fired a single arrow. One shaft after another slammed foursquare into the carcass, penetrating

the thick hide and crunching through bone and flesh. Only two
arrows failed to find their mark, and eleven protruded from the
gently swaying carcass when Llewellyn stepped up and took aim.
His shaft whistled through the air, struck a fraction above the
breastbone and, as the crowd gasped in astonishment, protruded
a full eight inches from the other side.

Hawkwood leapt to his feet, roaring his approval. 'By Christ,
sir, that is as fair a shaft as I have ever seen!'

Llewellyn walked forward to the shattered carcass, retrieved
his arrow, wiped it on his breeches and, grinning from ear to ear,
executed a preposterously low curtsey. The crowd laughed their
approval and cheered wildly. Hawkwood applauded with the
best of them.

Llewellyn was clearly the winner and another Welshman,
Huw Griffiths, shorter than Llewellyn but every bit as broad-
shouldered, was adjudged to have come second. He and
Llewellyn were to be put to the final test. Distance, accuracy
and penetration were key attributes of the experienced longbowman, but rate of fire was a crucial element in the field.

A single straw target was set at a distance of one hundred and
fifty paces. Each bowman was required to draw and fire as many
shafts as he could in one minute. Only those that lodged in the
straw would count; all that failed to find the mark would be null
and void.

Llewellyn and Griffiths stood side by side. To the right of each
man, a leather quiver of arrows was fixed upright. Hawkwood
gave the signal and the crowd – or those of them who knew how
to count – began to chant the seconds.

Llewellyn stooped, snatched a shaft from the quiver, positioned it, drew, took aim and fired. The arrow had scarcely left
his bow when he stooped again and repeated the process. Again
and again.

'Fifty-eight . . . fifty-nine . . . sixty!'

The target was a pheasant's fantail of coloured feathers. The
judges walked forward and solemnly removed each, tallying as
they went. Llewellyn had loosed eleven arrows in the sixty

seconds. One had missed to the right. His count was ten. Griffiths had fired thirteen arrows. Two had missed left and a third had flown clean over the target. His tally was also ten.

Hawkwood approached the two men, signalling that the contest was over. It seemed to him that both had performed equally well. To his surprise, he saw that Llewellyn was holding Griffiths's arm high above his head. Hawkwood's eyes narrowed. Llewellyn is right, he thought, the test *was* one of speed and rate of fire. Griffiths might have missed the target three times, but he had fired more arrows. The big question was how he had accomplished it.

Llewellyn clearly had the same question on his mind. He took the bow from Griffiths's hand and weighed it in his own. 'In faith, my friend, this is as well-waxed and well-balanced a bow as I have ever encountered. Yet I fear it is too short for me.'

Too short? thought Hawkwood. Perhaps, perhaps not. The longbow's effectiveness relied almost as much on rate of fire as on accuracy and distance. It was something he would bear in mind.

The day ended with a feast which continued well into the night. Hawkwood moved among the crowd, clasping an arm here, clapping a shoulder there. He had rarely been happier.

Two days later, Captain-General John Hawkwood departed Calais at the head of the Free Company of Essex. In his wake were thirty-seven hundred men-at-arms.

Sible Hedingham, 30 January 1361

Margaret Hawkwood had risen at daybreak on the morning of her husband's departure, and had stood shivering in the half-light of dawn as he and his small complement of retainers readied themselves. The destriers, palfreys and packhorses were marshalled into line and Hawkwood moved among them, checking a girth here, cinching a strap there.

He was in his element, she had thought, and who could blame him? At last, he had regained some purpose. A renewed dignity.

To her surprise, Margaret had mixed feelings about his departure. A great blow had been dealt to his pride, and he had become even more withdrawn than usual. He had said little, but she knew how unjustly he had been treated by the king and how he had brooded over that injustice. She had suffered with him.

He had left now, and she had no way of knowing when – or if – he would return. She was strangely saddened by the thought. He had spent an unusually long time at home and she had come to see him in a different light. Coarse, gruff, short-tempered as ever, yet curiously diligent in his ways. An honest man, a man of his word, a man who treated his people fairly, who helped where help was needed and who was mindful of his responsibilities.

She was still afraid of him, but she respected him more than she could express. Her husband was a man of honour, that much she now knew. He had left for a place she had never heard of and about which she cared little. And she would miss him.

Margaret felt bile rise in her throat. She hurried indoors, her hand clasped over her mouth. It had been like this for many weeks now, every morning. Her breasts were heavy and her waist had thickened. She was with child.

She had not spoken of this to Sir John. He had too many other things on his mind.

Palazzo della Signoria, Florence,
6 March 1361

An inscription on an atrium wall in Pompeii is attributed by some to Gaius Plinius Secundus, the Roman military commander, historian and savant who perished in the lava flow which engulfed that ancient city in AD 79. The inscription holds that 'A secret shared is a trust betrayed'. Most would be tempted to agree, although a cynic might add that a secret remains a secret provided it is transmitted to only one person at any one time.

Like other Italian city states, Florence had, throughout its turbulent history, witnessed the temporary ascendancy of one political group after another as alliances were formed and broken, as tenuous allegiances shifted and as the knife-edge balance of power between rulers and ruled swung first one way then another. With the possible exception of papal Rome, however, none of the city states of the Italian peninsula had sustained a more comprehensive or more effective network of scouts and informants than Florence.

Within three days of Pisa's decision to despatch Gennaro Altobardi to England to solicit Hawkwood's services, the details of his 'secret' mission were known to Florence and were the subject of heated debate by the city elders. By what means the information had been ferreted out was no longer of consequence: at issue was how to respond.

The consensus was that Florence must respond and must respond quickly. The need to take Pisa was paramount and should be addressed without delay, especially now that Pisa had called upon this English *condottiere*. Florence and its allies in Montepulciano, Bologna and Orvieto were in agreement: nothing would give greater satisfaction than to bring Pisa to its knees and, with it, Pisa's Ghibelline allies in Siena, Pistoia and Arezzo.

'Pisa and its allies must fall, of that I am persuaded,' said the council's president, Giancarlo Boninsegna. 'But I counsel prudence. We know little of this Hawkwood other than that he sells himself for booty and blood money. We do not know the man and are in no position to assess the threat he poses. But time is on our side. Hawkwood may reject Pisa's offer out of hand, or he may accept it but fail to raise an army. Even should he be successful, he will have to traverse half of Europe before he can come to Pisa's aid. We must be ready, but there *is* time.'

The elders were silent.

Only one raised his voice in muted protest. 'I am by nature a prudent man,' ventured Pietrangelo Bellisario, 'but there is a fine line between *prudenza* and inaction.'

'The point is well taken,' replied Boninsegna, 'and I concur. Let me say only that I counsel *prudenza* but not *passività*. We must determine more of this Hawkwood and his intentions. We must deploy informants to assess his numbers, ascertain his strengths and probe his weaknesses.'

'Hawkwood is a mercenary,' snorted Bellisario. 'He fights for money, not principle. We have money. Why not simply buy him off? Better still, why not purchase his services ourselves?'

'If that is an option, then it is one we shall exercise if and when the opportunity presents itself,' replied Boninsegna. 'For the moment, however, I propose we watch and wait.'

Watch and wait. The Council of Elders reluctantly bowed to Boninsegna's decision, as he had known they would. As they always did.

Abbaye de la Couronne, near Angoulême, 8 March 1361

The two men circled, each eyeing the dagger in the other's hand.

One was tall, fair-haired and loose-limbed, the other short and thickset. The tall one had stripped off his surcoat and wound it tightly around his left forearm. The thickset one was the older of the two by several years. His nose had been broken more than once and his pock-marked features were made even uglier by a jagged scar down the left side of his face. The younger man was the more mobile, repeatedly stepping in close, feinting with his dagger, then arching back away from his adversary's shorter reach. The older man came steadily and flatfootedly forward, imperceptibly closing the gap between himself and his opponent.

The onlookers did not know why the two men had squared off. No matter: the prospect of a fight was one they relished, the more so since this had all the makings of a fight to the death. They shouted encouragement as the younger man lunged forward, aiming at the other's head. There was a clash of steel as the other warded off the blow and jabbed his own weapon wildly at his adversary's midriff.

The crowd jeered derisively as he missed, losing his balance and stumbling to his knees. The younger man saw his opening and stepped in smartly. For once, his height put him at a disadvantage. As he stooped to strike, the thickset man rose on one knee and thrust his dagger sharply upwards, drawing blood from high on the other's thigh, only inches from his private parts. The wounded man backed away in expectation of the inevitable follow-up, but his adversary simply got to his feet and stood there, glowering at him and panting from his own exertions. He is mine now, thought the blond man. He drew a deep breath and moved swiftly in for the kill.

The older man stood his ground. He punched his dagger forward and up, dropping down on one knee as he did so. The young man's dagger scythed past his ear and he felt the jolt as his own weapon angled upwards and buried itself deep into his adversary's ribcage. It was a fatal blow and the thickset man knew as much. He released his dagger and rolled to one side, glancing up to see his opponent drop his weapon and clutch his chest with both hands. There was a look of surprise on his face as he pitched forward and lay still.

The victor walked over to the body, extracted his dagger, wiped it on his tunic and returned it to his belt.

The crowd was silent. Much as they had delighted in the confrontation, they were stunned at how quickly it had been brought to this deadly conclusion. Some turned away, while others hastened forward as if to satisfy themselves that one of the combatants was well and truly dead. The thickset man retrieved his helmet and walked slowly away.

When the incident was reported to Hawkwood, he knew he must take action. Immediately. Fights had broken out several times on the march from the coast, but he had elected to look the other way: when all was said and done, these were fighting men. This latest episode was different, however. One of his men had been killed – by a comrade-at-arms.

The thickset man was brought before him, and Hawkwood demanded an explanation. It transpired that the quarrel had been triggered by a simple remark. The dead man had been Welsh, the survivor was English. The Welshman had made a disparaging comment about the English and their virility and the Englishman had reacted accordingly.

The killer showed no remorse. He had been called out, he explained, and had defended his honour.

'Honour?' exclaimed Hawkwood. 'What honour is there in this, that you slaughter a comrade?'

The man looked at the ground, shuffling his feet. He muttered something that Hawkwood did not catch.

'You oblige me to repeat myself,' said Hawkwood. 'I ask again: what honour is there in this?'

The man said nothing.

Hawkwood looked around at those who had closed within earshot. They waited expectantly. He raised his voice. 'This is an army, a free company of men. You are here to fight when I say fight, and not before. You are hired to fight against an enemy, any enemy, not among yourselves. I will not brook such behaviour within our ranks. I have vowed to enter Pisa at the head of an army, not at the head of an undisciplined rabble.'

The man looked up hopefully. His eyes gave him away. Was this all? A reprimand? Words of censure? Was that to be his punishment?

'You have taken the life of one of my men,' continued Hawkwood. 'Your own life is forfeit. That is all.' He turned away with a gesture of disgust. 'Hang him.'

John Hawkwood was not a man of letters but he was an avid student of history and of the art of war. He had marvelled at the courage of the Spartans at Thermopylae. He had devoured chronicles of Alexander the Great's Persian campaigns. He had read the *Histories of Rome* by Polybius and Titus Livius, studied the tactics of Scipio Africanus, and read and re-read Caesar's *De bello gallico*. He particularly admired Hannibal's victory at Lake Trasimene and Caesar's victory over the Nervii. And he had many times replayed in his mind the victory of Emperor Otto I over the rampaging Magyars at the battle of the River Lech in 955.

He had concluded that strategy and tactics could be readily assimilated – after all, they were no more than the tools of the trade. What Alexander, Hannibal, Caesar and Otto had demonstrated was less easily achieved but every bit as vital: the military imperatives of unity, cohesion, discipline and singleness of purpose.

A few moments ago he had said, 'I have vowed to enter Pisa at the head of an army, not at the head of an undisciplined rabble.' His mind was made up. He, too, would forge unity, build cohesion, enforce discipline and develop singleness of purpose.

And he would do so without delay.

VI

Karl Eugen

You are my trusted friend, as none can doubt

Florence, 10 March 1361

Karl Eugen August Wilhelm von Strachwitz-Wettin was the third
son and the black sheep of a Polish-German family who had come
to prominence in the early twelfth century and whose lands now
extended across large tracts of the margraviate of Meissen. The
principle of primogeniture provided that Karl Eugen's eldest
brother, Harald Günther, would succeed to the Strachwitz-
Wettin estates. The second son, Werner Sigismund, had taken
holy orders and was a devout man of the cloth.

Karl Eugen August Wilhelm's destiny lay elsewhere.

Of all her children, Karl Eugen's mother had favoured her third
son, a beautiful child and now an exceptionally handsome young
man. That she had doted on him from infancy was, in his father's
considered view, the principal reason why the young man had
strayed so frequently from the straight and narrow. His mother
had looked the other way when, as a twelve-year-old, Karl Eugen
had cheerfully lopped the heads off a dozen or so chickens 'to see
how much blood was in them'. She had also looked the other way
when, as a fifteen-year-old, he had impregnated not one but two
of the family servants. And, yet again when, at twenty, the apple
of her eye had torched one of the peasant cottages on the Wettin
estates because a tenant's daughter had rejected his advances. She
attributed these and other episodes to youthful high spirits, and
soon forgave and forgot. Her *Liebling* could do no wrong.

Karl Eugen's father was less tolerant. He had thrashed his son
repeatedly from a very early age. After Karl Eugen's reprehensible
debut as a firebrand, he had ordered him horse-whipped, but had

thought better of it when his strapping son squared off against him, challenging him to do his worst.

The lad was now twenty-four, and had put the petty deeds of his youth behind him. Karl Eugen August Wilhelm von Strachwitz-Wettin had bigger fish to fry.

It was a glorious spring day and he had time on his hands. He had started out early from the Oltrarno, the poorer district of Florence on the opposite bank of the Arno river, and was heading for a palazzo near the Ponte Vecchio where he was to meet Giancarlo Boninsegna. Karl Eugen meandered through the streets, pausing to admire once more the cathedral, the ancient baptistery and Giotto's magnificent campanile with its great bell, intended to be rung *a stormo* when danger threatened. He sauntered down the bustling Borgo degli Albizi, one of the oldest thoroughfares in Florence. He spent a few moments in the Orsanmichele church, conceived originally as a grain market but now graced with Andrea Orcagna's stunning altarpiece. He strolled past the heavily fortified façade of the Bargello town hall, the beautiful church of Santa Croce with its incomparable Baroncelli Chapel frescoes by Giotto and Taddeo Gaddi, and the Dominican church of Santa Maria Novella, its cemetery wall lined with *avelli* grave niches.

Karl Eugen had spent time in Rome and Venice and had concluded that, though both were remarkable, neither rivalled Florence, the flower of Tuscany. Conscious of its destiny and proud of its heritage, it embodied the spirit of the age, both culturally and politically. It had a glorious past and was on the brink of an even more glorious future. It was a city after his own heart, a city of art and commerce, of opportunity and intrigue, a city he would be proud to serve.

As he approached the Ponte Vecchio, Karl Eugen heard the clamour – and breathed in the familiar stench – of the butchers' stalls, tanners' vats and blacksmiths' forges that lined the bridge and cantilevered out over the Arno on *sporti* brackets fashioned from stout timber.

The Palazzo Boninsegna stood on the west side of a piazza no more than fifty paces from the bridge. It was an imposing brick and marble structure topped by fishtail battlements. As he waited to be admitted, Karl Eugen reflected that Giancarlo Boninsegna must be a very wealthy man indeed, bearing in mind he did not belong to the Florentine aristocracy but was merely a *consigliere* to that city state. Karl Eugen was heartened by this fact. As he had come to know, there were fortunes to be made as an adviser.

Boninsegna received his visitor in the *cortile*, the cool inner courtyard typical of Italian palazzos. He was courteous but came quickly to the point.

'Your services come well recommended.' Boninsegna did not specify from which quarter the recommendation had come.

Karl Eugen said nothing.

'Well recommended and, as I understand, at some cost,' continued Boninsegna.

'As come most services of value,' replied Karl Eugen.

Boninsegna looked the young man over. Handsome, certainly, in the Teutonic mould: tall, with a full head of blond hair and an air of self-confidence that belied – or attested to – his youth. Boninsegna had some difficulty in reconciling the image with what little he knew of him. Could this conceivably be the same Strachwitz who had served so effectively as an informer on behalf of the Doges of Venice? Who had negotiated a truce with the German and Hungarian mercenaries who had threatened to sack Milan only eighteen months previously?

Karl Eugen waited.

'The cost of your services is not at issue here. You will be paid as agreed,' said Boninsegna.

A nod from Strachwitz.

'What *is* at issue is whether you can provide the service we require. It is a matter of some delicacy and one that is not without danger to your person.'

'Of that I am aware,' said Karl Eugen.

Boninsegna was uncertain whether to be impressed by the young man's calm acceptance of the dangers involved or irritated by his ill-concealed arrogance. He pursed his lips and continued.

'We have knowledge of one John Hawkwood, who is in the pay of Pisa. Our sources report that he is at present in France, at the head of a force of over three thousand men.'

'You wish me to confirm this?' asked Strachwitz.

'There is no need,' said Boninsegna impatiently. 'We are fully apprised of his whereabouts and the numbers at his disposal. What we expect of you is this: to attach yourself to his Company and find favour with him, then report back to me concerning his disposition and intentions. How well is he equipped? How is he regarded by his men? How loyal are they? Can Hawkwood himself be bought?'

Karl Eugen nodded again. 'I understand. And where is he now?'

'Our last reports say somewhere east of Bordeaux.'

'And his planned route to Pisa?'

'That is not certain. He may take care to avoid Bordeaux itself. It is a city in English hands and, as the renegade we believe him to be, he will not wish to fall foul of the English garrison there. He will strike inland across country, towards Arles or Nîmes, and from there eastwards along the coast.'

'Is it your intention to oppose him by force?'

Boninsegna raised a cautionary finger. 'Our intentions remain to be decided. What is vital is that you do what we ask. And with all speed.'

'There is little time,' ventured Strachwitz, betraying the first sign of hesitation and uncertainty.

'That is true,' said Boninsegna. 'But there is surely time enough for a man of your qualities and resolve.'

Karl Eugen realised he could do only one of two things: accept the mission or decline it. To do the latter was unthinkable, for his reputation was at stake and, with it, his future. Besides, he had always responded to a challenge.

'It shall be as you command,' he said.

Boninsegna extended a hand. 'I wish you success, Herr von Strachwitz.'

There was nothing more to be said. Karl Eugen left the palazzo and made his way back across the river to Oltrarno, conscious he was about to play for the highest stakes of all – his own life – yet comforted by the thought that the financial rewards and the possibilities for advancement would be beyond his every expectation.

Milan, 14 March 1361

Donnina Visconti was not privy to the negotiations that preceded her betrothal. She knew little of them and cared even less.

It was to be a *matrimonium ad morganaticum* between two noble houses; a morganatic marriage between herself, a daughter of Bernabò Visconti, Duke of Milan, and the half-brother of the Duke of Florence, the key provision of which was that their offspring would be precluded from acceding to their father's hereditary rank or property. In essence, then, a 'left-handed' marriage, a marriage of convenience to serve a strategic purpose: namely, forging a tenuous link between Milan and Florence, two great city states with a history of mutual antagonism.

Had Donnina taken a closer interest in the negotiations, she would have been aware that the conditions attaching to the marriage implied that she was of lesser rank than her husband-to-be. What had never been publicly disclosed – not even to Donnina herself – was that she was illegitimate, the product of a liaison between her father and a willing lady of the court.

She was undaunted by the prospect of being given in marriage to a man almost three times her age. After the nuptials and a night of doubtless peremptory consummation, she would in all probability return to live in Milan and her new husband would remain in Florence. When all was said and done, this was a marriage of convenience, the *most* convenient aspect being that, once married, she could enjoy certain discreet freedoms which had recently been largely denied her.

Besides, she loved her father; and his word was law.

**Near Bergerac, east of Bordeaux,
27 March 1361**

Hawkwood's company had bivouacked for several days outside Angoulême before striking camp and moving south-east.

That the forced march from Calais to Angoulême had been without major incident was as Hawkwood had expected. He knew the French must already have word of his ultimate destination and he was aware that his progress was being closely monitored. But he knew also that the French had insufficient forces in the region to check his advance and, in practice, no good reason to try to do so. His force posed no immediate threat to them or to the countryside through which he passed.

To Altobardi's surprise, Hawkwood's men now behaved impeccably. On the captain-general's orders, there had been no looting apart from a few isolated instances. The perpetrators had been caught and summarily punished. Even more surprising was Hawkwood's insistence that his men be provisioned against full payment to the towns and villages through which they marched.

'Our quarrel is no longer with the French,' explained Hawkwood, 'nor theirs with us. And do not forget, Gennaro, we may well travel this way again.'

The captain-general had rested his men near Angoulême in preparation for the push south. They were already close to the territories of the Limousin and Périgord ceded in 1259 to Henry III of England under the terms of the Treaty of Paris. They were also deep into lands which had surrendered *de facto* to Edward III and whose formal cession to England was currently the subject of treaty negotiations in Brétigny, near Chartres. From La Rochelle in the north to Bayonne in the south, virtually the whole of south-western France was English in all but name.

Hawkwood had considered giving Bordeaux the widest possible berth but had decided otherwise. It seemed unlikely that the garrison in Bordeaux would have reason to venture out against him. Like the French, they understood that his Free Company posed no threat. What was more, he was an Englishman – and an Englishman at the head of a modest but battle-hardened English force. Granted, there was a degree of risk in passing so close to Bordeaux, but that risk was more than offset by the directness of the route he had determined to follow: south through Bergerac towards Agen, then sharply east, along first the Garonne then the Tarn rivers, before striking south-east again towards Arles.

For the first five days out of Angoulême, it appeared that his decision was justified: there was no sign of the Bordeaux garrison. On the morning of the sixth day, however, his outriders returned with reports of a large force on the other side of the hill to the west.

Hawkwood was in two minds. He could continue on his way and try to outrun this new enemy, at the risk of being harried at every turn. Or he could make a stand and face them. He elected to do the latter.

He chose his ground well: a narrow draw flanked by steep inclines on both sides, which would afford his bowmen both protection and a clear field of fire. The opposing force would be able to enter the *défilé* no more than twenty or twenty-five abreast and the soft ground of the valley floor would oblige their cavalry to dismount and advance on foot.

Altobardi interrogated him as to his intentions and Hawkwood patiently explained that he wished to avoid a confrontation but would not shirk one. The Company was a fighting force. This would prove a test of its prowess. It was time for it to be blooded.

The archers took up position on the steep slopes and the ranks of pikemen massed in the valley below, with the cavalry behind them. The pikemen were under orders to check the opponents' advance and inflict as much damage as possible before, at a pre-arranged signal, they suddenly broke ranks and dispersed to the adjoining slopes, creating a gap through which Hawkwood would lead his cavalry in a final, victorious charge.

When the first riders appeared on the crest of the small hill to the west overlooking the valley, they approached only at a leisurely pace. One after another, they dipped slowly from view as they descended the slope. Behind them came large numbers of footsoldiers who followed suit, jostling each other as the valley narrowed. Hawkwood could discern no pattern, no clear plan of battle. Still more footsoldiers followed, squeezing into the bottle-neck below.

Hawkwood gave a sign to Llewellyn on the right flank and Griffiths on the left. Both longbowmen signalled that their men were ready.

The advancing column halted. Four riders detached themselves and rode forward sedately. Hawkwood frowned. His own battle lines were drawn and he had not expected a *pourparler*. He urged his mount to the front, gesturing to three of his knights to accompany him. The pikemen parted to let them through, and they made their way slowly towards the four riders, who had reined in no more than fifty paces from the Company's front ranks.

At a distance of ten paces, one of the riders drew his sword and held it upright before his face. The other three did likewise.

'Be you Sir John de Hawkwood of the Free Company of Essex?' asked the lead horseman.

'I am he,' answered Hawkwood.

'Then let it be known that we are freemen of England come to join a Free Company.'

Hawkwood glanced beyond the four men. Close behind them, the 'enemy' had come to a standstill. Hawkwood saw the expectancy on their faces.

'How are you in number?' said Hawkwood.

'By my count, seventeen hundred, of whom six hundred are skilled Welsh archers.'

Hawkwood nodded. 'Be advised I have twice that number on the slopes above, awaiting only my command.'

The horseman looked slowly up to his right, then to his left. He laughed. 'Then God forbid, sir, that you should so command.'

With that, he sheathed his sword, opened his visor, dismounted and walked towards Hawkwood, extending an arm in greeting. 'I am Sir Wilfred Perry of Winchester. I have the honour to place these men and their arms at your disposal and under your command.'

Arles, 3 April 1361

Karl Eugen von Strachwitz had often heard travellers sing the praises of the Camargue, but he found little there to his taste, save the distant sight of wild horses or the occasional glimpse of a savage bull grazing defiantly on the salt marshes.

The city of Arles was another matter entirely. Karl Eugen spent a full day walking the streets of this ancient and beautiful city – once regarded as the 'Piccola Roma' of the Western Roman Empire. He revelled in the vestiges of its Gallo-Roman past – the mosaics in the thermal baths of the Emperor Constantine, the imposing columns of the antique theatre, the carvings on the eleventh-century façade of the church of St Trophime, and the magnificently intact first-century BC *arènes*, a twenty-thousand-seat arena and amphitheatre reputed to have been at one time the largest Roman building in Gaul.

He walked the streets of Arles in unstinting admiration, but also with a purpose.

Arles had been an important Mediterranean port for close on fifteen hundred years and it was still an important gateway to the Rhône delta and beyond. And where there was a port, Karl Eugen knew, there would be sailors, vagrants and down-and-outs eager to do anything, however dangerous, in exchange for monetary reward.

He found what he was looking for on the morning of his second day in Arles. The man was in his late thirties, a beetle-browed, broad-shouldered hulk in soiled clothing, whose breath reeked of cheap wine and garlic. He looked up menacingly as Karl Eugen approached, taking in the elegant attire that looked so out of place on the Arles quayside, then remarking the German's physique and confident swagger. This, he concluded, was not a man to be trifled with.

The discussion was brief. A modest sum changed hands and it was agreed they should meet again late that evening, this time at the tomb of Genesius in the Alyscamps, the sprawling sarcophagi-lined cemetery that had once served as a clandestine meeting-place for the early Christians under St Trophime. Karl

Eugen smiled at the thought that the Romans had avoided the cemetery, afraid not of the dark but of the vapours of the night to which they superstitiously attributed all manner of disease; he harboured no such fears. His new acquaintance would be punctual, he was certain, and would bring three other able-bodied men with him, as instructed. They had everything to gain and little to lose.

Florence, 5 April 1361

Giancarlo Boninsegna was uneasy. Although he had no reason to believe that von Strachwitz would fail to worm his way into Hawkwood's confidence, he had every reason to believe this was asking a lot of the young German. Too much, perhaps; especially since Boninsegna had received intelligence from other sources which confirmed that the Englishman had made swift and unimpeded progress through France and that somehow – Boninsegna's informants were unable to establish precisely how – Hawkwood was now at the head of a mercenary force numbering five thousand or perhaps even more. Given his progress to date, it would be only a matter of weeks before he reached Pisa.

Boninsegna confided his fears to the Duke of Florence and urged him to act. 'My lord, we must move on Pisa before Hawkwood can marshal a coherent defence,' he said. 'In a word, we must act *now*. We must march on Pisa before Hawkwood and his mercenaries arrive.'

The duke paced the room, anxious not to be coerced into a decision he would later regret. There were too many imponderables. Did Florence have the military assets to mount a full-scale attack in such a short time? Could he be certain – *absolutely* certain – that Pisa could be taken quickly? When this Englishman finally arrived, would he be capable of mounting a resolute defence? Or, if he arrived too late to defend Pisa, would he have the resources – and, above all, the will – to counter-attack and regain the city?

'There are many issues here,' said the duke eventually.

'There are indeed,' agreed Boninsegna, 'but one issue stands above all others. Can we take Pisa once Hawkwood and his troops have arrived? That is possible, I concede. But is it not more opportune to strike before his arrival? If Hawkwood should discover his paymasters are dead or languishing in our prisons, would he continue to act in their interests?'

'Those are questions,' said the duke, clearly irritated. 'My concern is to find answers.'

'Measures are in place to ascertain Hawkwood's intentions,' ventured Boninsegna.

'Measures? *Measures?*' bellowed the duke. 'What good are *measures?*'

Boninsegna flinched. The duke glared at him.

It was time to equivocate, thought the *consigliere*. 'We cannot be certain—' he began, but the duke cut him short:

'I do not ask for certainty, I ask for a considered opinion.'

Boninsegna gulped a deep breath into his lungs. 'Then my considered opinion is this. We should proceed at once to assemble a force capable of marching on and capturing Pisa. Their defences are weak – why else would they have retained this *condottiere?*'

Why else indeed? thought the duke. 'Very well. It shall be so ordered.'

'And Hawkwood?' queried Boninsegna.

'Hawkwood is still an unknown factor, I grant you,' replied the duke. 'But we can make it clear to him that his longer-term interests lie with Florence. He can be bought – men of his kind can *always* be bought. He is a mercenary, a man without principle, a man without honour even in his own country.'

That, thought Giancarlo Boninsegna, remains to be seen.

Arles, 11 April 1361

'I say again, let me go in your place,' urged Sir Wilfred Perry for the third time in as many minutes. And, for the third time in as many minutes, Hawkwood would have none of it.

The Free Company was encamped on the banks of the Rhône little more than a mile north of Arles. Latrines had been dug, fires had been set, lookouts posted. In all, there were now over five thousand in the camp: Hawkwood's Company proper, their ranks bolstered by Perry's volunteers, together with several hundred camp followers – masons, wheelwrights, farriers, whores and assorted hangers-on. There were many mouths to feed and provisions were running low.

As he had done several times since leaving Calais, Hawkwood had announced his intention to approach the nearest town and negotiate with its burgomaster or municipal council, declaring his peaceful resolve and offering full and prompt settlement in return for victuals and other supplies. He saw no reason to depart from this procedure here in Arles and he was puzzled by the sudden concern expressed by both Perry and Altobardi.

'It shall be as I have ordered,' he said. 'I shall travel lightly armed and in the company only of a squire. It is vital that our peaceful purpose be made evident to the citizens of Arles, that they understand we mean them no ill.'

'You risk—' began Altobardi.

'I risk nothing,' interrupted Hawkwood. 'I shall come to no harm. I have near five thousand men under my command but a stone's throw from their city walls. Should I fail to return by nightfall, the Arlésiens will know only too well what to expect at dawn tomorrow. Enough of this. I ride at noon.'

He was received in Arles by members of the city council, who were nervous and hesitant at first but, as he had predicted, soon reassured by his conciliatory approach. They were quick to appreciate the benefits that would accrue overnight to the town's tradesmen and merchants. In less than two hours, Hawkwood had secured undertakings that food for his men would be forthcoming, together with fodder for his animals. He also purchased a large quantity of plain white twill. His purchases would be delivered by ox-cart to the encampment later that day.

Terms of payment were agreed and met, hands were shaken, and parting pleasantries were exchanged. By late afternoon, Hawkwood and his squire had emerged once more into the afternoon sunlight of Provence.

'The day went well, young Bertrand,' said Hawkwood, clapping his squire on the shoulder. 'We shall feast this night.'

The three men came out of nowhere.

Two wielded cudgels, the third menaced with a dagger. They circled Hawkwood and his squire. Their intent was evident.

Common thieves, thought Hawkwood. 'Stand aside,' he roared, drawing his short sword.

The three men fell back, suddenly unsure of themselves. Perhaps they had not expected to come face to face with a giant such as this.

Hawkwood heard a muffled sound behind him and whirled about to confront a fourth adversary. Too late: the man swung a double-headed axe which landed high on Bertrand's shoulder, crunching through his collarbone and cleaving his upper torso virtually in half. The young man uttered no sound as he slumped forward onto the cobblestones.

A cudgel swung at Hawkwood's head. He stepped back a pace to take stock of the situation. To his left, the axeman had wrenched his weapon free of Bertrand's body. He turned to face Hawkwood, rotting teeth bared in a contorted grin.

Hawkwood wore no armour and he knew his sword was no match for an axe. There was little he could do other than wave his sword in short, sweeping arcs in a bid to keep the quartet at bay. The odds were very much against him and his only hope lay in reducing those odds. He backed slowly against the stone wall behind him, swinging his sword this way and that. The four men pressed home their advantage. They moved in, tentatively at first, then with growing confidence.

Hawkwood waited until they had closed in a half-circle round him, then leapt suddenly to his right and lunged forward. The move was totally unexpected. The man on the far right looked down in astonishment as Hawkwood's sword pierced his belly and was withdrawn in a single motion. He screamed in pain, dropped his cudgel and clasped his abdomen. Rich, dark blood oozed through his fingers as he slid to the ground.

A shower of sparks flew off the stone wall as the axe slammed into it only a hand's breadth away from Hawkwood's head. The axeman quickly regained his balance and came on again. The other two hesitated, but the axeman urged them forward. The axe scythed through the air once more, mercifully well off target. But Hawkwood sensed the axeman had the distance now. The next clumsy blow might prove fatal. He could not repeat his earlier manoeuvre: the element of surprise had been lost. What the trio least expected, however, was that he would single out the axeman, the most dangerous of his assailants, as his next target.

He gauged the distance between them, preparing to step well inside the next blow and absorb its force before delivering a counter-thrust. The axeman divined Hawkwood's intentions. His eyes beaded and he stepped warily back a fraction.

Without warning, the axe clattered to the ground. The axeman's eyes glazed as he looked down at the point of a sword that had entered his lower back and protruded below his sternum. He stood there, literally transfixed. The sword was sharply withdrawn and he fell to his knees. A thin trickle of blood formed round his mouth and dribbled into his thick beard. Hawkwood did not hesitate. He took a quick pace forward and slashed his sword across the man's exposed neck. The man's mouth gaped as if in protest. The stench of cheap wine and garlic was palpable.

The other two thieves turned and ran.

Hawkwood looked at the tall, fair-haired young man who was nonchalantly wiping his sword-blade on the coarse tunic of the axeman. The man looked across at Hawkwood and grinned, revealing a row of dazzling white teeth.

'Welcome to Arles,' said Hawkwood's deliverer. 'Allow me to present myself – Karl Eugen August Wilhelm von Strachwitz-Wettin. *Zu Euren Diensten*. I am delighted to have been of some service.'

Everything had gone more or less according to plan, thought Karl Eugen. Well, perhaps not quite everything, but near enough. He had not foreseen the unfortunate death of Hawkwood's squire but, all things considered, that had probably added an extra touch of authenticity to the proceedings. The pair who had escaped would count themselves fortunate, for their reward would now be shared two ways rather than four. As for despatching the axeman, that had been the plan all along.

Karl Eugen detested the stench of stale garlic.

VII

Pisa

Swear and give your hand never to attack this land

East of Carrara, 26 May 1361

They were deep into northern Italy, encamped by the Carrione river in the foothills of the Alpi Apuane. For Hawkwood and the vast majority of his force this was unknown territory, and he found himself relying increasingly on the counsel of young Gennaro Altobardi, at whose insistence the Company had marched inland from the Ligurian coast, giving Genoa and the Genoese a wide berth before striking out to the south towards La Spezia. Pisa was now only some forty miles distant, and Florence lay less than a three-day march to the east.

They had encountered no resistance up to this point, and Altobardi assured Hawkwood there would be none from Carrara: 'The Carraresi present no threat except to themselves. They live in constant fear of Milan and Venice. And of each other.'

'That is so,' said Strachwitz. 'I have heard it said they are a family of cutthroats and murderers.'

'Their reputation is well deserved,' said Altobardi. 'Marsigliello Carrarese was murdered by Jacopo di Niccolò, then Jacopo was murdered by Guglielmino, and *his* successor, Jacopino, was removed by Francesco il Vecchio—'

'Enough,' broke in Hawkwood, a broad grin on his face. 'Is there no end to this tale of treachery?'

Altobardi shrugged. 'This is Italy, not France or England. Italy is not a nation. It has no national sovereign, no sense of nationhood. We Italians are united only in mutual antagonisms and in the will of each city state to assert and protect its independence.'

'But you all answer to the Pope, do you not?' asked Perry.

'In some matters, yes, but not in all. Besides, there is one Pope in Rome and another in Avignon.'

Altobardì was on dangerous ground and he knew it. Openly questioning papal authority – however divided that authority might currently be – was imprudent at best.

He changed tack. 'You must understand how the city states are governed,' he said. 'Many are ruled by one man or by one family. The *signori* have absolute authority and they wield that authority to consolidate and extend their power. There are many examples of this: the della Scala family in Verona, the Gonzaga in Mantua, the Visconti in Milan. And, only a few miles from here, the Carraresi. They all stand above the law. They *are* the law.'

'And what of Pisa?' asked Hawkwood.

'Pisa is a republic,' answered Altobardì, 'like Venice, Siena, Lucca. Like Florence, even, although I am loth to admit as much. Pisa is ruled by consensus, by an elected merchant guild, not by a despot or a *podestà*.' He hesitated, realising he had spoken out of turn and hoping that Hawkwood and the others would not ask the inevitable question.

'*Podestà*?' said Hawkwood. 'Explain, if you will.'

Altobardì felt the colour rise to his cheeks.

'A *podestà*, Sir John, is a person – an outsider – retained by a city state to ensure order. A captain of the people, if you will.'

'A *condottiere*, then?'

'Not exactly.'

'In what way "not exactly"?'

'A-a *condottiere* leads an army hired by a city state to . . . to ensure its protection,' stammered Altobardì.

'A man such as myself?'

'Yes, Sir John, such as yourself.'

'But I am not a *podestà*?'

'No.'

'And why not, pray?'

'A *podestà* is political.'

'Whereas I and those I lead in the service of Pisa are not?'

'You are appointed for political reasons, certainly, but you are not a member of the body politic.'

'In other words, we serve but do not lead?'

'In other words, yes.'

Hawkwood laughed out loud and clapped Altobardi on the shoulder to show no offence had been taken. He turned to Perry. 'Take good heed of young Gennaro's words, Sir Wilfred. We must never forget we are mere hirelings. We may serve, but we may not lead.'

'There is honour in service, Sir John, if the cause is just.'

'Well spoken, Sir Wilfred. Should the cause prove just, we shall indeed serve honourably.'

Hawkwood admired Altobardi's candour and respected him the more for it. He glanced at the young Pisan and then at Karl Eugen von Strachwitz. He liked them both immensely, yet they were very different. Altobardi: tallish but slender, with a natural elegance in and out of the saddle. His shoulder-length dark hair and smooth olive complexion made him appear almost effeminate, yet there was an air of resolve about him, particularly when he spoke of Pisa and his family.

Strachwitz towered above Altobardi, his rugged features, close-cropped blond hair and reddish beard contrasting with Altobardi's delicate features. Strachwitz carried himself with an athlete's grace and was the epitome of strength and virility. His courage, as Hawkwood had every cause to know, was evident. He spoke little, but always to the point.

Hawkwood was barely more than a decade older than these two young men, but he regarded them with a father's pride. One day, perhaps, he might have a son of his own . . .

'Come, let us address the affairs at hand,' said Hawkwood. 'We are at most a day's march from Pisa. It is my wish that we approach that city in the best of order. We shall make permanent camp outside the city walls on the banks of the Arno river and shall immediately build such fortifications as I deem necessary for the defence of the city and for our own comfort and protection.' He looked enquiringly at Perry.

'The men stand in readiness,' said Sir Wilfred. 'They are equipped and clothed as ordered.'

Hawkwood nodded. The white twill purchased in Arles had been fashioned into thigh-length surcoats which identified each member of the Company by rank and function. Diagonal strips of coloured cloth had been attached front and back – green for the longbowmen, blue for the pikemen, black for the footsoldiers and crimson for the cavalry. The surcoats served a dual purpose, both imparting a uniformity and coherence to the Company when arrayed in battle order and also enabling friend to be readily distinguished from foe. At Crécy and Poitiers, many lives had been lost among the Welsh archers, who had been mistaken for the enemy by their English comrades because, in the heat of battle, they had spoken their own language. Hawkwood had vowed that would never happen under his command.

Under the supervision of Llewellyn and Griffiths, the classic longbow had been shortened. A marginal loss of distance and penetration had resulted, but the bow was now easier to handle and gave a better rate of fire. The cavalry saddles had been redesigned to lower the conventional backrest which, in Hawkwood's view, was better suited to providing support in a formal joust than to combat in the open. There was slightly less protection for the rider's back, but this was offset by considerably improved flexibility in the saddle.

On the approach to Pisa, lances and swords had been sharpened and re-pointed. Polished pikestaves glinted in the Tuscan sun. Chain mail had been burnished and oiled. The Company was battle-ready.

It remained only for Hawkwood to ascertain whether any troop movements had been detected from the direction of Florence and to determine that Pisa was prepared to receive him and his men. Gennaro Altobardi was the logical choice to ride ahead to Pisa and inform the city fathers of the Company's imminent arrival. He would report back to Hawkwood the following day.

Karl Eugen von Strachwitz immediately volunteered to travel to Florence, where he would assess Florentine intentions. Hawkwood knew the dangers involved in such a mission, but was secretly proud that his German second-in-command had volunteered with such alacrity.

Karl Eugen insisted on going alone. 'I know the city well,' he said, 'and I have friends there. Have no fear. I shall come to no harm.'

Sible Hedingham, 28 May 1361

Margaret Hawkwood had been in labour since daybreak over seventeen hours ago. She understood little about the process of childbirth, but had been repeatedly assured it was natural and spontaneous. To her mind, there was nothing natural or spontaneous about the intense pain she was experiencing. Not to mention the indignity of it all.

Concern showed on the faces of the three women attending her. Each knew instinctively that something was wrong, but their rudimentary knowledge of midwifery was limited to births that progressed without incident. They could see that the initial phase of labour had been completed and that Margaret was fully dilated, but they were at a loss to explain why the baby had not emerged. They exhorted Margaret to bear down even harder and she did her best to comply.

The sprig of silver birch wedged between her teeth chafed her mouth and gums. Sweat coursed down her back. The pain was unbearable.

At last, the baby's head emerged, followed by a shoulder. The three women exchanged glances. Perhaps it was going to be all right after all.

The oldest of the three was the first to recognise that something was far from all right. Margaret's face and body were rapidly turning blue, and her breathing was sporadic. She was no longer screaming. Her eyes had rolled back in her head and her upper body was strangely still.

The midwife grasped the infant by the head and shoulders and pulled with all her might. The tiny body came free with a rush of blood and birth fluids. The baby was safe.

Margaret Hawkwood's eyes flickered open and something akin to a smile crossed her face. With an effort, she raised her head a few inches from the cushions and whispered something the women did not catch. The oldest leant over her, holding her ear close to Margaret's lips.

'John . . . Antiochus . . . Hawkwood,' muttered Margaret. 'John . . . Antiochus . . . Hawkwood.'

The women looked at each other in bewilderment.

Margaret made a final effort. 'My husband . . . Tell him . . . Tell Sir John . . . John Antiochus Hawkwood . . . His son . . . His first-born.'

She fell back against the cushions, closed her eyes and died.

The youngest woman wrapped the infant in a linen shawl. John Hawkwood's baby daughter was already fast asleep.

Pisa, 8 June 1361

Gennaro Altobardi took immense pride in the city of his birth and in its republican past. He had seldom travelled beyond the city walls and found even the briefest of absences difficult to endure. It was many months since he had left Pisa on his mission to recruit Sir John de Hawkwood, and his pulse quickened as he entered the magnificent sweep of the Campo dei Miracoli and was confronted by the familiar sight of the Torre Pendente.

He had been born and raised within a stone's throw of the Field of Miracles. As boys, he and his friends had watched in wonder as the final bellchamber storey was added to the octagonal Byzantine cylinder of the Leaning Tower. Like everyone else on that day in 1350, they had held their breath as the seven great bells were winched up and suspended from their massive supports, adding the final touches to the white marble tower. It had been commissioned almost two centuries before, in 1173, as a pendant to the imposing Duomo with its intricate array of marble inlays and arabesques.

All Pisa had held its breath that day until the tower bells rang out for the very first time. There were those who predicted the tower would one day collapse, signalling an end to Pisa's glory;

others, less superstitious, questioned the wisdom of the city fathers and the competence of the architects: the latter for failing to make due and proper allowance for the unstable soil on which the tower stood, the former for having permitted work on it to continue beyond the third storey.

None of that had mattered on inauguration day. The thousands gathered on the Campo dei Miracoli had known they were bearing witness to a signal event in Pisa's history.

Today, however, the Campo was almost deserted. Puzzled, Altobardi reined in and dismounted. The pace of life in Pisa was serene by comparison with the bustle of Rome and Florence, but at this time of day – almost noon – the Campo should be busier than this. The few citizens who were out and about seemed to be in curious haste, and their faces betrayed an unusual concern.

Something was seriously wrong.

Altobardi suddenly knew what it must be. He made his way quickly to Tommaso Gracchi's modest palazzo, only to be informed that Gracchi was not available, because an extraordinary meeting of the Council of Guilds had been convened that morning.

Something *was* seriously wrong.

The guildsmen looked up in surprise as Altobardi burst unannounced into the Council Chamber. Gracchi sat at the head of the cedarwood table. He rose at once and came round the table to greet Altobardi.

'Is he here?' asked Gracchi.

'He is here,' replied Altobardi. 'Less than a day's march away.'

The councillors' relief was palpable.

'And is he how they say he is?' continued Gracchi.

'He is all that, and more besides,' replied Gennaro.

Several members of the council crossed themselves.

'What has happened?' asked Gennaro.

'We have learnt that the Florentines are readying to march on Pisa,' said Gracchi.

'When?'

'Within a week at most. They have assembled a force which

our sources report in excess of four thousand men. We need Hawkwood here and we need him now.'

'The captain-general is encamped outside Carrara,' said Gennaro reassuringly. 'He will be in Pisa by the end of the week.'

'That, I fear, may be too late.'

Altobardi looked round the room. His fellow guildsmen looked up at him expectantly. He understood at once what had to be done.

'I shall return this instant and request him to proceed to Pisa without delay.'

'Let it be so,' said Gracchi.

Florence, 9 June 1361

'Let it be so,' said Giancarlo Boninsegna. Karl Eugen von Strachwitz had made his report and Boninsegna was in no doubt what had to be done next. 'Let it be so,' he said again. He waved his hand in dismissal.

General Malatesta inclined his head and swept from the room. He had his orders, and his men were ready. They would move on Pisa immediately.

Boninsegna turned back to Karl Eugen. 'You have acquitted yourself well,' he said.

Karl Eugen nodded. 'I have done what I said I would do, no more, no less.'

Boninsegna paced the room. The information provided by this arrogant young *tedesco* was invaluable. The Company was at most a day's march from Pisa, but Hawkwood now intended to delay his entry for several days. This was excellent news. Pisa had no defences to speak of, no real military resources with which to oppose Florence in the field. If all went to plan, Hawkwood would arrive in Pisa to find the city had fallen and his would-be paymasters captured and executed. It remained to be seen how he would react.

Strachwitz had provided exhaustive details of Hawkwood's force and its present composition and deployment. He had said little, however, about its leader.

'Tell me about this Hawkwood,' said Boninsegna.

Karl Eugen hesitated. He had expected the question but was uncertain how to respond. Eventually he said, 'He is a man of great physical strength, a handsome man, I venture to say, although not of refined taste and habits. A soldier first and foremost, fair yet uncompromising, a disciplinarian but not without wit. In all, a good man and an honest one.'

'And what of his men?'

'They come from every corner of England and Wales. There are some Germans among them and a sprinkling of Magyars and Catalans. They are a diverse crew but no rabble. They respond to Hawkwood. They respect and like him. They serve with him for booty and fortune, but they serve with him gladly.'

Boninsegna rubbed his aquiline nose between thumb and forefinger. To his mind, Strachwitz was exhibiting all the characteristics of a loyal follower rather than those of a paid informer. 'And what of you?'

'Myself?'

'Yes. Would you yourself follow him?'

Karl Eugen hesitated again. He sensed what this scheming Florentine had in mind and knew he must choose his next words with care. 'Hawkwood is a man who can be trusted.'

'Yet, unlike yourself, Herr von Strachwitz, a man who cannot be bought?'

This was the opening Karl Eugen had hoped for. 'I beg to differ. Hawkwood has been bought – by Pisa.'

'You avoid my question.'

'On the contrary, I have answered it.'

'But not entirely. I repeat: would you yourself follow him?'

'Yes.'

'And will you?'

'I cannot, for I have already betrayed him. To you.'

Boninsegna held the young man's gaze for a moment, then turned away. 'That is true, and he will not thank you for it.'

No, thought Karl Eugen, he will not. In that moment, he realised what he had done and how guilty he felt on account of it. Hawkwood had been deceived into accepting him at face value and had responded with unstinting generosity and the hand of friendship. He resolved that on his return to Carrara he would confess to Hawkwood what had transpired between himself and Boninsegna. Honesty – a precept Karl Eugen had found inconvenient all his life – would be the best and only policy. He would confess, and Hawkwood would understand and, perhaps, forgive.

Boninsegna's eyes bored once again into his. 'You are aware, are you not, Herr von Strachwitz, that we have assembled a force to strike at Pisa?'

Karl Eugen nodded. He had observed the preparations that had been made and had been present when Malatesta was briefed. Now he understood why he had been thus privileged.

'Then you must also be aware that I cannot permit you to reveal this to Hawkwood?'

Scheisse, thought Karl Eugen. 'Do you imply that I would break your confidence?' he asked.

Boninsegna laughed. 'You are a man of numerous talents, Herr von Strachwitz, but I do not count loyalty among them. You will forgive my lack of faith in you, but I fear that lack of faith may be more than justified. I have already given instructions. You are to remain here in Florence until Pisa falls. You shall be our guest and will be accorded all the privileges that implies. When Pisa is taken, it may well be that Florence can avail itself of your services once again. Until then, you will remain here, as I said, as a guest of the city of Florence.'

Bastard, thought Karl Eugen. But he knew it was pointless to protest. 'I am grateful for your hospitality,' he replied, confident that he would be able to seize the first opportunity to escape.

'I regret to say that, should you elect to abuse that hospitality, the consequences for your person will be, shall we say, severe?'

'I understand.'

'I am certain you do,' answered Boninsegna with an unctuous smile. He stamped his foot twice on the wooden floor and the door immediately opened to admit four armed guards.

'Escort Herr von Strachwitz to his quarters,' instructed Boninsegna, 'and make certain he is well provided for.'

The guards formed up round Karl Eugen and he was firmly but politely marched from the room.

'*Auf Wiedersehen,*' said Boninsegna as the door closed behind him.

Auf Wiedersehen, my arse, thought Karl Eugen von Strachwitz. I swear by all that's holy, you have seen the last of me.

Carrara, 9 June 1361

Gennaro Altobardi and his three companions had ridden through the night. They arrived at Hawkwood's camp shortly after dawn. Hawkwood's pleasure at seeing Altobardi again was plain, but his look became puzzled as he took in the Italian's lathered horse and drawn face.

'Pisa is under attack, Sir John,' croaked Altobardi.

Hawkwood poured fresh spring water into a wooden goblet and handed it to the Italian. 'Drink this and compose yourself,' he said curtly.

Altobardi drank the water down in a single gulp.

'Now tell me what has happened,' ordered Hawkwood.

'The Florentines have readied an attack on Pisa. They are only days – perhaps even hours – from the gates of the city,' stammered Altobardi.

'Days?' queried Hawkwood. 'Or hours? Which is it, man, hours or days?'

Altobardi slumped onto a bench, drew a deep breath and replied more calmly. 'They are poised to leave Florence. My informants say they will be within striking distance of Pisa at most four days from now.'

'That's better,' said Hawkwood. 'And what of their number?'

'It is estimated at four thousand, perhaps even more – at all events, large enough to sack Pisa and murder all those in it.'

Hawkwood turned to Perry. 'Ready the Company, Sir Wilfred. We march within the hour.'

Thank God, thought Altobardi. He smiled weakly at

Hawkwood. '*Deo volente*, we shall arrive in time, Sir John. Pisa is but a day's march away.'

'That is true, Gennaro, but we do not march on Pisa.'

'But . . .'

'No. We march on Florence.'

Pisa, 12 June 1361

The city gates had been closed since noon the previous day and Pisa's poorly equipped City Guard had been thinly deployed along the wooden battlements in the vain hope of repelling the advancing horde.

Beacons had been lit and the Torre Pendente's bells pealed erratically, signalling the approach of danger. The forward lookouts strained their eyes against the morning sun as rank after rank of the hated Florentines approached slowly but inexorably. The tally varied from one lookout to the next, but there was a degree of consensus: upwards of eight hundred cavalry on the horizon, with as many as two thousand footsoldiers, four hundred pikemen and at least as many crossbowmen. The best Pisa could hope for was to hold out until Hawkwood arrived.

With this in mind, Gracchi had urged every able-bodied man in the city to take to the walls to bolster the defences. The Pisans had grasped the seriousness of the situation and had responded in considerable numbers. True, many were armed only with pitchforks and like implements, but their presence on the walls might – Gracchi hoped – give the Florentines pause.

Where is that *bastardo* Hawkwood? thought Gracchi. Where is he? And where is Gennaro Altobardi? Those cowardly whoresons should be here by now. Had Gennaro failed to reach Hawkwood? Or had Hawkwood sold them out? Had this so-called *condottiere* failed him and failed Pisa?

'There is still time,' Gracchi explained to the guildsmen clustered beside him on the north wall, anxiously scanning the flat countryside for Hawkwood's arrival.

'Time, you say?' shouted Massimo Mastrodonato, the eighty-year-old who had been so vociferous in his opposition to

Hawkwood's appointment. 'How mean you, sir? There is no time. The Florentine pigs are here and we have been left powerless to defend ourselves. Where is your accursed *condottiere* now, I ask you? Tell me that, if you will.'

Gracchi rounded on him – it was almost as if the old fart was enjoying this. 'There is time, I tell you,' said Gracchi. 'There are formalities to be observed. The Florentines will make camp today and send an advance party to parley. They will invite us to surrender under threat of attack tomorrow. We shall ask for time to consider our position. We must hold out until Hawkwood and his force arrive.'

Mastrodonato snorted his derision. 'Then we can wait until hell freezes over,' he said. 'We are lost. Pisa is lost.'

Gracchi turned away in disgust but, deep down, he understood the old man's pessimism. Altobardi had assured them Hawkwood and his men were only a day's march away. That solemn assurance had been given on 8 June. Four days ago.

Hawkwood had failed them.

VIII

Florentia

He must dwell in prison, locked away

Florence, 13 June 1361

Giancarlo Boninsegna was a creature of habit. He rose each day exactly one hour after dawn and sipped a glass of boiling water laced with lime, a potion his personal physician had assured him was a simple yet highly effective laxative. By mid-morning he had already spent a full three hours at his desk, sifting credit applications, approving, rejecting, annotating and initialising contracts, appending conditions, stipulating rates of interest, drawing up repayment schedules and specifying late-payment penalties.

By the time the late-morning sun started to filter through the ogival window behind him, Boninsegna was ready for a *prima colazione* – a late breakfast, as it were. He ate sparingly: green olives macerated in balsamic vinegar, a chunk of coarse rye bread, a plump tomato and a portion of wafer-thin air-cured ham, the whole washed down with a goblet of full-bodied red wine. He then slept for two full hours before settling down to receive visits from colleagues and clients or attending to his many civic duties.

Boninsegna brooked no departure from this daily schedule, no disruption to a rhythm which he had developed over the years and which he found both comfortable and comforting. Today was no exception. He worked steadily and methodically, unconcerned by the fact that a few days previously he had committed Florence to waging war on Pisa. The wheels had been set in motion, ducal authorisation had been secured and delegated as appropriate, and the matter would soon be settled without further direct involvement on his part.

Salvatore Balducci had been in Boninsegna's service for over twenty years. He knew and respected his master's routine and had never had cause to deviate from it. As a result, Boninsegna was genuinely startled when Balducci entered the chamber in a rush and without knocking.

Boninsegna glared at him. Balducci was too early. Worse, he had come empty-handed: no green olives, no wine, no bread.

'They . . . they are at the city gates,' stuttered Balducci. 'At the gates. Thousands of them.'

Boninsegna stood up and came out from behind his desk. 'Compose yourself, Salvatore, and explain. Who is here? Who is at the gates?'

'An army,' said Balducci, 'a whole army. An army all in white.'

Boninsegna could make no sense of this. He pushed past Balducci and left the chamber.

Balducci followed, gesticulating wildly. 'They are at the north-east wall,' he said. 'There – outside the north-east wall.'

Boninsegna bounded down the marble staircase and wrenched open the brass-studded door that opened on the piazza.

Florence was in uproar, its citizens scurrying this way and that. Bells pealed, dogs yapped, and wide-eyed mothers herded frightened children. Market vendors had taken to their heels, leaving their precious stalls unattended. A vegetable cart had overturned, sending melons, aubergines and pumpkins careering across the cobbles. The horse, thrown down by the weight of the cart and pinioned by the rigid wooden shafts, lay on its back, legs threshing the air, eyes glinting white with fear.

The noonday sun reflected from the helmets and breastplates of a handful of guards rushing wildly to and fro on the north-east wall. Boninsegna ran to the base of the wall and scrambled up the stone steps to the wooden boardwalk. He found the battlements virtually deserted. Discarded weapons littered the area. A sergeant-at-arms screamed shrill commands which went unheeded by the sprinkling of guards remaining on the wall.

Boninsegna grasped the edge of the parapet and peered out over it. His throat constricted as he took in the sight below.

Deployed on the north bank of the Arno was an army several thousand strong, stretching almost as far as the eye could see. An army in white, just as Balducci had said.

Hawkwood.

It was only with great difficulty that Boninsegna was able to regain his composure and take stock. To the left, close by the river bank, he made out white surcoats embellished with diagonal strips of black cloth. Footsoldiers. In the centre, the surcoats boasted green stripes. Longbowmen. On the right were deployed pikemen, the white of their surcoats broken by a deep blue band. In the centre, behind the longbowmen, he saw mounted cavalry, several hundred at least, in white and crimson. And on a rise behind the cavalry Boninsegna saw what he feared most: siege engines.

Two siege towers on massive wooden wheels had appeared some five hundred paces from the city wall. Between them stood a *bélier*, a battering-ram fashioned from a stout tree trunk tipped with iron, suspended from chains and protected by a wooden housing sheathed in animal skins. To the right were two small trebuchets, catapult-like devices capable of launching large rocks and infected animal carcasses at and over the walls of the city. In the distance, behind the cavalry and safely out of crossbow range, Boninsegna saw the A-frame, counterweight and sling of another trebuchet, at least three times as large as the other two.

Boninsegna was a man of politics, unversed in military matters. He was astounded at the appearance overnight of these huge and complex weapons. How could they have been constructed so quickly? Hawkwood must have transported them in sections, and ordered them reassembled under cover of darkness.

He croaked an order to Balducci. 'Convene the Balia. Assemble the Emergency Council. Here – now.'

Balducci nodded and disappeared down the stone steps two at a time.

The ranks of the longbowmen parted, and a small group of mounted men advanced slowly towards the walls. The lead horseman sat tall in the saddle. He wore no helmet and next to no armour; as he rode nearer, Boninsegna could make out his coarse beard and thick black hair. Immediately behind and to the right of him came four riders trailing between them a large square of white cloth. The four fanned out, releasing their respective corners of the cloth and laying it flat on the ground a hundred paces or so from the city wall. They reined their mounts to the left and took up position flanking the lead horseman. The group halted within hailing distance of the north-east wall and two figures rode forward several paces.

'I speak for Captain-General Sir John de Hawkwood and his Company,' called Gennaro Altobardi, 'who present their compliments to the city of Florence and to its worthy citizens.'

Several members of the council – at last – came rushing up the steps to join Boninsegna on the boardwalk. He waited until they had taken up positions left and right of him before replying.

'The city fathers of Florence welcome Captain-General de Hawkwood and his Company, and seek to know his intentions.'

'Those intentions are honourable,' said Altobardi. 'The captain-general wishes to serve due notice on Florence and its citizens that this fair city is to be razed to the ground.'

'By what authority?' asked Boninsegna.

'By the authority vested in the captain-general by the city state and Council of Guilds of Pisa, whose cause he is sworn to uphold.'

'The city state of Florence will not yield to threats from a foreign *condottiere*.'

'Nor will the city state of Pisa yield to the aggression of Florence,' came the reply.

A stalemate had been reached and Boninsegna knew it. Florence was virtually defenceless, certainly when faced with an armed force in such numbers. He must stall for time to negotiate.

'Does it please the captain-general to discuss terms?' he called.

The bearded figure next to Altobardi raised his sword high above his head and rotated the blade in the sunlight. Instantly there was movement in the ranks behind him as the longbowmen primed their weapons. The sword dipped and a hail of arrows darkened the sky. Boninsegna flinched as the barbed shafts reached their apogee and arched earthwards, thudding into the square of white cloth.

'Those are our terms,' shouted Altobardi.

Boninsegna turned to his companions. They looked at him in dismay, but offered no comment.

'Then hear this,' shouted Boninsegna. 'The armies of Florence are at the gates of Pisa and await only orders to sack that city. I and only I can countermand those orders. Is it thus you would best serve the interests of your paymasters?'

Again the sword was raised and rotated. Again the longbowmen stooped as one man, notching fresh arrows onto their bowstrings, again the sword fell, and again the sky darkened. This time, however, the trajectory was different. The arrows rained in on the battlements. One councillor took an arrow clean through the chest; the impact sent him staggering backwards off the boardwalk and he plunged into the cobbled piazza below. Another took an arrow through the throat. He fell without a sound.

Boninsegna cowered behind the parapet, waiting until the last arrow had fallen to earth. He looked around and saw that the councillors were alone: the guards had long since deserted their posts, and the piazza below was empty. Florence had gone to ground.

Cautiously, he inched his head above the parapet. The horsemen were still there.

'I offer these terms,' he shouted. 'I shall despatch riders to Pisa to order our armies to break off the siege and return to Florence. With immediate effect.'

There was a pause as the two lead horsemen conferred.

'It shall be so,' said Altobardi. 'The captain-general and his Company will remain in position until such time as your forces return from Pisa and until we ascertain that the siege has been lifted. We seek no confrontation with you, but neither do we fear it. We shall depart from Florence by the northern route to Pisa. Your armies shall return to the south.' He paused. 'Are the terms agreed?' he demanded.

'The terms are agreed,' said Boninsegna.

The riders turned and rode back towards the main force.

Altobardi looked over at Hawkwood and saw that he was pleased.

'In truth, Gennaro, this has been as bloodless a battle as I have ever witnessed,' said Hawkwood.

'Yet victory is yours, Sir John.'

Hawkwood nodded in acknowledgement, but his mind was troubled. He had welded his Company into a compact and well-disciplined force, but it had not yet been exposed to the heat of battle. Sooner or later, the men would crave real action. They were fighting men, and would lose their edge if not tested in combat.

'Pray God, Gennaro, that all our victories are not as hollow.'

Hawkwood stood the Company down and gave orders to set pickets. All they could do now was wait.

Karl Eugen von Strachwitz heard the commotion in the hallway outside but was at a loss to account for it. He hurried over to the window, and thrust his head against the wrought-iron bars. In the inner courtyard far below, people were running aimlessly hither and thither. His first thought was that the palazzo was on fire, but he saw nothing to confirm it – no water pails, no flames, no hint of smoke. Whatever had happened, he must make it work to his advantage.

He was confined to two well-appointed rooms on the fourth floor of the palazzo. Not only were the windows barred, but the doors were secured on the outside by massive bolts which clunked back into place each time his guards left the room. He had been treated well – wined and dined unstintingly – but, despite these courtesies, he remained very much a prisoner. He could only guess at Boninsegna's intentions, but he suspected his future in Florence might be short-lived.

It was time to escape.

Karl Eugen had not been idle. The bars were solid enough, but he had contrived to prise away some of the mortar securing the central bar of the window in his bedchamber. He had also wrenched free of the stucco wall one of the sturdy iron lamp-brackets, afterwards pushing it back into place so that the guards would notice nothing.

He hurried into his bedchamber and pulled the bracket free. He wedged it against the central window bar and, using it as a lever, strained against the bar. He felt a slight movement – of perhaps an inch – but the bar remained in its socket. He removed the bracket and repositioned it higher up, threading it past the bar and bracing it against the stone window frame. Placing his right foot on the windowsill, he heaved with all the strength he could muster. The bar still held but he felt it bend very slightly. He heaved again, and it bent another inch. Then again and again. With a jolt, it came free of its socket. Karl Eugen fell flat on his back on the floor.

The lower part of the bar was jutting free. He leapt to his feet and worked it feverishly to and fro, hearing a gratifying crunch as the mortar flaked. Suddenly, the bar came away in his hands, for all the world like a rotten tooth wrenched from an abscessed gum.

He thrust his head and shoulders through the opening. He judged the drop to the courtyard to be all of forty feet – too far to jump, too far to risk breaking an ankle or a leg. He glanced right and left. The palazzo's interior walls were smooth and unornamented and, as he had feared, offered no convenient hand- or foot-holds. No matter: he had made allowance for this.

The windows in his rooms were flanked by long velvet curtains elegantly draped into position and secured by thick silk cords. Four windows: eight cords, each some six or seven feet long. He quickly detached all eight and knotted them together, creating a rope some twenty-five feet long. Too short to reach the ground, but possibly long enough.

He sacrificed another foot or so by tying one end round the bar he had dislodged. Then he climbed out on the window ledge and pulled the bar tight, horizontally, against the remaining bars. Cautiously, he looked down: the courtyard was now empty. He lowered himself into space, leaning out from the wall and planting his feet against it. Foot by foot, he 'walked' down the wall, using the rope's thick knots as hand- and foot-holds. Within seconds, he had reached the end of the rope. Karl Eugen did not hesitate. He dropped the final twelve feet to the ground, cushioning his fall by bending his legs and rolling on impact.

He stood up and looked around. One of the doors off the courtyard must lead to the street outside. But which one? A servant appeared, seemingly from nowhere, clutching a silver soup tureen. He pulled up short on seeing Karl Eugen, then flung open a door and dashed through it. Karl Eugen wasted no time on speculating why the servant should be running off with household silverware, but assumed the servant was making for the street. He followed. They traversed an empty chamber, then ran down a long wood-panelled corridor which did indeed lead to the main entrance to the palazzo.

The great double doors were ajar and Karl Eugen ran out through them into the street beyond. There, he paused for a second or two to get his bearings, then slowed to a brisk walk, heading towards Oltrarno.

He had no notion as yet of what was happening. All he knew was that he was free again. He must now decide how best to exercise that freedom.

Pisa, 14 June 1361

The pale pink of dawn tinged the uppermost levels of the Torre Pendente and crept inexorably over the flamboyant sandstone and majolica façade of the Duomo. Watching on the walls, Tommaso Gracchi and the men under his command shielded their eyes as the sun eased over the horizon, casting into ever sharper relief the unique contours of a city where Corinthian capital and elegant arabesque proudly attested to the twin influences of classical antiquity and Islam.

Gracchi was inordinately proud of his city and a zealous guardian of its history. He stood on the east wall, looking out towards the massed Florentine army silhouetted against the morning sun. He knew Pisa was doomed. This small city state whose powerful navies had once dominated the entire western Mediterranean and the coasts of North Africa would soon be no more.

The Florentines had been at the gates of the city for two full days. They had proposed a *pourparler* under a flag of truce and had called on Pisa to surrender. Gracchi and the Council of Guilds had defiantly rejected the call: Pisa would defend itself to the last, although the outcome was clearly inevitable.

Gracchi had ordered some of Pisa's most prized possessions removed from the city and concealed in the crypt of San Piero a Grado, a church built three centuries earlier on a spot east of Pisa where St Peter was believed to have first set foot on Italian soil. Simone Martini's *Madonna and Child* polyptych had also been concealed there, as had a *Virgin and Child* carved in ivory by Giovanni Pisano for the high altar of the Duomo, and a bronze statue of the mythical hippogriff – half-horse, half-gryphon – sculpted by Islamic artists over four centuries previously. The statue had been captured by Pisan armies at the time of the Saracen wars and was arguably the most potent single symbol of the city's glorious past. Gracchi hoped these and other treasures would somehow escape the Florentines' clutches and be saved for posterity.

There was a stirring on the hill to the east. Gracchi and his men exchanged nervous looks. As they watched, squinting against the sun, the Florentines formed ranks and unfurled their battle standards. The besieging army cranked into motion.

The Pisans watched and waited.

Gracchi took a square of soot-darkened glass from his doublet and held it to his eyes. It was too early to be certain, but it appeared the Florentines were moving southwards. That was strange. Gracchi and his military advisers had expected a frontal assault on the east wall. An attack from the south made little tactical sense: the Florentines would be constrained by the River Arno on their left flank and would have to attack uphill.

Puzzled, Gracchi passed the glass to a young captain of the City

Guard, whose eyesight might be sharper: 'They move to the south, do they not?'

The young man peered through the glass.

'Well?' said Gracchi. 'Do they? Move south?'

The captain did not reply, but continued to observe. Gracchi was about to wrest the glass back when he saw the captain's hand begin to tremble. Not in fear, but in excitement.

'Yes – yes! They move south, and then they move east! They're withdrawing!'

The men on the wall waited, uncomprehending. The first ranks of the Florentine army gradually receded over the hill. Other ranks followed. The cavalry took up the rear, moving ponderously but incontrovertibly *away* from Pisa.

Gracchi could contain himself no longer. 'They have withdrawn!' he shouted.

Jubilant cries echoed along the battlements. Men knelt and crossed themselves. Some embraced, others wept.

For an hour or more they held station on the battlements, but the Florentines did not return. Gracchi sent riders to confirm their inexplicable departure. The riders returned and reported no trace of the armies of Florence apart from the grass scorched by their cooking fires and the earth churned by their siege engines. Pisa was safe – for the time being at least.

An exhausted Tommaso Gracchi climbed down from the wall. He was unable to explain what had occurred. It must, he concluded, have been divine intervention – a miracle.

What other explanation could there possibly be?

IX

Donnina

The freshness of her beauty strikes me dead

Near Florence, 16 June 1361
The English sergeant-at-arms anticipated the blow and arched his head away. Too late. Delicate fingers, dripping with ornate rings, balled into a fist which caught him full on the mouth and split his lower lip.

He wiped away the salt taste of blood and grinned from ear to ear. 'What have we here, then?' he said. 'A little wildcat?'

His men laughed.

'Lay a hand on me again at your peril, you vermin!' Donnina Visconti's eyes glittered in anger as she surveyed the soldiers crowding round her and her carriage. To her right, her retinue of eight outriders had been herded at pikestaff-point into a compact group. One or two of them eyed her sheepishly, aware that they had failed in their duty; the others looked down at the ground, ashamed and fearful.

'A wildcat indeed, by God, and as pretty a one as I'll ever hope to see,' opined the sergeant-at-arms.

'Aye,' said another voice, 'a proper beauty. And I warrant there's something soft and juicy for us all beneath that splendid gown.'

Donnina feared for her life. It had all happened so suddenly. One moment her carriage had been proceeding sedately towards Florence; the next, it was surrounded by this whooping pack of animals who had materialised seemingly out of nowhere. Her guards had been overpowered in a matter of seconds and she herself had been yanked unceremoniously from her carriage.

The men had spoken in English. Donnina had been tutored in that language and she responded in kind.

'I am the Lady Donnina Visconti of the Visconti of Milan,' she said with as much hauteur as she could muster. 'Who, pray, are you?'

'We, my beauty, are Essex men of the Essex Free Company, come to rid this land of Florentines and all those who would do harm to Pisa.'

'I am a Visconti of Milan,' she repeated. 'And I demand to know by what right you detain me here.'

The sergeant-at-arms spoke again, his voice more threatening this time. 'Right? You ask by what right? Then let me tell you straight. We detain you as a spy for Florence.'

Donnina laughed contemptuously and her captors looked at each other in some confusion.

'A spy? You numbskulls! I am no spy, nor am I in the pay of Florence. I am a loyal subject of Milan, and these men are my guards.'

'Call them guards if you will. I call them milksops – and spies and turncoats, to boot.'

'Then you, sir, are a fool – and an ugly one, to boot.'

The men laughed uncertainly, but they were impressed.

'Ugly I may be, but I am no man's fool,' retorted the sergeant.

'Then you must surely have the wit to comprehend that I, Donnina Visconti, do not treat with fellows of your base rank.'

He hesitated. If this woman was indeed a spy, the information she carried might be valuable. Her arrogance certainly held conviction. He felt somewhat intimidated by her. His men were looking at him expectantly and he took the only course that seemed open to him. He would do as soldiers the world over have always done: pass the decision to someone of higher rank.

'Secure these prisoners and guard them well,' he ordered. 'And escort the lady to the captain-general's pavilion.'

'Escort me as you wish,' said Donnina, 'but I shall ride in my own carriage. A Visconti does not travel on foot.'

The sergeant-at-arms bowed mockingly. 'If that is your wish, Your Highness.'

Donnina got back into her carriage. One man clambered in

beside her and two others sat up top. She leant forward and rapped with her knuckles on the carriage roof.

'Drive on,' she commanded.

The sergeant watched as the carriage, rocking gently from side to side, gradually disappeared from view. 'Sir John will have both hands full with that one,' he predicted.

His men laughed. Sir John de Hawkwood was the match for any mere woman, Visconti or no Visconti.

Florence, 16 June 1361

At Hawkwood's command, the Company had held station until the fourth day following his *pourparler* with Boninsegna. That morning, outriders reported the armies of Florence to be at most five leagues from the south wall of the city, approaching in good order. At noon, Hawkwood ordered the Company to stand down and prepare to strike camp.

'And what, pray, Sir John,' said Perry, grinning, 'is to become of our invaluable siege engines?'

Hawkwood returned the grin. 'We shall put the torch to them, Sir Wilfred,' he said. 'It would be imprudent, would it not, to let such precious engines of war fall into Florentine hands?'

Perry laughed. The captain-general's ruse had succeeded spectacularly. Only one of the siege engines – an assault tower – had actually been completed; the others had merely been rigged to look as if they were battle-ready. It would indeed be most imprudent to permit them to fall into enemy hands. The Florentines must never know how they had been duped.

Hawkwood was elated that this first confrontation with Florence was virtually at an end and that the Company would leave the following morning for Pisa. At the same time, he was troubled by the continuing absence of Karl Eugen. He could only assume that the mercurial German had been detained by the Florentines. God forbid that any harm should have come to him. But there was nothing Hawkwood could do at present – he had no knowledge of Karl Eugen's whereabouts and could not be certain whether his second-in-command was dead or languishing in a Florentine jail. He felt a twinge of guilt at his readiness to allow Strachwitz to venture alone into the snake-pit that was Florence.

He was jolted out of his reverie by the leisurely approach of a preposterously ornate gilded carriage drawn by four splendid jet-black horses and flanked by a number of English pikemen. A burly sergeant-at-arms called the small cavalcade to a halt and came forward to salute him.

Hawkwood acknowledged the salute. 'What have we here, Sergeant?'

'I cannot say for certain, Captain-General, but it is my belief we have captured a spy in the pay of Florence.'

'Then you have done well.'

The carriage door opened, and one of the pikemen stepped forward to help the occupant alight. Hawkwood was astonished to see a trim ankle emerge, followed by the sweeping folds of a satin gown. He caught his breath as Donnina Visconti shrugged aside the pikeman's arm and cautiously descended from the carriage. He took in the thick mane of chestnut hair, the gracefully curved back, the slender waist. She turned to face him. Flawless pale olive skin, high cheekbones, a firm jawline, a nose which bordered on the aquiline. And then the eyes: eyes which caught and held his gaze. He had rarely – no, never – seen a woman so beautiful.

Or so angry.

Donnina strode purposefully up to him. He greeted her in Italian. She answered in English.

'Your accent is execrable,' she said dismissively. 'But that is only to be expected of one with the manners of a *sporcaccione*. How dare you treat a Visconti with such disrespect?'

'In my country,' replied Hawkwood, 'swine do not have the power of speech. It is perhaps otherwise here in Italy.'

Her right hand balled into a tiny fist and Hawkwood thought for a moment she was going to lash out at him. But then she smiled and abruptly changed tack.

She said, 'There is doubtless much in Italy that is different from what you are accustomed to in your own land.'

'Not least, my lady, that we *sporcaccioni* do not permit our women to meddle in the affairs of men.'

'Whereas we in Italy respect our women and show them every courtesy.'

'May I ask that you explain in what manner you have been treated discourteously?' said Hawkwood.

'Clearly, sir, I am held here against my will.'

'But not, as yet, against mine. I am sworn to serve the interests of Pisa, and if you are indeed in the pay of Florence you must understand that you are my enemy.'

'I am in no man's pay,' retorted Donnina. 'Unlike yourself, Captain-General, I am no hireling.'

'But, also unlike myself, you have yet to demonstrate your *bona fides*, to prove you are no spy.'

Donnina was on shaky ground. At her own insistence, she had travelled to Florence to be presented at the ducal court and, not least, to meet the duke's half-brother, to whom she was betrothed. To disclose as much was tantamount to admitting to a tenuous but undeniable link between herself and Florence. And doing that might give credence to the allegations made against her by Hawkwood's men.

'I was seized on the approach to Florence,' she protested. 'I have no knowledge of that city and owe no allegiance to it.'

Hawkwood was already persuaded that this beautiful firebrand was no spy. Even if she were, he judged her to pose no real threat now that the initial confrontation with Florence was over. Besides, she was breathtakingly beautiful.

'You and your escort shall accompany us to Pisa,' he said. 'You will be detained there only until such time as I am convinced of your intentions. I shall then return you safely to Milan.'

'That is intolerable,' said Donnina.

'Perhaps,' said Hawkwood. 'But it is also prudent. And I am a prudent man.'

He dismissed the sergeant-at-arms and his pikemen, ordering them to release the escort but keep them under close watch. He then turned again to Donnina.

'My lady, quarters will be readied for you until we leave tomorrow. We are in the field and I regret are ill placed to accommodate you as befits your rank. You shall dine with us.'

'I do not dine with hirelings,' said a petulant Donnina.

'As you wish.'

'And I have no appetite.'

'Then perhaps you will do us the honour of gracing our table with your presence and your discourse?'

Donnina hesitated, weighing the alternatives. Accept? Or spend the rest of the day and all the night alone and incarcerated in a draughty field tent? She decided to accept. Perhaps she could charm this *condottiere* into releasing her, or at least into sparing her the tedium of travelling to Pisa. He was not an unreasonable man, this *condottiere*. He had treated her with courtesy and he was not without wit. Besides, he was exceptionally handsome.

'I shall dine at your table,' she said. 'But on one condition and on one condition only.'

'And that is?'

'That you do not attempt to speak Italian.'

Hawkwood laughed. 'I accept.'

She expected the meal to be a frugal affair, but was proved quite wrong. They dined on succulent saffron-flavoured guinea fowl accompanied by *polenta concia valdostana* – thick maize-flour cakes grilled over an open fire – and complemented by richly spiced *polpette* of veal and *bresaola*, thin slices of dried beef macerated in olive oil and lemon. The wine was of excellent quality – not Italian, she concluded, but a French *clairette* she thought she recognised as one of her father's favourites.

Donnina was seated directly across from Hawkwood, with Gennaro Altobardi to her left and Sir Wilfred Perry to her right. Sir Wilfred was both an elegant *raconteur* and an attentive listener. Altobardi said little but scarcely took his eyes from her. Hawkwood also said little at first but, gradually, was persuaded to talk of England, of the war against France, of his first impressions of Italy.

To her chagrin, Donnina realised she was enjoying herself.

From time to time, her glance fell on a cylindrical ivory ornament that rested on the table near Hawkwood's elbow. It was
small – no more than six or seven inches high – but carved exquis-
itely with articulated leafage and a script she could not decipher.

Eventually, her curiosity got the better of her. 'What is that?'
she asked.

'A box,' Hawkwood replied unhelpfully.

'A box, you say?'

He hesitated. 'Yes, a box. A small box. A *puxidion* – a
diminutive of the Greek *puxis*, meaning a box.'

'You speak Greek, Sir John?' asked Donnina, leaving him in no
doubt that she was teasing him.

'Some,' he answered gruffly. 'Almost as well as I speak Italian.'

'And what is the box's purpose?'

'It has none, except to serve as a *telesmon* – a *talismano*, I
believe you say in Italian.'

Donnina was unrelenting. 'And the inscription on this *talismano*?'

'The box is of Moorish origin. The Arabic inscription merely
says that it was crafted in Cuenca in our tenth century.'

'And how did you come by it?'

'It was given to me by King Edward's eldest son – the Black
Prince, as he is sometimes known – after the siege of Narbonne in
1355. I was wounded there—'

'Saving the prince's life,' put in Sir Wilfred.

'I was wounded there,' continued Hawkwood, ignoring the
interruption. 'The prince gifted me the box as a charm to ward off
evil and ensure good fortune and good health.'

'And has the charm worked?'

'Well enough, I wager.'

From Hawkwood's tone of voice, Donnina sensed she might
have raised a sensitive issue, perhaps even given offence. 'I meant
no offence, Sir John. I was merely curious.'

'None is taken. And curiosity is no vice.'

'Then tell me if you will, for I am indeed curious: what fresh
treasures do you hope to find here in Italy?'

Hawkwood met and held her eyes. 'There is much to admire and there will be much to treasure. There is, I warrant, great beauty before my eyes at this very moment.'

There was an awkward pause. Donnina felt the colour rise to her cheeks. She looked away, then back at him again. He was still gazing at her, unsmiling.

Sir Wilfred cleared his throat. 'Let us drink a toast to beauty,' he said.

Hawkwood raised his goblet. 'To beauty.' He drank the wine down in a single gulp, set the goblet back on the table and stood up abruptly.

'I have things to do before the morrow,' he said, and then, turning to Altobardi, 'Escort the Lady Donnina to her quarters, and guard her well. I would not forgive myself should harm come to her.'

X

Bella Figura

He bore himself well in peace and war

Pisa, 9 July 1361

'Remember, Caesar, thou art but mortal.'

Sir Wilfred's admonition made Hawkwood smile. He countered with a line from Plutarch: 'Rather the first man here, than the second in Rome!'

But Perry had a point. In ancient Rome, the Senate used to place a slave in the chariot of a victorious general to accompany him and his legions on their triumphant parade through the city streets to the Capitol. The slave's sole duty was to whisper repeatedly that injunction, reminding the hero of the day that he was a man, not a demi-god.

Hawkwood had little need to be reminded of his own mortality. He had witnessed the brutalities of war and the ravages of peace, the triumphs of Crécy and Poitiers and the horrors of the Black Death, the indignities of promises broken and the pain of loyalties abjured. If any man were conscious of his own mortality, it was he, John Hawkwood, *condottiere*.

As the token force rode into Pisa, however, he felt an irrepressible surge of pride. Pride in his Company. Pride in what his men had achieved and the manner in which they had achieved it. The pride felt by any commander who has successfully led from the front. And with that surge of pride came an awareness of power – and of all that power implies.

They entered by the Santa Maria portal. It seemed as if all Pisa had crowded into the Campo dei Miracoli to catch a glimpse of their deliverers and to welcome them. Banners and bunting decorated every inch of the colonnaded Duomo, the imposing

Campanile and the Battistero. Fathers held children aloft on their shoulders, and women dressed in their finest waved coloured silk shawls and threw garland after garland. The clamour was deafening as Pisa gave vent to its admiration and relief. A ritual chant went up:

'*Acuto! Acuto! Acuto! Acuto!*'

Hawkwood, Sir Wilfred Perry and Gennaro Altobardi had set out riding three abreast, but Perry and Altobardi had imperceptibly reined in their mounts, with the result that Hawkwood spearheaded the procession. Behind them came a detail of mounted cavalry and small detachments of footsoldiers, pikemen and archers. The bulk of the Company had been billeted for some three weeks outside the city walls but, paradoxically, their absence seemed to make the small escort force even more impressive.

As they approached the cathedral, Hawkwood saw that a large table draped in scarlet and gold had been set up on the steps leading to the main entrance. At the table sat the city fathers – his employers.

Tommaso Gracchi could contain himself no longer. While his fellow guildsmen stood and applauded, he dashed forward, his face flushed with pleasure. Almost before Hawkwood had time to dismount, Gracchi was upon him, pinning Hawkwood's arms to his sides in a warm embrace, pounding him on the shoulder and then, to Hawkwood's astonishment, attempting to kiss him on both cheeks. This last manoeuvre was initially unsuccessful on account of Gracchi's diminutive stature and Hawkwood's height, but the Pisan was not to be denied. Grasping Hawkwood's head in both hands, he yanked it down and planted a kiss on his brow.

'Thank you, Sir John!' he said. '*Grazie! Mille grazie – mille, mille grazie!*'

This effusive greeting left Hawkwood initially at a loss for words. All he could do was nod and gently disengage himself.

He stepped back, bowed and said calmly, 'John Hawkwood, sir, at your service and at the service of the city state of Pisa.'

The bystanders roared their approval and the chant started up again: '*Acuto! Acuto! Acuto! Acuto!*'

Hawkwood turned to face the throng. With a swift movement, he drew his sword and held it up, the hilt against his face in a gesture of salute. He brought the sword down in a graceful arc, held the pose for a brief moment, then re-sheathed it.

Again the crowd bellowed its approval.

Hawkwood clasped the hand of each member of the Council of Guilds in turn. Altobardi had told him their names and functions, but he did not know who was who. It was of little consequence. To a man, they greeted him without reserve.

Gracchi gestured in vain for the crowd to be silent. Hawkwood turned to face them. He raised his arms high above his head, and the noise immediately subsided.

'Citizens of Pisa,' said Gracchi, with a nod of acknowledgement to Hawkwood, 'it is our great honour and privilege to express our immense debt of gratitude to Sir John de Hawkwood, who has delivered our fair city from the grasp of an evil neighbour. We thank him for the courage he and his men have shown and we—'

The rest was drowned out: '*Acuto! Acuto! Acuto! Acuto!*'

Gracchi smiled indulgently. He waited patiently for the better part of a minute, then shrugged, turned away and sat down. He had intended a lengthy speech but it was destined to go unheard.

At the ceremonial banquet that evening, Hawkwood sat at the table of honour with Donnina Visconti beside him. Altobardi had counselled against her presence, discreetly pointing out that she was the daughter of none other than Bernabò Visconti, known throughout Italy as the Tyrant of Milan. Hawkwood would have none of it. 'She is my guest and as such shall be made welcome,' he had snapped. 'I take pleasure in her company and little heed of her father's name or reputation.'

The guests rose time and again to drink Hawkwood's health, as one guildsman after another heaped praise on him and his Company. One of the last to speak was the octogenarian Massimo Mastrodonato. Unlike the previous speakers, he not only lavished praise on Hawkwood but was also at pains to introduce a note of caution.

'*Salus populi suprema lex*,' he intoned. 'Yes, I grant that the safety and well-being of the people is indeed the supreme law. But mark my words well: an immediate danger has been averted but there is danger still. Danger from without and danger from within.'

Hawkwood set down his goblet and smiled wryly at Donnina. He had expected this from one quarter or another. He listened attentively as Mastrodonato continued.

'The danger from without remains real, but is for the present in abeyance. As to the danger from within, I recall the words of Tacitus.' He paused for effect.

To Donnina's astonishment, Hawkwood softly but distinctly matched Mastrodonato word for word: '*Atque ubi colitudinum faciunt pacem appellant*. They create a desolation and call it a peace.'

The old man had had his say. He sat down abruptly. The guests looked at each other in bewilderment. What point was he trying to make? Was he challenging Hawkwood? Criticising him?

Hawkwood himself was in no doubt. The celebrated line from Tacitus had been spoken by Calgacus, a leader of the ancient Britons who had dared question the *pax romana* imposed by Roman military might on his land and people. He made to respond, but Donnina laid a hand on his arm.

'This is not the moment,' she whispered. 'The time may come soon enough.'

The celebrations lasted until late. It was close on midnight when the first guests started to take their leave, and later still before Hawkwood and Donnina could depart. Ritual required them to be among the last to leave.

They were quartered in the Palazzo Gracchi on the far side of the Piazza dei Cavalieri close to another Pisan landmark, the Palazzo dell'Orologio, a wing of which served as the city jail. For Hawkwood's edification, Gennaro Altobardi had earlier re-counted a grim episode in the Orologio's history. Some sixty years previously, a burgomaster of Pisa, Count Ugolino, had been charged with treason, convicted and, together with the entire male issue of the Ugolino family, walled up inside the prison and left to rot.

'It would be well, then, to give the place a wide berth,' Hawkwood had observed.

'That it would,' said Altobardi.

A carriage awaited them, but Hawkwood dismissed it. 'It is a night of great beauty,' he said. 'Does it please you to walk under the stars?'

Donnina linked her arm through his. He could feel the warmth of her body against his and the pressure of her firm breast against his forearm. She looked up at him and smiled. 'It pleases me.'

As Christ is my witness, thought Gennaro Altobardi, they make a handsome couple. His eyes followed them until they disappeared into the balmy Tuscan night.

Pisa, 9 July 1361

Karl Eugen von Strachwitz stood in the shadows as John Hawkwood and the beautiful creature on his arm strolled towards the Piazza dei Cavalieri. He was tempted to follow but, on second thoughts, decided there was little to be gained.

He had been in the Field of Miracles that afternoon, his distinctive white-blond hair concealed under a makeshift turban. He had shared in the crowd's intense excitement, had even cheered along with them. But in his heart he had scant cause to rejoice. He was an outcast now, a traitor in all but name.

The young man had asked himself repeatedly how Hawkwood might have reacted to his sudden disappearance. He would have been concerned – that much was certain – and perhaps would have thought Karl Eugen had been taken and held by the Florentines. With certainty, Hawkwood would not have suspected his duplicity. There was no way Hawkwood could know that, from the outset, Karl Eugen had been an informant in the pay of Florence, nor, for that matter, that he had effectively reneged on his commitment to Boninsegna, telling the Florentine next to nothing. When all was said and done, thought Karl

Eugen, his report to Boninsegna had been superficial, a compound of half-truths and unhelpful generalities.

Clearly, what Hawkwood would also not know was that, had the Company not presented itself so unexpectedly at the gates of Florence, Karl Eugen would have been unable to make good his escape and save his own hide.

Bile rose to his throat. What manner of man was he? The duplicitous Karl Eugen von Strachwitz: outsider, outcast, traitor, man without conscience or honour. And what of John Hawkwood? A friend deceived, a friend betrayed.

Karl Eugen had been self-seeking and self-serving all his life. He understood that now and despised himself for it. It was time to set the record straight, at whatever cost to himself.

Pisa, 10 July 1361

An insipid morning sun filtered through the draperies and traced its path across the bedchamber, illuminating garments that lay scattered where they had fallen and silk sheets that were rumpled and stained, redolent of the previous night's exertions.

Hawkwood was astonished to discover that Donnina was still completely naked – and even more astonished to discover that he was, too. He had never seen a woman's body totally exposed and he cautiously ran his eyes over her. She lay face down, one arm cradling her head, the other resting casually on his midriff. Her ample breasts were flattened against the firm mattress and her generous buttocks formed a graceful semi-circle. Chestnut hair fanned out across the pillow. Olive skin glinted in the pale light.

He was suddenly conscious of his own battle-scarred body, the dense, dark hair of his chest and the thick undergrowth at his belly. He felt coarse and somehow inadequate next to this immaculate creature. Yet he could only smile at the naturalness of it all.

Shortly after midnight they had been welcomed to the Palazzo Gracchi by a deferential servant who had shown them to their respective chambers above the *piano nobile*. Hawkwood had hesitated at her door and was on the point of wishing her a formal goodnight when she put a finger to her lips and beckoned him to follow her. She secured the door, turned to him and opened her arms. Hawkwood embraced her, breathing in the musky perfume of her hair and shoulders. They kissed. Her lips parted, moist and soft on his.

He drew her quickly to the bed. She fell back across it as Hawkwood fumbled at his breeches. He entered her at once, pinning her shoulders to the bed and thrusting urgently into yielding flesh. It was over in a matter of seconds. She said nothing as he rolled off her and lay on his back, his breathing uneven and laboured.

Hawkwood felt deeply ashamed. He had treated her like a common whore, a cheap vessel of no consequence. He grappled for words to explain, to break the ominous silence between them.

Donnina raised herself on one elbow and gazed at him. A smile played about her lips. She slowly lowered her head to his chest and lay there, absolutely still at first until he felt her hand explore his buttocks and the inside of his thigh. Very gradually, she moved closer to him, her breasts pressing into him, her long legs straining against his. He offered no movement as she straddled him, reaching down and pulling him back into her. She rocked this way and that, leaning forwards to brush her mouth against his, then arching back to anchor her hands against the tops of his thighs. It was she who was thrusting now, drawing him into her, subtly shifting her weight to release him, then plunging down again, driving him deep inside. Hawkwood felt an exquisite pain start somewhere in the small of his back and gradually infuse his entire frame. He reached up to clutch her buttocks and strove to match his rhythm to hers. The pain intensified until it became almost unbearable. His back arched from the mattress as he climaxed. He was only vaguely aware that she, too, was shuddering and crying out.

They remained locked together until he felt himself go limp and contract. Donnina released him and he fell back against the pillows, his throat dry and constricted. It was only then that she had fully undressed him, stripping off his *blouson* and breeches. He had felt no guilt, no shame. She lay back down beside him, her fingers tousling his chest hairs and her breath cool on his shoulder. He turned to speak, but she held a finger to his lips. Smiling, John Hawkwood slept.

Now he looked at her again, marvelling at her casual sensuality and willing himself to recall each and every detail of the previous night. He watched while the sun inched up the bed, moving gradually up her narrow back until it fell across her face and brought out the highlights in her hair. She stirred, opened one eye, then closed it again. She murmured something, more to herself than to him, it seemed, then edged even closer. Hawkwood was uncertain what to do next. He had never been in a situation like this. It was first nature to him to take the initiative in everything, to make the first move. He felt a twinge of guilt at the thought of his wife, but put her from his mind.

Donnina's mouth was on his belly now, her tongue darting this way and that. Her hand cupped him, massaging with a gentle firmness. He felt himself come gradually erect. He longed to see her face, but could see only her mane of chestnut hair draped over his belly and his upper thighs. He gasped as she took him in her mouth. It was pure sensation now, a sensation unlike any he had ever experienced. Her mouth worked on him unrelentingly. She moaned softly, her body bucking and rearing in concert with his. When it was over, she held him for a time, then gently released him. She turned her head and her eyes met his. She slowly uncoiled from between his legs and lay alongside him, her head once again on his chest. Hawkwood silently stroked her hair.

'You and I have much to learn from each other, my *condottiere*,' said Donnina.

'That we have,' he said, 'but I warrant it is I who have most to learn from you.'

'Then we shall learn together, you and I.'

Without warning, she bounded from the bed. 'But first, Sir John, we shall break our fast together. Come, stir yourself. You have whetted my appetite.'

And you mine, thought Hawkwood, reaching for his breeches.

Pisa, 14 July 1361
Acuto.

Now that he understood the epithet's connotations, Hawk-wood had come to accept it with good grace. *Acuto*: subtle, sharp, shrewd, decisive, quick-witted. Resourceful, too, and cunning. All these were qualities attributed to the Odysseus of legend. Yet there were other connotations: devious, unscrupulous, destructive, capable of trickery and deceit. Those, too, were qualities frequently assigned to Homer's hero.

Hawkwood could not deny that there were distinct parallels between himself and Odysseus. Hawkwood, too, was among the dispossessed, a wanderer in foreign lands at whose snares and perils he could still only guess. His own future was as uncertain and fraught with danger as that of Odysseus and his companions caught between the dual menace of the twelve-footed, six-headed siren Scylla (Florence?) and the treacherous whirlpool that was Charybdis (Pisa?).

Questions flooded his mind. Would Pisa prove a Land of Lotus Eaters, inducing lethargy among those under his command? Who were the cannibal Laistrygones and when and how would they strike? For how long would the Company respond to his orders before they yielded to temptation and bit the hand that fed them, much as Odysseus' companions had turned on the Cattle of the Sun? Not least, what would become of Margaret Hawkwood – *his* Penelope – and his own lands?

Of one thing, however, Hawkwood was already certain: the reincarnation of the enchantress Calypso in the guise of Donnina Visconti . . .

Acuto?

Only time would tell. For the present, there were more practical matters to be attended to.

'A bagatelle, Sir John, a trifling matter, no more.'

Sir Wilfred Perry sat in the command pavilion facing Hawk-wood and Altobardi. At issue was the construction of fortifications to reinforce Pisa's outer defences and the building of permanent quarters to house the Company. In this, Hawkwood was heavily reliant on the older man's knowledge and experience.

'A bagatelle, you say, Sir Wilfred?' he replied. 'Would that it were!'

'You are a fine general, and I am the first to bow to your excellence in the field. I ask only that you take me at my word, that you acknowledge my skills in this regard. I have presided before now over the building of such fortifications, at both Bordeaux and Calais.'

Hawkwood knew this to be true. He had only a passing knowledge of Bordeaux, but he had seen a second Calais – a town in its own right – spring up virtually overnight to accommodate the English armies garrisoned there. To him, the task was daunting; to Sir Wilfred, it seemed, it could be accomplished swiftly and effectively.

'My needs are plain, Sir Wilfred, and I have set them out as best I can. I need earthworks and stone ramparts to the east of the city. I need living quarters for the Company. I need kitchens and stabling blocks, storehouses and granaries, latrines, lookout towers, direct and unfettered access to the city walls—'

Perry held up a hand, cutting him off in full flow. 'I know your requirements, sir, and they shall be met. You have my word on that.'

'I shall hold you to it. And tell me, pray, when will all this be in readiness?'

'Before the year is out – on that, too, you have my word.'

Hawkwood frowned. Less than six months to build new defences and an entire new town? It was scarcely credible, yet Sir Wilfred's confidence was reassuring.

'So be it,' he said.

He turned to Altobardi, who was clearly taken aback by, if not incredulous at, the nonchalance with which Sir Wilfred had acceded to Hawkwood's demands.

'What say you, Gennaro? Can Sir Wilfred achieve in Pisa more than Caesar Augustus achieved in Rome?'

'I do not understand you, Sir John.'

'Come, come, Gennaro. You must know your Suetonius!'
Altobardi still looked puzzled.

'Caesar Augustus professed to have found Rome brick and left
it marble. Is that not true of what we plan for Pisa?'

'We in Pisa already have the marble, Sir John,' replied Altobardi with a show of spirit, 'but it seems we now also have need
of brick.'

Hawkwood and Sir Wilfred roared with laughter at the riposte,
but Altobardi could muster no more than a grim smile. Altobardi
believed Hawkwood's intentions to be honourable but, in his
anxiety to safeguard his beloved Pisa, he had not thought ahead
to the prospect of a permanent encampment only a stone's throw
from the city walls.

Altobardi knew in his bones that it was only a matter of time
before the Council of Guilds came to share his misgivings.

Pisa, 16 July 1361

Karl Eugen's reappearance could scarcely have been more un-
timely. News had come that day from England, and the news was
anything but good.

Hawkwood sat at his desk in the Palazzo Gracchi and took
stock. For all that his treatment at King Edward's hands had been
harsh and, to his mind, unjustified, he was still an Englishman at
heart and, as such, was dismayed to learn that the king's most
recent incursion into France – ostensibly to compel acceptance
of the Treaty of London signed more than a year previously –
had been signally unsuccessful. Edward had been outraged at
France's repudiation of the treaty's provisions with regard to the
surrender of French territories and at the continuing reluctance of
the French citizenry to ransom King Jean, who was still comfor-
tably ensconced in the Savoy Palace in London.

Edward had sailed to Calais and marched on Burgundy, where
he had been repelled by the French. He had then retreated north
and east and had been constrained to set his signature to a
precarious Peace of Brittany, the terms of which appeared to
Hawkwood to be less favourable to England than to France. The

document provided that Edward renounce his claims to the French throne in exchange for sovereignty over the whole of Aquitaine – a territorial gain, as Hawkwood readily conceded, but one which did not translate into sorely needed revenue. Moreover, Hawkwood believed that the gain would be of only short duration.

That the English exchequer remained depleted was beyond question. The most recent members of the Company spoke of an England whose economy was in disarray, of cities like London, York and Bristol decimated by the Black Death and its aftermath. The England they had long taken for granted was now no more, they reported. Bakers' ovens were cold. Physicians had deserted their vocation or died at their posts. The stench of death and putrefaction was everywhere. Cemeteries and mass grave pits were filled to overflowing. Priests were conspicuous by their absence, many of them having fled the cities and townships to escape the tide of pestilence, many others having already succumbed to it, infected in the course of their futile ministrations on the plague-infested streets or in the close confines of monasteries they had erroneously believed safe.

Peasants who had left the land to find fortune in the cities were dismayed to find they too had miscalculated. The Statute of Labourers, enacted in 1351, was still *in* force but only sporadically *en*forced, with the result that prices soared while wages were largely pegged at pre-plague levels. Those who had the wherewithal took to their heels and sought refuge in the 'clean' air of the countryside, only to find pastures and farms deserted, with livestock wandering aimlessly in search of fodder or lying dead in the fields, their bellies bloated and maggot-ridden. Orphaned children drifted disconsolately from one village to the next, and robbers and highwaymen roamed the countryside in search of modest pickings.

It was fervently believed that the Black Death had abated somewhat, but sporadic outbreaks of pestilence continued to ravage both city and countryside. Feudal society was collapsing and, with it, the old order. Serf rebelled against master as the plague took its merciless toll of rich and poor alike.

Hawkwood Manor had also suffered, he was informed. In his absence, ploughing and harvesting had been neglected. Trespass was now the rule rather than the exception as serfs foraged far and wide for food to sustain their families. The social hierarchy was crumbling and self-interest was the rule. In this respect, Hawkwood Manor had weathered the storm better than most. The reeve had absconded but had been replaced by Sir John's father-in-law, who had assumed responsibility for managing the estate. Revenues had remained stable – no mean feat in the circumstances – and the tannery continued to generate a modest profit. Not least, Hawkwood's stud had been zealously guarded, and remained by and large intact.

The worst news of all was that Margaret had died in childbirth. Hawkwood took some comfort from the fact that his baby daughter – Antiocha – was safely in the care of his mother-in-law.

He was in a quandary, asking himself repeatedly whether or not he should return to England. To do so would mean breaking his contract with Pisa, however, and he concluded he could not in all conscience go back on his word.

Little wonder, then, that John Hawkwood was in a vile humour, a humour compounded by the knowledge that Donnina had announced her intention to honour her father's wishes and travel to Florence the next day to meet her future husband. Hawkwood's guilt at their adulterous relationship had intensified on the news of Margaret's death. Although not a deeply religious man, he was a Christian and he had knowingly transgressed against the Seventh Commandment. For a moment, he even considered the possibility that his wife's death might be a punishment for his adultery, but he dismissed the thought: after all, he had transgressed in many other ways, too, infringing Commandments as a matter of course by virtue of his chosen profession.

He greeted the peremptory rap on the door with a gruff 'Enter!'

When he saw who stood on the threshold, a broad smile etched his features.

'Karl Eugen! By all that's holy!'

Hawkwood embraced the young man, then held him at arm's

length, looking him over. He noted that Karl Eugen's face was pale and that his eyes had lost their habitual sparkle.

'Out with it, man! What became of you?'

'There is much to be said, Sir John.'

'That is so, I warrant. Where have you been these long days?'

'I have been in Florence. And, for some days now, in Pisa.'

Hawkwood's eyes narrowed. There was something amiss. 'For some days now? Then why . . . ?'

Karl Eugen had prepared himself for this encounter, rehearsing what he must say and how he must say it. But his mind suddenly went blank. *Tabula rasa*. He hesitated for a moment and then it all came spilling out.

As Sir Wilfred entered the corridor leading to Hawkwood's quarters, he heard a roar akin to that of a beast in agony. Fearing the worst, he broke into a run, unsheathed his sword, and burst into the room.

He was unprepared for the scene that confronted him.

Blood coursed down Karl Eugen's face as Hawkwood rained blows upon him. The German reeled from the onslaught but kept his feet and made no move to retaliate. An uncomprehending Sir Wilfred thrust himself between the two, forcing them apart. Hawkwood's face was contorted with rage, and spittle leaked from the corners of his mouth. Hawkwood reached for the squat dagger in his belt, but Perry clamped a restraining hand over his.

'What is the meaning of this?' shouted Sir Wilfred.

'Meaning?' bellowed Hawkwood. 'You ask what meaning? If you wish meaning, ask it of the traitorous dog that stands before you!'

Karl Eugen still had not moved. There were deep cuts on his face where Hawkwood had struck him. He had taken the blows and he expected worse would follow. But, for once, he had done an honourable thing: he had told the unblemished truth.

Suddenly, the anger drained from Hawkwood. His hand withdrew from his dagger-hilt and his shoulders sagged. He shook his head violently as if to clear it, then sat down heavily in his chair. He muttered something that Sir Wilfred failed to catch.

'Sir John?'

Hawkwood shook his head slowly. He did not look up, but his voice was steadier now. 'Remove this vermin from my presence. The stench of treachery is too much for me to bear.'

Sir Wilfred looked at Karl Eugen. The German was in pain and it showed.

'It is for the best that you leave,' said Sir Wilfred.

Karl Eugen nodded but remained where he was.

After a moment or so, Hawkwood spoke again, softly this time. 'Leave! Leave now, I say!'

'At your orders, Captain-General.' Karl Eugen saluted, turned on his heel and left the chamber.

Sir Wilfred gazed in bewilderment at Hawkwood, who was slumped in his chair, his head in his hands, his grief palpable. What had transpired between the two men? Sir Wilfred elected not to ask. All in good time, he thought.

Eventually, Hawkwood looked up. 'He was like a son to me.'

Perry nodded. He waited. There would be more.

'Like a son, I tell you,' repeated Hawkwood. He cleared his throat. 'And he betrayed me as no son should betray a father.'

'I do not understand you, Sir John.'

'Then understand you shall. It is a tale of such deceit and double-dealing as no man of honour may either countenance or condone.'

Hawkwood spoke for close on half an hour. Of Karl Eugen's recruitment by the Florentines, his feigned rescue of Hawkwood in Arles, his subsequent dealings with Boninsegna, his imprisonment in Florence and his escape. And of Karl Eugen's reluctance to confront Hawkwood and confess all.

'But confront you he did,' Sir Wilfred pointed out, 'and he confessed all, freely and openly. To my mind, that speaks to his honesty – and to his courage.'

'Honesty, you say? Courage? Would that were true! He wormed his way into my confidence and into my affection. Then he betrayed me.'

'You are wrong, Sir John. He told the Florentines nothing their spies had not already reported.'

'He betrayed me. For money.'

Perry raised an eyebrow. 'He did no more than you yourself have done. He accepted a *condotta* – a contract – in good faith, as you have done here in Pisa. He had no knowledge of you when he entered the service of Florence. He is a *condottiere*, as you are. He broke faith, certainly, but if with anyone then with the Florentines. You are wrong in this matter, Sir John. You do him an injustice.'

Karl Eugen had vowed he would not leave Pisa until Hawkwood formally released him from all further obligation. The penalty for betrayal was death: if that was to be his fate, he would accept it.

He was in the stables, grooming his horse, when Hawkwood sought him out.

'It is your intention to leave the Company?' asked Hawkwood.

'I await your command, sir.'

'I wish you to remain. We have much to discuss.'

He held out his hand.

Karl Eugen stared incredulously for a moment, then clasped it.

'I fear I have wronged you,' said Hawkwood.

'No more than I have wronged you, Captain-General.'

'Then let that be an end to it.'

Hawkwood pulled Karl Eugen close, and the two men stood locked in each other's embrace.

After a few moments Hawkwood disengaged himself. 'There is much work to be done,' he said. 'I need a . . . a son by my side.'

Karl Eugen felt the salt sting of tears. 'I left your side once, Sir John. I give you my solemn oath I shall never do so again.'

'Your hand will suffice,' said Hawkwood, turning abruptly away.

Pisa, 17 July 1361

Donnina Visconti rose at dawn. Her legs ached and her *mons Veneris* felt bruised and tender. The sensation was not unpleasant.

She had slipped from Hawkwood's bed as the first rays of sun flooded the bedchamber, while he lay there still, sleeping off the exertions of the night. By Christus, she thought, he is a fine man. Her eyes caressed his powerful frame, taking in the corded muscle and tracing the countless scars that etched his arms and shoulders.

He is mine now, she thought.

She found it well-nigh incredible that they had met a scant four weeks previously and had been lovers for no more than a week. She had been attracted to him from the first. He had almost everything she wanted in a man, not least the sexual aura that inevitably comes with power. When Hawkwood moved among his Company, she admired his easy manner as he greeted many by their first names, offering words of advice and encouragement. The men responded to him with equal ease – coarse, cynical, battle-hardened veterans and fresh-faced, unseasoned youths alike, each and every one devoted to his captain-general. She had seen the pride he took in those nearest to him – Perry, Altobardi, the colossus Llewellyn, the diminutive Griffiths – and had seen tears in his eyes when he spoke of his reconciliation with Karl Eugen von Strachwitz. She had been touched by his grief on hearing of his wife's death.

There was more. To her initial astonishment, Hawkwood had gradually revealed his considerable erudition. True, he was sadly unversed in the fine arts, but he spoke excellent French and was fluent in Latin and Greek and – although she had not conceded as much to him – spoke more than acceptable Italian. His knowledge of history was as broad as his taste in literature was eclectic, and his way with horses was nothing short of extraordinary. He had his faults, of course – not least a distinct lack of *finesse* in the bedchamber – but those were rough edges she could smooth and soften over time.

That she was on the point of leaving for Florence to wed a man of whom she had little knowledge and for whom she could understandably muster no affection did not trouble her unduly. That was the way of the world. It was a political union, nothing more. Hawkwood bitterly resented her impending departure and she had delighted in his repeated attempts to dissuade her. It was her father's wish, however, and that wish must be respected, irrespective of her own misgivings and her distinct lack of enthusiasm for the match.

Donnina and Hawkwood had said their farewells the previous night and she was anxious to leave before he woke. There was little more to be said and Hawkwood's sense of decorum and propriety would in any event preclude more than a few perfunctory parting words in public. That, she reasoned, would only cause both of them more unwanted discomfiture and grief.

Servants drew her bath and she luxuriated in its warmth, feeling the ache in her legs gradually ebb. She dressed and went downstairs to where her carriage and escort were waiting. She got in and settled herself for what would be a tiresome journey.

On the seat opposite lay a small blue velvet bag fastened with a gold silk cord. She opened it to find a cylindrical ivory ornament identical to the one she had admired on the night she and Hawkwood had first met. She turned it over in her hands, inspecting the exquisite carving and the Arabic inscription. There could be no doubt: this was no copy, it was Hawkwood's 'small box', his *puxidion*, the precious *talismano* given to him by the Black Prince. Given – how had he phrased it? – as a charm to ward off evil and ensure good fortune and good health.

There was a piece of parchment in the velvet bag. She carefully unfolded it.

'*Per sempre.*'

For ever.

Donnina Visconti was not given to tears, but she found herself sobbing uncontrollably. She craned her head out of the carriage window and looked back at the Palazzo Gracchi and the window of Hawkwood's bedchamber. She could not be certain, but she thought she saw him standing there.

The carriage turned a corner and the Palazzo Gracchi disappeared from view.

Hawkwood stood at the window and watched the carriage leave. There was a lump in his throat. She is mine, he reassured himself. Not now, perhaps. But one day soon.

XI

Pisa Nuova

Where stood the sovereign mansion of King Mars

Pisa, 18 November 1361
John Hawkwood watched and approved as a second Pisa took shape. To the south, where the River Arno already formed a natural barrier against any invading force, little had been done other than to heighten the parapet walls by the simple expedient of affixing covered wooden galleries and hoardings – *brattices* – to create *allures*, wall-walkways which afforded lookouts and sentries a secure yet commanding view of the wetlands beyond the Arno. To the north of the city, however, the outer defensive walls had been heavily reinforced and gradually integrated into a chain of fortified towers extending fully sixteen hundred paces from Pisa's erstwhile limits before looping westwards towards the sea.

Sir Wilfred Perry was in his element. Building a walled city almost from scratch was no mean undertaking, but he had direct experience of the logistics involved. Besides, he had admired, and learnt from, the many fortifications masterminded by Maître Jacques de Saint-Georges, the Savoyard mason and architect whose fortress design at St-Georges d'Esperanche had been the model for a succession of fortified towns and castles commissioned by Edward I to secure the inland and coastal defences in Wales. It was Master James, as he had become known at the English court, who had extended the Norman castle of Beaumaris built on drained marshland at the north-eastern end of the Menai Strait on the Isle of Anglesey. And the same Master James had elaborated the concentric walls-within-walls concept that had revolutionised castle-building towards the end of the previous century.

Hawkwood was careful to mask his disappointment during the early weeks of the project, when Sir Wilfred's own 'castle' was little more than an earthwork mound surrounded by a wide ditch. But that disappointment soon gave way to admiration as encircling walls appeared at the foot of the mound and inner wards – baileys – took shape. The *fossatori* excavated the land beyond the *enceinte* outer wall to create deep and imposing moats; the *cementarii* added barbicans and other advance fortifications, then interpolated bastions, towers and turrets.

Hawkwood marvelled at the skill of the stonecutters and layers as they fashioned notched crenels and saw-tooth *merlons*, narrow *meurtrière* arrow loops, drum towers, bartizans, and embrasures and machicolations which would prove invaluable in repelling besiegers. What impressed him most was how quickly all this was accomplished. Sir Wilfred modestly shrugged off any suggestion that he had worked a miracle, pointing out that he had access to a very large contingent of unskilled and semi-skilled labour in the guise of the Company, together with a complement of skilled artisans from Pisa itself. The new Pisa – Pisa Nuova – would be ready more or less on time, he insisted.

It was not a thing of great beauty: much still remained to be done in terms of providing gatehouses, drawbridges, cross-walls, arcades and screens and, not least, outfitting the all-important *magna turris*, the *donjon* or tower keep. Projecting corbel stone brackets and putlog holes had to be cut to take beams; loopholes had to be added to provide light and air; ashlar facings of smooth, square-hewn stone had to be cemented into place to revet and reinforce the walls; and ornamental finials had to be applied to decorate roofs, pediments, gables and towers. Then – and only then – would the new fortifications seem a natural extension of Pisa's existing defences rather than a squat and ugly adjunct to a beautiful city.

At present, the contrast between the raw, ungainly new fortifications and the pristine filigree architecture of Pisa was both striking and disturbing. Hawkwood was aware of this – and also of the fact that the members of the Council of Guilds were even more conscious of the disparity between Pisa Vecchia and his Pisa Nuova. They were in a quandary. They respected Hawkwood's judgment and Sir Wilfred's experience and skill, yet they were in two minds as regards what was happening to their beloved city.

Soon after his arrival, Hawkwood had been voted into membership of the Council of Guilds in his capacity as the 'saviour' of the city. On the face of it, the gesture was both appropriate and well deserved, but he appreciated it for what it really was: a means by which his intentions could be monitored and his actions subjected to strict supervision. All well and good, he had concluded, since a seat on the council also afforded him an opportunity to keep a finger on the pulse of the council and gauge its collective response to his actions.

In this, he was mindful of Gennaro Altobardi's admonition on hearing of Hawkwood's plans for the city's continued defence: *We in Pisa already have the marble, Sir John, but it seems we now also have need of brick.* At the time, Hawkwood had found the remark amusing. It appeared, however, that the prospect of a permanent encampment as an extension of the city walls did not sit well with the council.

He solicited Altobardi's advice. The young man was hesitant at first and, so Hawkwood thought, altogether too deferential. But when the subject turned to the essential role of *condottieri* and their dealings with the Italian city states, Altobardi would prove as outspoken as he was informative. For all that, the young Italian listened patiently as Hawkwood waxed lyrical on the role mercenary armies had played throughout history.

'Had it not been for mercenaries,' Hawkwood argued, 'there would have been no spread of Hellenistic civilisation after the death of Alexander the Great.'

Altobardi nodded.

'And what of so-called "Roman" legions? Need I remind you they were drawn in the main from mercenaries recruited from within the conquered territories and *paid* to serve under the Eagle?'

Altobardi nodded again.

'And would Carthage have ever dared challenge Rome in the absence of a powerful mercenary force?'

Another nod. Hawkwood was warming to his subject now, thought Gennaro.

'There were Turkish hirelings in the service of the T'ang dynasty in China – that was in the eighth century. And what of the Rajputs, the "warrior sons of kings", who held sway in central and northern India in the ninth and tenth centuries?'

'I know little of them,' said Altobardi.

Hawkwood droned on, recalling tales of Flemish mercenaries who had served England's King Stephen in the twelfth century in his protracted battle against the Plantagenets. And Henry II, the Plantagenet king: where would *he* have been without mercenaries to put down successive challenges to his throne?

Gennaro Altobardi was left in no doubt that Hawkwood was knowledgeable about and manifestly proud of his chosen profession. But Altobardi cared little about Turks and warrior kings and Plantagenets. For him, the salient fact was that mercenaries were rarely citizens of the states on whose behalf they fought. They were hirelings, paid specialists in the art of warfare. Such hirelings had been in Italy since the beginning of the century – and had not always been welcome.

'The city states have long since considered war a vital element in the development of commerce and in ensuring prosperity,' explained Altobardi, tiring of Hawkwood's history lesson. 'They are prepared to engage in war and to finance war, but they themselves have lost the taste for it. They prefer to hire others to serve on their behalf. They see war as a continuation of commerce, but they scorn brute force and consider it a mark of the uncivilised.'

If Hawkwood took offence at the implications of Altobardi's remark he showed little sign. What interested him was the use of *foreign* mercenaries. 'Is it considered unworthy, then, to take up arms on behalf of one's own country?'

'Unworthy, no,' replied Altobardi, 'but unnecessary, given the circumstances.'

'Which are?'

'Which are that Italy's city states – Venice, Milan, Florence, the Papal States, Pisa and others – generally have the financial resources to purchase an army rather than serve in one. In Florence, for example, bearing arms is required of every citizen whose annual income exceeds a specified level, but any man is free to nominate and pay someone to serve in his stead.'

'Then, pray, why not retain Italians?'

'There is grave danger in that.'

'Danger? In what way, danger?'

'Allegiances are fragile and fluid. They can be swayed by political considerations and personal sentiment. Loyalties are never permanent.'

It was Hawkwood's turn to nod. 'But this must also hold true of foreign mercenaries?'

'Certainly,' replied Altobardi, suddenly unwilling to meet Hawkwood's gaze. 'There have been . . . troubling moments.'

'Continue.'

'In Florence, not so very long ago – in 1342 – Gauthier, Count of Brienne was retained to restore civil order. He held the city to ransom and bled it dry.'

Hawkwood could scarcely believe his ears. 'Brienne was once in the pay of Florence?'

It was Altobardi's turn to be surprised. 'You had no knowledge of this?'

'None,' replied Hawkwood.

'But it was his death at your hands that helped persuade Pisa to recruit you.'

Hawkwood suppressed a smile at the irony of the situation. Had the Council of Guilds known of his despairing efforts to keep Brienne alive after Poitiers, they might have been less willing to hire him.

'There were others?' he persisted.

'Yes,' replied Altobardi. 'The Germans spread terror in central Italy in 1334, and they stripped the region bare. In 1339, other German mercenaries – *Söldner*, they called themselves – carried the banner of St George and fought for Lodrizio Visconti.'

The words were tumbling out now. 'We have seen it again and
again. In 1342, another German, Werner von Urslingen, declared
himself an enemy of God, piety and pity. Then there was
Montreal d'Albarno—'

'An Italian, at last?'

'No, a *bastardo* from Provence at the head of a rabble of
drunken Frenchmen, Hungarians and Germans. But he was
captured and beheaded – in Rome, as I recall. And then—'

'Enough,' said Hawkwood.

Altobardi paused, his face flushed. 'There is more,' he said,
'much more.'

'Of that I am now certain,' replied Hawkwood with a grim
smile.

He had heard enough to realise that, in terms of role and status,
a *condottiere* was someone to be respected and feared rather than
admired and liked. If Altobardi – whose loyalty to Hawkwood
had thus far proved unswerving – felt this way, what of the other
council members? How long would it be before they turned on
the saviour of Pisa?

The thought troubled him more than he cared to admit.

XII

Alarms and Excursions

Crawling for ransack 'midst the piles of slain
And stripping accoutrements for gain

Borgo San Donnino, west of Parma,
22 November 1361
'Burn it!'

Árpád Károly was in the foulest of foul moods. His men had swept into Borgo San Donnino at dawn, surging through the narrow streets of the township and scything down men, women and children alike. They had dismounted in the piazza and stormed into the Duomo, confident there was booty to be had. But the pickings had been lean, just as they had been some days earlier in Fontanellato. And elsewhere before that.

Somehow, the townspeople had got wind of their imminent arrival. Many had fled, but not before they had carefully hidden what meagre possessions they could not take with them. Except for a couple of tattered wall-hangings, the cathedral was stripped of ornament. The modest houses were empty save for a few sticks of furniture.

His men were angry and Károly could scarcely blame them. They had taken their anger out on what was left of the populace of San Donnino, torturing the men and raping any female they could lay their hands on, irrespective of age. They had foraged for food and uncovered next to none. The livestock had been spirited away and there was only the occasional scrawny chicken to be had.

Quarrels broke out over a woollen blanket, a discarded pair of boots or a rough peasant smock. One man proved more fortunate than most and laid hands on a tiny silver crucifix, another stumbled on a modest cache of low-denomination coins. The looting was short-lived, however: there was nothing of real value to be found. The men vented their spleen on the survivors, killing some outright and playfully roasting alive others less fortunate.

Károly watched his men pile bales of straw against the high altar. A torch was lit and, in seconds, the church was ablaze, the dry wood of the choirstalls fuelling the flames that tongued up the off-white walls and fanned across the wooden beams. A priest lay face down on the flagstone floor, his head split open and leaking blood which rapidly congealed and darkened in the heat.

Károly turned away. He crossed the square and entered the two-storey building he had chosen as his command post. In one corner of the downstairs room a woman lay motionless, her legs splayed and bruised, her eyes staring uncomprehendingly at the ceiling. Next to her was a young girl, no more than ten or eleven years old. She was curled into a tight ball, and whimpered incessantly.

Károly crossed the room and kicked the woman twice, then once again for good measure. She continued to stare at the ceiling. He drew a dagger and ran it across her throat, stepping back sharply as the blood spurted. She tried to cry out but emitted only a low gurgling. Her body convulsed and then she lay still.

He turned to the girl. He had raped her twice already. The mother had been accommodating – no doubt in the vain hope he would spare her daughter – but the girl was more to his taste. The dagger flashed again in his hand, but he checked himself. Perhaps he should let the girl live? Her dark eyes and olive complexion reminded him of his young sister. Besides, he told himself, he was not *entirely* without feeling.

Árpád Károly knew instinctively he had reached a crossroads. The men under his command were a heterogeneous rabble – Magyars mostly, but with a large contingent of Germans and a sprinkling of disaffected Frenchies. Cutthroats and cowards to a man, but none the less a force to be reckoned with. They had ranged north and west as far as the outskirts of Avignon, then turned east and south again, seeking out isolated villages and townships in north-eastern Italy, pillaging as they went. Thus far, Károly had succeeded in imposing and maintaining some semblance of discipline, but time was running out. The men remained together because there was safety in numbers, but shortage of food and scarcity of plunder had sapped their morale. It was only a matter of time before they broke ranks and went their separate ways.

Károly was honest enough to accept much of the blame. His judgment had been flawed. He had the numbers – close on two thousand – to attack larger towns, but he had consistently chosen the easier option. It was time to review his strategy. Time to hunt for bigger game.

Károly reminded himself that he was a Magyar, the descendant of a warrior race which had terrorised whole regions of Europe and Asia Minor ever since the ninth century. It shamed him that he had been reduced to this, burning defenceless towns and scrambling for scraps of sustenance.

The immediate task was to keep his force intact until his Catalan reinforcements arrived, at which point he could cast around for a more ambitious and more affluent target. Avignon? No, not Avignon: it offered rich pickings, certainly, but the papal defences were well organised and the risks correspondingly high.

To the south-east, however, lay one of the most inviting targets of all: Florence. It was a city of enormous wealth, defended – if rumours were to be credited – by a craven army which had turned tail and fled at the merest hint of battle; an army which had given up without a fight when confronted by an untried English *condottiere* called Hawkwood.

Pisa, 22 November 1361

John Hawkwood bathed, shaved and put on a fresh *blouson* and breeches. He left his quarters in the Palazzo Gracchi in good time for that morning's meeting of the Council of Guilds.

He relished the prospect. To date, he had been content to attend council meetings as little more than an observer, responding only to specific questions asked of him. Today would be different. Today, he at last had something of his own to say.

At previous meetings he had sensed growing opposition among some members to the changes being imposed on Pisa. Now that Pisa Nuova was nearing completion, he hoped the council would understand that he had acted in his employer's best interests and would endorse his long-term plans for Pisa's defence. He knew he could count on the support of Tommaso Gracchi and Gennaro Altobardi, and also, to some degree, on that of Pisa's senior magistrate, Giacomo Albertosi. Massimo Mastrodonato continued to oppose him at almost every turn, and there were others who could best be described as being in two minds.

In the course of his discussions with Altobardi, Hawkwood had come to realise that his standing with the council was precarious on two counts. First, the council was unnerved by the very notion of a *condottiere* – and a foreigner, to boot – who might desert them or, worse, turn against them at any moment. Second, Hawkwood and the Company were a drain on the city's resources.

There were other minor concerns, including the issue of the Company's day-to-day conduct. There had been incidents – mercifully none particularly serious – when men had breached Pisa's hospitality. In the main, these incidents were attributable to alcohol-fuelled excess or to the men's less than subtle approaches to Pisan women. Hawkwood had resolved that particular problem by declaring Pisa Vecchia off limits to the Company except in specific circumstances and subject to his written orders. He had also ensured that Pisa Nuova included an ample number of whorehouses. To his amusement, those places now offered services provided not only by the Company's contingent of female camp-followers but also (and increasingly) by young and not-so-young Pisan women who, he could only assume, were not among those the council deemed to be in need of protection from his men's uncouth advances.

The most pressing issue of all was that of morale. Almost the entire Company had been conscripted into service as *minutii* – labourers or semi-skilled workers – to help in the construction of Pisa Nuova. This had provided an outlet and a distraction for a time, but they were professional fighting men whose allegiance to him was conditional upon their being allowed to do what they did best. The initial confrontation with the Florentines had been bloodless and booty-less, and there appeared to be no immediate prospect of action. The men were restless – Llewellyn and others had confided as much – and spoiling for battle. There was urgent need of a new enemy.

Hawkwood entered the Council Chamber and acknowledged the guildsmen's perfunctory greetings. They took their seats and Tommaso Gracchi called the meeting to order. Hawkwood waited patiently, knowing that one or other of those round the table would provide him with the opening he needed. It came sooner than he had expected.

Massimo Mastrodonato – who else? – formally entered a motion that payments to the Company and its *condottiere* be reviewed, bearing in mind that those payments were an onerous financial burden on the state exchequer.

Before the motion could be seconded and passed to a vote, Hawkwood claimed the floor. 'The annuities that accrue to the Company and to myself are as contractually agreed and set out in the *condotta*,' he said, 'and the *condotta* is invalidated if its terms are altered or broken.'

'Continue,' said Gracchi.

'It is to my mind in the best interest of both parties that the *condotta* be honoured both in letter and in spirit,' Hawkwood went on. 'Thus, I propose not that the terms of the contract be reviewed, but that the *condotta* itself be seen in a different light and amended accordingly.'

Mastrodonato made to protest but was forestalled by senior magistrate Giacomo Albertosi.

'There is some merit in that,' said Albertosi.

Not to be outdone, Mastrodonato intervened. 'Am I to understand that you – a hireling and a *straniero* – have the impertinence to suggest that our laws and customs be amended in your favour?' he spluttered.

'As a hireling and foreigner in your midst, I suggest only that the financial burden on my employer could most readily be alleviated should this council review the *condotta* with an open mind.'

Albertosi leant forward. 'We are listening.'

'I apologise for my inadequate command of your language,' said Hawkwood, 'and ask that Consigliere Altobardi intervene as necessary as my interpreter.'

Altobardi nodded his agreement.

'What I propose is this,' continued Hawkwood. 'That I and my Company shall continue in loyal service to the city state of Pisa under the terms and provisions of the original contract. We shall honour those terms until such time as the *condotta* is deemed by both signatories to be irrevocably at an end. In other words, we shall serve Pisa for a predetermined period to accomplish a predetermined task or tasks in exchange for a predetermined payment.'

He paused to allow them time to take in what he had said.

Albertosi looked puzzled. 'But, Condottiere, those provisions are already enshrined in the existing contract – the *locatio operarum et rei* convened between our two parties.'

'That is so,' replied Hawkwood. 'But the terms of the contract do not preclude Pisa from hiring out my services to a third party.'

Mastrodonato could contain himself no longer. 'It is as I feared all along,' he expostulated. 'Our noble *condottiere* seeks to feather his own nest.'

Hawkwood smiled. 'On the contrary, what I propose is that Pisa feather *its* own nest. I and my Company are pledged to serve Pisa and we shall honour that pledge – on that you have my most solemn word. But, I ask you, is it not to the advantage of Pisa that our annuities be paid by another?'

Gracchi intervened. 'Explain, if you will, how this can be accomplished?'

'Quite simply,' replied Hawkwood. 'By selling our services to a third party for a sum equivalent to or greater than that which Pisa currently disburses on our behalf.'

There was silence round the table.

'It would be for this council to negotiate an agreement between

Pisa and a third party,' continued Hawkwood, 'and to specify the number of men put at the third party's disposal for a specified or extended term—'

'*Ferma o di rispetto*,' whispered Altobardi.

'—whereby the city state of Pisa would be the employer—'

'*Datore*—'

'—and all revenues with respect to my services would accrue to Pisa.'

Silence.

Hawkwood looked around at the key members of the council. Predictably, Massimo Mastrodonato was apoplectic, but Gracchi, Albertosi and Altobardi were clearly intrigued by his proposal.

He got to his feet. 'This is a matter of considerable import and one that should be resolved by this council in closed session,' he said. 'Gentlemen, I await your response and reassure you of my most honourable intentions.'

He looked at each guildsman in turn, bowed slightly and left the chamber, withdrawing to an anteroom to await the councillors' response.

To his surprise, their deliberations lasted less than half an hour. As he re-entered the room he sensed immediately that he enjoyed their respect and, possibly, their trust.

'We have reviewed your proposal,' said Tommaso Gracchi, 'and we consider it has much to commend it. In principle, that is. What we are anxious to discover is how you believe it should be implemented in practice.'

'In practice?' said Hawkwood.

'Indeed,' said Gracchi. 'To which third party do you propose we hire out your services?'

This was the moment of truth.

'Florence,' he replied.

**Near Artimino, west of Florence,
22 December 1361**

Károly's advance guard crested the rise and stopped in its tracks. Arrayed in tight battle formation on the hill opposite was a small but compact force of pikemen and mounted knights whose light armour glinted in a pallid winter sun.

Károly immediately surmised that the Florentines had guessed his intentions and had interposed this token force between him and the city gates. At a rough estimate, the Florentines numbered scarcely one thousand, of which no more than fifty or so were mounted cavalry. They must be mad, he thought: his own force alone was twice that number and he could now count on the six hundred or so seasoned Gascons and Catalans who had joined him some ten days previously. He shaded his eyes and surveyed the terrain between the two armies. The ground was a touch soft, certainly, but by no means impassable.

Jean de Grailly, more commonly known as Captal de Buch, reined in alongside him, and together they took stock of the situation. De Buch, whose small cavalry troop had fought on the English side at the battle of Poitiers, was not one to throw caution to the winds. 'I warrant these are not the most Florence can muster,' he said, scanning the woodland to the left for tell-tale signs of ambush. 'Their main force may lie beyond the rise.'

Károly did not share these misgivings. 'They stand in our path and block our way to Florence,' he countered. 'I say we attack now!'

On the hill opposite, Hawkwood and Karl Eugen von Strachwitz watched their adversaries form battle ranks and advance.

'It is as you predicted, Sir John. They intend to attack us.'

Károly's force reached the low ground and came on confidently and at a measured pace. Footsoldiers were to the fore, closely followed by Károly's cavalry, with Captal de Buch's regiment of horse bringing up the rear.

At a signal from Hawkwood, his pikemen fell back several paces. Encouraged, the attacking footsoldiers broke into a half-run. The pikemen broke ranks and retreated up the hill, spreading out left and right; Hawkwood and his mounted knights did likewise. With a roar, Károly's men pounded up the incline, confident now that the Florentines were on the run.

From his vantage point high on the hill, Hawkwood adjudged

the enemy to be little more than a hundred and fifty paces distant. He raised his broadsword and swept it slowly right to left, then back again. Llewellyn and Griffiths were positioned on the brow of the hill; they saw and relayed Hawkwood's signal. The longbowmen angled their bows and fired blind from beyond the crest of the hill. Skein after skein of arrows hissed high and fell relentlessly on the attacking footsoldiers, shredding their ranks. Their advance checked, and they turned to flee, only to find their retreat impeded by Károly's cavalry, which had kept close order.

Hawkwood held his sword high above his head. Two units of horse exploded out of their woodland cover, cutting off Károly's retreat. The longbowmen discarded their bows, drew their stubby swords and raced over and down the hill. The pikemen did likewise, ploughing into Károly's flanks.

Károly waited in vain for Captal de Buch to join the fray, but the Gascon gave his men no such order. He had observed the simple-mindedness of Károly's tactics. What was more, he had seen enough to know these were no Florentines. Those arrows had been launched from English longbows, of that he was certain. Their signature was as readily identified as the figure of the lead knight who now charged down the hill at the head of his cavalry: Sir John de Hawkwood.

Árpád Károly was no coward. He urged his destrier forward, trampling his own men and those of the enemy as he drove straight for the adversary who had out-thought and out-fought him in the field. Hawkwood saw his intention and steadied himself for the inevitable clash of man and horse.

At the last moment, Karl Eugen spurred his mount in front of Hawkwood and across him. His sword-hand described a graceful arc, neatly severing Károly's head from his body. Hawkwood was conscious only of the spray of crimson blood and the bizarre sight of a headless Károly thundering past him and disappearing over the hill behind.

Captal de Buch had seen enough. He stood his cavalry down and waited for the slaughter to end. He would pay his compliments to Sir John and be on his way.

Hawkwood had already dismounted when Karl Eugen rode up, grinning from ear to ear. Together, they watched the Company gleefully searching for booty. Some would come away empty-handed, but no matter: they had reasserted themselves as a fighting force and regained their pride and self-respect.

At his own insistence, Hawkwood had not been present at the protracted and vituperative negotiations conducted between Pisa and Florence in the small town of Vinci in the early days of December 1361. Nor did he know the precise terms of the agreement hammered out between erstwhile arch-enemies Tommaso Gracchi and Giancarlo Boninsegna. What he did know was that he, John Hawkwood – Giovanni Acuto – had carried the day.

For Florence *and* for Pisa.

XIII

Cascina

Where men are as so many cattle,
Herded, captured, killed in battle

Cascina, 20 July 1364

It was no consolation to John Hawkwood that, for some three years, he had led his Company on successful forays against all who posed a threat to Pisa, committing his force to sporadic skirmishes and full-fledged engagements and invariably carrying all before him.

The Company had developed into a compact and supremely confident force of over three thousand fighting men divided into three battle groups which served in rotation, one assigned to the immediate defence of Pisa, the second held in reserve, and the third active in the field. The defensive unit was deployed behind the imposing fortifications of Pisa Nuova; the reserves were held behind the lines in semi-permanent readiness; and the offensive unit was a highly mobile force which moved on horseback but usually fought on foot. Saddles had been lowered and stirrups shortened to ensure greater comfort and manoeuvrability, and the traditional *arco longo* had been modified to produce a longbow which was substantially more effective at close quarters. Meanwhile, the Company's goat-greased and burnished light-weight armour had become its distinctive feature, a unifying element recalling the silver shields – the *argyraspides* – favoured by Alexander the Great. The Company was now known and feared throughout the length and breadth of northern Italy as the Compagnia Bianca, the White Company.

Today, however, for the first time in a long and illustrious career, John Hawkwood had tasted the acrid potion of defeat.

The White Company had been bested that afternoon on an undulating plain outside Cascina in the province of Pisa. Worse, it had been bested by a *Florentine* force under the command of a captain-general named Galeotto Malatesta, reinforced by troops led by Genoa's Count Grimaldi and a redoubtable squadron of Genoese crossbowmen.

Hawkwood roundly cursed his own folly in assuming that the brittle truce negotiated between Pisa and Florence would hold indefinitely and still Florence's ambition to subdue Pisa. That ambition had not been removed by Pisa's installation of Hawkwood and his Company, but merely held in abeyance.

For a time, the Florentines had acquiesced in the arrangement under which Hawkwood and his Company were occasionally retained to serve in their defence, but the truce with Pisa had lasted only until Florence again had enough troops to fend for itself. At that juncture, Hawkwood's occasional secondment to Florence had become irrelevant.

He also cursed his arrogance in assuming that his tactics in the field would enjoy uniform and sustained success. As a rule, the White Company fought defensively and in the open. Once a suitable defensive position had been established – typically on an upslope – his men-at-arms dismounted and sent their horses to the rear. Fifteen-foot stakes would be driven into the ground and each of these so-called 'lances' secured by two men. Some way behind, the longbowmen would take up position, ready to expedite their murderous hail of arrows against an opposing cavalry as it attacked uphill.

Between the 'lances' and the longbows, other men-at-arms – the 'blades' – would wait in readiness, venturing forward only as and when the armour-piercing shafts of the longbowmen had blunted the first attacking wave and brought down substantial numbers of men and horses. The 'blades' would then work swiftly and without mercy, driving their short swords into the interstices in the fallen knights' armour, gouging eyes out and slitting throats before retreating to security behind the wall of 'lances' until a fresh wave of enemy footsoldiers finally laboured up the incline, only to be met by yet another deadly shoal of arrows. Hawkwood usually held in reserve a small contingent of cavalry, ready to swoop in and mop up the remnants of the opposition force when the moment was opportune.

Over the years, these tactics had served Hawkwood and his Company well.

Until today in Cascina.

Hawkwood had arrived that morning from his encampment near the abbey of San Savina, some five miles distant, but had waited until early afternoon, when the enemy would be staring into the glare of a summer sun and subjected to a dust-storm blowing from the west across the Pisan plain.

The White Company had ostensibly abandoned its defensive tactics and moved aggressively on the Florentines and Genoese entrenched in Cascina. Hawkwood was largely unconcerned by the fact that his men were substantially outnumbered, but he had moved cautiously, ordering three probing attacks in a bid to entice the Florentines and Genoese out from behind their defences and lure them into attacking his typical – and, as he now realised, predictable – defensive/offensive battle formation.

This time, the tactic had not worked. The Florentines and Genoese had held station, refusing to be enticed into open-field confrontation. Frustrated, the White Company had moved forward again, its eagerness for battle fuelled by the expectation of rich booty and the juicy prospect of ransom monies to be had from the capture of what they assumed to be the cream of young Florentine and Genoese nobility. To Hawkwood's alarm, they had taken the enemy's reluctance to venture out as an indication that the Florentines and Genoese had no stomach for a pitched battle. The Company's impetuous and ill-advised frontal assault breached the enemy defences with suspicious ease, and it seemed for a moment that it would once again rout a significantly superior force.

But Grimaldi's crossbowmen, secreted in safe positions at the windows of houses on the outskirts of the town, were primed to unleash a withering crossfire. The Company's ranks quickly thinned as a number were killed outright and many others wounded, some seriously. Their repeated attempts to withdraw were frustrated by a large force of Florentine cavalry which swept left and right to outflank them and pen them in a pincer movement that left no option other than to fight to the death or to surrender.

Hawkwood, Karl Eugen von Strachwitz and a handful of cavalry had had no choice other than to charge into Cascina in a bid to support their over-eager footsoldiers. They were soon surrounded. For a time, they held their own against the Florentines who came at them from all sides, but Hawkwood knew only too well that the longer the battle was joined the greater would be the number of his Company slaughtered. He reluctantly yielded and lowered his sword, signalling that the battle was over. All around him, his men laid down their arms. Some lay dead, others were dying, others still waited in vain for treatment. They were disarmed, and their armour and precious longbows confiscated.

A number of the wounded, some all but naked, were allowed to return in ignominy to Pisa. Hawkwood and his officers, among them Karl Eugen, had been marched in triumph to Florence, together with several hundred of the Company, who now faced the dismal prospect of years of captivity and forced labour. Meanwhile, a large detachment of Florentines had marched on Pisa, where they paraded in front of the city walls, bared their backsides in a gesture of contempt, and hurled abuse at the defenders before returning, honour satisfied, to Florence.

Hawkwood had long dreamt of entering Florence, albeit as a general at the head of a victorious army rather than as a captive soldier of fortune. He had never seen the inner city, and he was wholly unprepared for its unabashed splendour. He could readily understand why it was named Florentia, the Flourishing City. Given the present circumstances, however, he found he could not share Karl Eugen's elation at the sight of its Etruscan ramparts, its magnificent palazzos and *castelli*, its Roman baths and amphitheatres, its bustling markets and its imposing banking houses. Nor could he share Karl Eugen's undisguised admiration for the partially completed Cathedral of Santa Maria dei Fiore, for Giotto's campanile or for the church of Santa Margerhita de' Cerchi, where the exiled and discredited poet Dante Alighieri was believed to have caught a first fleeting glimpse of his muse, Beatrice Portinari.

Hawkwood had too many other things on his mind.

They were conveyed through the city streets to the Piazza dei Priori, whose slender square tower – the Palazzo dei Priori – had succeeded the Bargello palace fortress as the seat of Florentine government. Jeers and insults rang out as Hawkwood and the others descended from the ox-drawn carts, but the city fathers greeted them politely as they were ushered into the main Council Chamber. Chivalric custom decreed that they be formally regarded as 'guests' rather than prisoners. They were accorded every courtesy and afforded every honour due to their rank and reputation.

But prisoners they undoubtedly were.

Arrogance, cupidity and lack of discipline had been their undoing; he saw that now. He could not be certain what effect the shameful defeat at Cascina might have on his Company and, not least, on his own standing. Although Pisa could by no stretch of the imagination be regarded as easy prey for Florence and its allies, the disastrous events of the day would in all likelihood undermine Hawkwood's credibility as Pisa's *condottiere*.

That said, Galeotto Malatesta's decision to take them prisoner rather than kill them came as no surprise: their capture dealt a body blow to Pisa and boosted Florentine morale. It remained to be seen what the Florentine city fathers had in store for them.

Giancarlo Boninsegna stepped forward and bowed very slightly. Hawkwood returned the salutation but said nothing. Boninsegna glanced briefly at Karl Eugen and smiled a thin-lipped smile of satisfaction.

'It is an honour to meet one's adversaries and servants face to face,' said Boninsegna.

'As it is always an honour to meet those one has faced in the field,' replied Hawkwood.

The sarcasm was not lost on Boninsegna, but he elected to ignore it. He went on, 'I offer you the hospitality of Florence, and my own. Your loyal service to Pisa is admired by many. I am privileged to count myself among them.'

Hawkwood did not reply and Boninsegna changed tack. 'There are those in Florence who deem you an enemy. I, for one, do not.'

'I do not take your meaning.'

'I have long considered you a potential ally,' said Boninsegna. 'And, indeed, you have already served Florence well many times in the past.'

'With the greatest respect, I still do not take your meaning,' answered Hawkwood. 'I am Pisa's man and am pledged to serve as such.'

'And I – with equally great respect – submit that you are at this moment poorly placed to serve your masters and that they, in their turn, are poorly placed to serve you.'

'That may be,' countered Hawkwood, 'but my Company is at the disposal of Pisa and shall serve in my stead.'

'Come, come,' said Boninsegna, gesturing to Hawkwood to take a seat. 'We are men of reason and experience, you and I. You must accept that your Company is nothing without you at its head.'

Hawkwood made no reply. He suspected this to be true and was unwilling to protest to the contrary.

'You and I, Sir John, have much to discuss, and I suggest that as men of reason and experience we can doubtless resolve our differences.'

That remains to be seen, thought Hawkwood, wondering how.

Pisa, 7 August 1364

The Pisans watched in fear and despair as the tattered remnants of the White Company limped into the city all day long, their bare feet shredded by the stony ground, their wounds already festering and suppurating, their hangdog expressions eloquent testimony to their shame and humiliation.

Sir Wilfred and his men hurried out to meet them, hoisting the survivors onto their shoulders or fashioning litters for those who could walk no further. Perry had no need to ask what had happened: the details would emerge over time. For the present, wounds must be bound and amputations carried out.

It was evident that the Company had suffered a major defeat. So much had been made clear when the jubilant Florentines had descended on Pisa some days previously and paraded backwards and forwards a stone's throw from the city walls, hurling scorn and invective at the defenders. The Company's offensive force had been wiped out, and its commander had surrendered in the field and been taken as captive to Florence. Sir Wilfred was now the nominal head of the Company. It was a position he did not relish. He could only assume that the Florentines would move on Pisa any day now and that his first priority as Sir John's deputy must be to attend to the city's defences.

Nowhere was the panic more acute than in the Council of Guilds, where Hawkwood's defeat and capture had spawned impotence and outrage in almost equal parts. Tommaso Gracchi was unstinting in his efforts to reassure his fellow guildsmen that Hawkwood's release could be negotiated, subject to an appropriate ransom. But others, spurred on by Giacomo Albertosi, protested that Hawkwood had failed in his duties as *condottiere* and that his fate should be left to the Florentines' discretion. At the same time, they proposed no solution to Pisa's immediate predicament. Gennaro Altobardi, although he feared for the lives of Hawkwood and his fellow prisoners, argued that Pisa must await developments from the Florentine side before deciding on a course of action.

While the debate flowed back and forth, it dawned on one councillor that the situation could be turned to his personal advantage. Giovanni Agnello had long aspired to the title of Doge but that aspiration had consistently been frustrated for the simple reason that he was almost universally detested. His position on the council had been secured on the back of his enormous wealth – which many alleged to be in direct proportion to his duplicity – and to his unquestioned talents as a negotiator.

The would-be Doge of Pisa recognised that his moment had come. To the utter astonishment of Gracchi and Altobardi, he informed the council that the Virgin Mary had appeared to him in a dream and instructed him to assume full responsibility for securing Hawkwood's release by paying, from his own pocket, the ransom that Florence would undoubtedly exact. In exchange for doing so, Agnello petitioned the council for a 'modest' reward, namely that he be accorded the title of Doge for a period of one year. Incredibly, the Council of Guilds voted a resolution in his favour and on those terms.

Enraged, Gracchi immediately resigned his post as president of the council. Altobardi and two others also relinquished their seats in protest at what they regarded as a patent absurdity and a blatant bid for power. On behalf of the council, Giovanni Agnello graciously accepted their resignations, inwardly delighted his principal detractors had been so easily removed.

It was decided that Agnello should proceed to Florence under a flag of truce in order to discuss the terms and conditions of Hawkwood's repatriation and reinstatement as captain-general of the White Company, in which capacity he would – naturally – report in future directly and solely to the new and self-styled Doge. Altobardi's request to accompany Agnello as a member of the negotiating party was politely but firmly rejected, as was Sir Wilfred Perry's proposal that the council assume collective responsibility for securing – and underwriting – Hawkwood's release.

Agnello and a small escort left for Florence the following morning.

Florence, 14 August 1364

Hawkwood and Karl Eugen were quartered together in the very chambers from which Karl Eugen had made good his escape three years previously. On entering, Karl Eugen noted with a wry smile that the draperies and their silk cords had been removed. The bars at the window had been repaired and reinforced, and the iron lamps, one of whose brackets he had used to prise those bars apart, had been replaced by tallow candles set in wooden bowls.

They were continually under armed supervision and, in any case, could not count on a distraction from without. As if to drive that point home, Boninsegna had instructed the chamber doors to be left unbolted: Hawkwood and Karl Eugen were confined to the palazzo but otherwise free to come and go as they pleased, he said. After all, they were his guests.

Neither of them could see any means by which they could conceivably escape Boninsegna's 'hospitality'. But saving their own skins was not their principal concern. Of far greater importance was the welfare of the soldiers captured at Cascina.

'I demand news of my men and their well-being,' Hawkwood said to Boninsegna.

'Demand? *Demand*, Captain-General Hawkwood? I think not. You are ill placed to issue demands. But you may *request* news of them and I shall be happy to inform you accordingly.'

'Very well. I *request* knowledge of my men and of their well-being,' Hawkwood repeated.

'They are fed and watered as befits their station. We hold them by night in the Bargello fortress. By day, they labour at our discretion.'

'They are soldiers, not farm labourers and slaves.'

'I beg to differ. They *were* soldiers. They are now prisoners.'

'As I am myself, and my officers.'

'Need I remind you, Sir John, of the rules of engagement in times of war? You fought and were defeated, and in defeat there is no choice but to accept the terms the victor imposes.'

Hawkwood held Boninsegna's gaze for a moment then turned away, shaking his head in resignation. 'Do your worst,' he replied.

'On the contrary, I shall do my best. Even as we speak, the terms of your release are the subject of intense negotiation. I say no more at present, other than to observe that your Pisan masters appear to hold you in continued high regard. As, I hasten to assure you, I do myself.' With that, Boninsegna turned on his heel and left.

'Can he be taken at his word?' Karl Eugen asked.

Hawkwood shrugged. 'Who can be taken at his word in this land of self-seekers and double-dealers?'

The young man made no reply. Not long since, Karl Eugen von Strachwitz had been among the most self-seeking and double-dealing of all.

Two days later the doors of the chamber were thrown open and Boninsegna entered, followed by two armed guards and an elegantly attired figure that Hawkwood at first failed to recognise.

'Gentlemen,' said Boninsegna, 'may I present His Excellency Giovanni Agnello, Doge of Pisa? I believe you are already acquainted?'

Agnello removed his plumed *capello* and bent low in a sweeping bow.

Hawkwood could scarcely believe his eyes. What manner of duplicity was this? The Doge of Pisa? This smug tub-of-lard who routinely smirked and simpered at the far end of the table at the Council of Guilds?

'Signor Agnello,' he said uncertainly, 'I confess I am surprised to meet you again under such circumstances.'

'I present my compliments, Condottiere. I bring you greetings from the council I am honoured to represent. It gladdens my heart that you are in good health – and you, too, Herr von Strachwitz.'

Karl Eugen bowed. His mind was racing. He had seen Agnello on no more than a couple of occasions and had found him overbearingly self-important. This must be a ruse. Perhaps Gennaro . . . ?

'It will gratify you to know, Sir John, that you, your officers and your English men-at-arms are to be released forthwith,' said Boninsegna. 'Doge Agnello has personally indemnified the city state of Florence in order to secure your repatriation to Pisa.'

Hawkwood chose his words carefully. 'The Doge does us great honour. My men and I are indeed grateful.'

Agnello gave a dismissive wave of the hand. 'Pisa looks after its own,' he said.

Hawkwood could only nod. He was utterly bemused by this turn of events.

'Orders have been issued that your English comrades-in-arms are to be released unharmed,' said Boninsegna. 'You are to depart at first light tomorrow. We wish you God's speed.'

Agnello bowed again and minced out of the room, followed by the armed guards.

Boninsegna remained. 'Doge Agnello has met our ransom demand from his own purse, Captain-General,' he said. 'In full. He has secured your release on payment of thirty thousand gold florins and that of your men for a further twenty thousand. Accordingly, you are free to go – as free to go, I would add, as you are free to return to Florence whenever you may wish.'

He paused, then fixed his eyes on Hawkwood and spoke slowly and distinctly. 'Those fifty thousand florins will be given into your safekeeping as you depart tomorrow. You may do with them as you deem necessary. Florence has no need of such a trifling sum. Florence has need of *you*.'

Hawkwood was uncertain whether he had been complimented or insulted. What he did know with some certainty was that Giancarlo Boninsegna was issuing both a warning and an invitation. He resolved to be cautious.

'We thank you for your gracious hospitality,' he said.

'It has been our pleasure,' replied Boninsegna. 'As I have said more than once, the gates of Florence are always open to men of honour and integrity.'

The remnants of the White Company left Florence the following day.

Vinci, 18 August 1364

Vinci lay no more than a day's forced march from the gates of Florence, but it was close on nightfall on the second day before Hawkwood and his men at last reached the fortified town and made camp on the field below the castle. He and his officers had horses put at their disposal by Boninsegna, but had quickly dismounted and proceeded on foot in order that some of the Company's more seriously wounded could ride. The pace had been correspondingly slow and they were relieved to break their journey.

Cooking fires were lit and the men set about preparing a rudimentary meal from the meagre rations they had been issued in Florence. Hawkwood moved among the Company, consoling those worst injured. He discovered, rather to his surprise, that most of the men were in good heart. They had been routed at Cascina, certainly, but had accepted their defeat with good grace. After all, they had survived and were on their way home – or, rather, to the comparative creature comforts of Pisa Nuova.

Some would not return. Among them longbowman Huw Griffiths, who had taken a crossbow bolt through the neck. Hawkwood sat beside the towering figure of Llewellyn – who had suffered an ugly wound to his left thigh – and mouthed words of comfort. Griffiths and Llewellyn had been inseparable ever since Calais, and there were tears in Llewellyn's eyes as he talked of the diminutive Welshman and his skill with the bow.

Hawkwood had words of comfort, too, for those who had lost an arm or a leg. They would be sent home to England, he assured them, and would receive backpay due to them, together with a modest stipend to help ease their way back into civilian life.

The men responded to his ministrations. Some were clearly convinced he himself had negotiated their freedom. He did not disabuse them of this notion, not least because – up to a point – it was almost true: had it not been for his previous service to the Pisans, they might not have responded so promptly to Florence's demands.

He still found it difficult to account for the unexpected appearance in Florence of Giovanni Agnello, not to mention the man's sudden and inexplicable elevation to the rank of Doge. He could only surmise that Gracchi and Altobardi had concocted some scheme or other to secure his and his men's release, and that

Agnello was part of that scheme. All would be revealed when they reached Pisa in three or four days' time.

The defeat at Cascina still rankled but he had accepted it and, above all, his failure to control his men as a *condottiere* should. What he could not fathom was Boninsegna's attitude, especially his parting words. The Florentine had, he was obliged to concede, behaved with great courtesy throughout their enforced stay in Florence, and he could not fault the man's conduct. But what was the reason for Boninsegna's remarkable gesture in refusing the ransom monies paid by Pisa and putting them at Hawkwood's disposal? Hawkwood asked himself that question over and over again, but could arrive at no plausible motive.

What Hawkwood found hardest to stomach was the ransom process itself. It was a procedure he had endorsed unquestioningly throughout his career – and it had been a major factor in his emergence as a wealthy man – but this was the first time he himself had been ransomed. He felt a profound resentment that the negotiations had been completed entirely without his involvement. To have no control over his own value, his own destiny, reduced him to a commodity – a mere chattel which could be bought, sold and bartered at the whim of others. That, he now realised, was part and parcel of his status as a hireling. He found it demeaning.

He stood deep in thought on a knoll a few hundred paces from the encampment. Night had fallen, but the air was balmy, with only a wisp of wind caressing the grass at his feet.

'It is a night of great beauty,' came a soft voice from behind him. 'Does it please you to walk under the stars?'

He whirled round, his hand dropping to his dagger-hilt.

Donnina Visconti stood there, tall and proud, the fullness of her figure silhouetted by the breeze that ruffled her dark silk cape and moulded it to her body. She watched expectantly, waiting for Hawkwood's reaction.

'It pleases me,' he said.

She took his arm and they walked silently some distance further from the encampment. They stopped at the fringe of a small copse.

Donnina looked up at him. 'You sent me no word,' she said.

'Nor you me,' answered Hawkwood brusquely.

She was astonishingly beautiful, more beautiful even than he remembered. And how he had remembered: the day they met, the first night they had lain together, the wrench of her departure, his conviction that one day she would be his. Soon, he had thought, it would be soon. But that had been three long years ago and he had since heard – and done – nothing. Yet now, seemingly out of nowhere, she had heard of his defeat and had come to him again.

'You are well?' he enquired, at once conscious of the banality of the question.

'I am well,' replied Donnina. 'But what of you, my dearest Condottiere?'

The endearment irritated him. His first thought was to turn on her and demand an explanation for her protracted silence. But he checked, reminding himself she was a married woman now. No longer his.

'And what of your husband?' he asked.

'To my knowledge, he is well,' replied Donnina. 'I have seen but little of him these three years.'

'Why is that?'

'He has many interests,' she said.

She was tempted to add that those interests did not include her. The marriage was indeed one of convenience – in every sense. Through no fault of hers, it had never been consummated. She had dutifully offered her body on their wedding night and had been brusquely rejected. It seemed her new husband preferred other outlets: young, slender, fine-boned – and male. She had promised herself she would confide this to Hawkwood one day, should the opportunity present itself.

Hawkwood recalled how coarse and ungainly he had always felt in her presence. He cast about for words that might alleviate the tense silence.

'You have been in my thoughts,' he said eventually.

'And you have always been in mine,' said Donnina.

They embraced with a tenderness Hawkwood had not thought himself capable of. He felt her tears against the stubble on his cheek. He held her for a long time, until tenderness gave way to urgency.

She convulsed as he entered her and cried out as he climaxed.

He had found her again, and he vowed that she would always be part of his life, whatever the years ahead held in store.

Pisa, 20 August 1364

Giovanni Agnello had the bit between his teeth.

The Council of Guilds could do nothing other than formally acknowledge their indebtedness to this upstart merchant who, out of his own pocket, had delivered their *condottiere* from the clutches of the Florentines and, what was more, had somehow negotiated a year-long extension to the truce with their arch-enemy. Voices which would otherwise have been raised in dissent were still, particularly now that Gracchi, Altobardi and two or three others who might have been expected to question Agnello's motives and aspirations had resigned from office.

Agnello wasted no time. He recapitulated in considerable detail his successes as Pisa's envoy to Florence, and proclaimed himself Doge for life rather than for the one year originally agreed. The council knew full well that this ran counter to tradition, but raised no serious protest: when all was said and done, Pisa was demonstrably in Agnello's debt. Moreover, Massimo Mastrodonato, whom many regarded as the conscience of Pisa and the guardian of its resolutely republican heritage, was not present: he was gravely ill and was not expected to last the week.

Hawkwood said little as the council went on to transact its everyday business. He waited until the meeting was almost over before claiming the floor.

'This council and all of Pisa owe much to the intervention of Doge Agnello,' he said. 'As for myself and my men, we owe him a debt of gratitude which can be repaid only in part by pledging to continue in the service of Pisa. But there is one portion of that debt we can discharge forthwith and in full. The ransom monies expended by Doge Agnello on our behalf shall be reimbursed to him. I regard this as a matter of personal honour.'

Agnello had not anticipated this. His jaw dropped, but only for a second. He quickly regained his composure. 'Condottiere Hawkwood is indeed a man of integrity,' he said, trying hard to keep a note of condescension from his voice. 'I am certain that this council will continue to recognise his honourable intentions and will duly propose a schedule of repayment.'

'That will not be necessary,' said Hawkwood. 'I have already given my instructions. Fifty thousand florins shall be conveyed to the Doge's quarters this very day.'

At a stroke, Hawkwood had diluted Agnello's new-found authority. The latter might retain the title of Doge, but his standing with the council was damaged beyond repair. He stood exposed as a self-seeking go-between, whereas John Hawkwood had turned defeat at Cascina into victory in Pisa.

Agnello called the meeting to order. 'I am grateful to Sir John—' he began.

'It is I who am grateful,' interrupted Hawkwood. 'In all conscience, I could not continue in Pisa's service knowing that the *condotta* to which I am a party had resulted in the imposition of an intolerable financial burden on a member of this council.'

Applause broke out all round the table.

'As *primus inter pares*,' continued Hawkwood, 'Doge Agnello has upheld the best republican traditions of Pisa. And, as the first among equals, he has done this city state a great service.'

The applause grew louder.

Bastardo, thought Agnello. *Bastardo, bastardo, bastardo!* He held up his hands, modestly disclaiming the applause he knew to be directed not at him but at Hawkwood.

The meeting was over. Hawkwood rose from the table and shook hands with each councillor in turn, including Giovanni Agnello.

Hawkwood at last understood. It is all a game, he thought, and I am rapidly learning that it is played with no rules or, better still perhaps, with rules that are made to be broken. He resolved then and there to learn to play the game in earnest and to the best of his ability.

XIV

Master of the Game

'Twas said that never since the world began
Had so few men made such a noble band

Florence, 22 May 1369

History had taught John Hawkwood that military men tend to be viewed by society at large as little more than dependable servants of the established order and upholders of the status quo. Hawkwood saw things differently.

To him, it was society that was reactionary and, as a result, less flexible and less well equipped to deal with sudden and unwelcome change. By contrast, the military was a closed society with a fixed hierarchical base and an established set of criteria and procedures. As such, it was often much better placed to adapt to changing circumstances and concepts and to develop and hone strategic and tactical responses.

An army might well be a servant of the *res publica*, but Hawkwood believed that in order to serve *any* state to the best of its ability, an army must also be a *res perfecta*, a body complete in itself, a body which was, in the Platonic sense, self-sufficient, self-contained, self-sustaining and – although he, like most soldiers, might be reluctant to admit as much, even to himself – self-perpetuating.

Hawkwood had long since concluded that his first allegiance must be to his men. In exchange, he demanded only loyalty. Desertion was punishable by death, and theft – as opposed to looting – by instant flogging. There were many who regarded the mercenary's calling as a malignant growth in the body of society and a corruption of chivalric tradition. Hawkwood had little patience with that view. Chivalry was all too frequently an illusion, as the gruesome excesses of the Crusades had shown. He preferred to think of his Company as a band of brothers-in-arms who respected the chain of command and an unwritten code of decency and integrity which counted for more – much more – than the artificial and verbose codes of military service formulated and promulgated typically by men who had rarely, if ever, taken up arms themselves.

Since his humiliating defeat at Cascina five years previously, Hawkwood had done everything in his power to mould the White Company into a compact and self-sustaining unit. There was a clearly defined command structure. There were fixed and generous rates of pay and bonuses. There was provision for free medical treatment. There was an army bank which held deposits from and even approved loans to Company men. His men or their dependants were indemnified in the event of serious injury or loss of life. Payments fell due to those who had faithfully served out their contractual tour of duty. The Company was well equipped, well housed, well fed and well watered. Training programmes encouraged advancement within the ranks from modest footsoldier to specialist pikeman or longbowman. Taverns and brothels and rest camps in the hills provided for amusement and sport. To serve in the White Company was a privilege.

Much of the credit for this devolved to Sir Wilfred Perry, whose abilities as an administrator were, in Hawkwood's experience, without equal. But Sir Wilfred's achievements were in no small measure a reflection of Hawkwood's unremitting commitment to build his White Company into a body of professionals who thought and fought as a cohesive unit.

He had been fortunate in one significant respect. There had been an unexpected but protracted lull in major hostilities between Italy's city states. True, there had been short-lived civilian uprisings in Venice and in the Papal States in 1366–7, and the Company had been seconded to help put them down. The following year, a small detachment had been deployed to help ward off incursions into Piedmont by a makeshift army of Germans and Magyars. And, in early 1369, an insurrection in the

Marches had been quelled – brutally and profitably – by the simple expedient of detaching a large force which met with next to no armed resistance.

The White Company had been involved in a series of other engagements of little consequence. In one, at Arezzo, Hawkwood had even been taken hostage, but was soon ransomed. As his men had come to expect, Hawkwood continued to lead them into battle, but his value to the Company was now largely as a figurehead and strategist rather than as a fighting man. To a degree, he regretted this.

Donnina Visconti had no such regrets.

The two were now inseparable. They lived openly together in Pisa and in Florence where, to his continuing bewilderment, Hawkwood had become a well-known and respected public figure and a close confidant of Giancarlo Boninsegna. Donnina's status as the nominal spouse of the duke's half-brother provided unfettered access to Florentine society, whose mild disapproval of their liaison was eclipsed by the general distaste for her dissolute husband. The latter was approaching his seventies, his incipient dotage accelerated by the ravages of the pox. He was not expected to live much longer.

As 'Giovanni Acuto', Hawkwood was still revered by the citizens of Pisa. Although the Council of Guilds disapproved in principle of his increasingly close personal ties to Florence and Milan, it accepted that he had consistently honoured his *condotta* and acted in what they conceded to be in Pisa's longer-term interests. Besides, his manifest acceptance by Florence appeared to work in Pisa's favour, since he served as a buffer of sorts between the two city states. Indeed, as a member of the Pisan Guild, he had successfully advocated a compromise which many Pisans judged both eminently sensible and long overdue: he had proposed that, in exchange for a substantial annual commission, Pisa should grant Florence access to its seaports to facilitate Florentine textile shipments abroad. For the time being, at least, an accommodation of sorts had been reached – and Hawkwood now stood revealed not only as Pisa's *condottiere* but as an honest broker acting to the mutual benefit of two erstwhile rivals. The arrangement had been greatly to Hawkwood's liking inasmuch as he had been remunerated by both parties.

What he still found difficult to accept, in view of the simmering rivalry between Florence and Milan, was that the Tyrant of Milan had been willing to marry his daughter to the Duke of Florence's half-brother. The marriage was, for reasons he had since learnt, doomed to be without issue. Moreover, it had lessened tensions between Milan and Florence to no perceptible degree. He had once – and only once – broached the subject with Donnina and had been taken aback by her angry response.

'Your father must be endowed with uncommon foresight,' he had ventured.

'In what way?' said Donnina.

'Your marriage . . .' he said, hesitating as he caught the unmistakable flash of irritation that crossed her face.

'A marriage decreed by politics.'

'Evidently,' said Hawkwood. 'But to what practical outcome?'

'That is for my father to know. It does not concern you. You should be aware that there are elements in Milan who openly challenge my father's authority, who *openly* conspire against his rule.'

'And?'

'*And*, for reasons of state best known to himself, my father considered the marriage appropriate and expedient.'

Hawkwood inwardly refuted any suggestion that Donnina's marital status was no concern of his. Nor did he consider that vague 'reasons of state' were an adequate explanation.

' "Reasons of state"?' he persisted. 'What "reasons of state", pray?'

'Reasons of which I have no knowledge. I am my father's daughter, and I obey as he commands. He is a man not unlike yourself, decisive, uncompromising, difficult to understand at times. He has his own way of seeing things, as have you.'

'And, like myself, he is not *always* incapable of poor judgment?'

'That remains to be seen. But no, not always.'

Hawkwood had decided to let the matter rest. The issue was sensitive and he did not wish to quarrel. He had not yet been presented to Bernabò Visconti, but he knew him by reputation. One day, he thought, we shall meet and I shall form my own opinion. After all, he is her father . . .

Donnina's anger subsided as quickly as it had erupted. 'I have great faith in your judgment,' she said, holding out an olive branch which Hawkwood graciously accepted.

'And I in yours, Donnina Visconti,' he replied. He had consistently refused to address her by her married name.

Hawkwood regretted that the exchange had taken place. He admitted to himself that, for some months now, he had been aware of his own shortcomings as a father. His daughter Antiocha must be – what? – almost ten by now, and he had never seen her, never even corresponded with her. What must she think of him? Indeed, did she think of him? Did she even know who her father was? Or, for that matter, where he was and what he did?

Time and again, his thoughts turned to England. Would he ever again see the country of his birth? Would he ever see Hawkwood Manor once more? Had England changed as much as he himself had changed?

These and similar questions could not be answered by the scant reports received at third hand from new recruits to the Company. What could those recruits know of the England he had known and loved?

Windsor Castle, 22 May 1369

Edward III, King of England and aspirant to the throne of France, stood at the window and looked out over Windsor Great Park, reflecting on his life and times.

He had been on the throne since 1327 when, as a mere stripling of fourteen, he had been obliged to step into his father's shoes on the latter's abdication. But his reign had not started in earnest until three or four years later, when he had at last cut himself loose from his French-born mother Isabella's apron strings and rid himself for good of John Mortimer, Earl of March, who had conspired against Edward's father and been an instrument of the latter's overthrow.

Edward sipped from a goblet of his favourite claret as he recalled the highs and lows of his reign. By the grace of God, he thought, it had all started so well. He had brought the perfidious Scots to heel at the battle of Halidon Hill in 1333, paying them back in their own currency for the ignoble defeat suffered by his father at Bannockburn. Yet he harboured a strong suspicion that his judgment might have been flawed when he decided to move against the French some four years later. God knows, he told himself, I had reason enough at the time: the Gascon question had been a perennial thorn in England's side, Brittany was a bone of contention gnawed in turns by England and France, and Flanders was . . . well, Flanders, a land that owed allegiance to the French crown yet was dependent for its livelihood on imports of English wool and vital exports of textiles to England.

He could not understand his father's attachment to the Capetian Queen Isabella, but that union had provided a convenient peg on which to hang his own pretensions to the French throne and contest the claim of Philippe of Valois. If nothing else, his declaration of war on France had fired the popular imagination. The fleur-de-lis of France still adorned his heraldic device, despite the fact that, deep down, he now doubted that his bid for the French throne would ever bear fruit.

In the early days of the French war, things had gone very much Edward's way. In 1340, English ships had sent an entire French fleet to the bottom at the battle of Sluys off the Flemish coast and, in 1346, French armies under Philippe VI had been virtually annihilated at Crécy. The latter had been a *very* good year, both at home and abroad. His armies had halted the Scots as they advanced on Northumbria and probed further south in support of the French. That was also the year when he had captured Scotland's David II, son of Robert the Bruce. And then – then! – came the glory of Poitiers in 1356 and the valiant rearguard action fought by his pride and joy – and his successor – Edward,

Prince of Woodstock, Prince d'Aquitaine, Prince of Wales, Duke of Cornwall and Earl of Chester. His Edward, his Black Prince.

But then it had all started to turn sour. The Black Prince's victories in the field had been more than offset by a series of crises. The situation in Aquitaine was spiralling out of control. Two years ago, in 1367, the Black Prince had fought a campaign which had culminated in a resounding victory at Najéra but which had ruined the prince's health and drained Edward's coffers. The prospects of sound English rule in Aquitaine were now bleak. It was reported that the nobles and prelates had appealed to Charles V of France to intervene and Edward had some difficulty in suppressing a chuckle as he recalled the Black Prince's response when summoned by Charles to appear before the parliament in Paris only two months ago: 'Gladly, but with sixty thousand men at my back.' To be sure, it was a reply worthy of a future king, but it was also a reply as hollow as it was spirited.

Meanwhile, the Black Death had ravaged the whole of Europe and had inflicted irreparable damage on Edward's realm. The balance of power in the kingdom had shifted – and shifted for good, it seemed – as the long-established feudal order was usurped by a new social reality where bloodlines were substituted by new-found wealth and property, and where commoners now vied with princes and kings. The ranks of the Church had been severely reduced by the plague and the Church as an institution had been greatly diminished in terms of its hierarchical power, spawning the likes of John Wycliffe and his 'mumblers', Lollards who preached the salvation of all believers.

England had needed a focus again and Edward III had attempted to supply that focus by redoubling his efforts against the French. War was a great catalyst. Lately, however, it seemed the Commons had lost its taste for war and was set to oppose him at every turn.

True, war was a costly business. Gone were the days when armies could be mustered as of right and as a matter of feudal obligation. Now everything had its price. Edward needed to raise money if he was to continue his crusade against the French. That meant only one thing: going cap in hand once again to the Florentines.

Château de Vincennes, 22 May 1369

Charles V of France sat in his library in the Château de Vincennes. Like his counterpart across the Channel, he was taking stock.

It was almost thirteen years since his father, King Jean, had been taken hostage by the English following the battle of Poitiers; Jean had since died unransomed in London. While still Dauphin of France, Charles – Jean's eldest son and successor – had weathered a number of storms, including a full-scale rebellion spearheaded by the States General under the leadership of merchant-provost Etienne Marcel, not to mention a series of peasant uprisings in north-eastern France – the so-called 'Jacquerie' – in protest against swingeing dues levied to pay for the refortification of Paris at a time when companies of mercenaries were systematically pillaging the French countryside.

Though a mere twenty-year-old, Charles had risen to these challenges. By 1358 he had quashed the uprisings, and by 1360 he had made short shrift of the ringleaders. Even before his accession to the throne in 1364, he had had every reason to believe he had acquitted himself well. But there was much still to be done. He had great plans: for a new defensive wall round Paris, for the beautification of the Château de Vincennes, for the construction of a *bastille*, and for the furtherance of the arts and natural sciences in France to rival those of the Italian city states.

The perennial thorn in France's side was England. And King Edward's obsession with the French crown. Charles knew Edward was in dire need of a popular war with France to keep in line the malcontents among his subjects. He also knew that war had so depleted the English exchequer that Edward would be decidedly *un*popular if he could not post another outstanding victory. Charles was determined such a victory would not be forthcoming. Accordingly, he had decided to temporise, alternating protracted negotiation with a campaign of discreet attrition directed at the remaining English presence in Calais and the Aquitaine.

Charles also needed to build alliances on the diplomatic front. He hoped his brother-in-law Galeazzo Visconti might prove an invaluable ally in Milan.

The burdens of kingship are at times intolerable, thought Charles. He turned to the other man in the room, Gilles Malet, a distinguished academic recently appointed Keeper of the King's Books and commissioned to draw up an inventory of the royal library to be housed in a remodelled Louvre Palace.

'There is no honour in the English soul,' said Charles.

Malet looked up from his annotations. He thought it prudent to agree.

Florence, 3 July 1369

'It is a matter of honour,' said John Hawkwood.

'It is a matter of necessity,' replied Giancarlo Boninsegna. 'You have many mouths to feed. You have friends, but you have made enemies, too. There are those who fear you and those who respect you. Some do both. You must choose and you must choose wisely. You have served Pisa well. You would serve Florence equally well.'

Hawkwood had to concede Boninsegna's point. For five years now, he had served first one master then another. He had been for a time in the pay of Milan, then in that of Florence and its allies against Milan. He had fought against Captal de Buch and alongside him, against the Germans of the Company of the Flower and together with them.

'It is a matter of honour,' insisted Hawkwood. 'I have given my word. In all conscience, I cannot enter into an exclusive contract with Florence at this time. I will not bear arms against Pisa and I fear that is the longer-term intention of Florence. I shall look south to Rome and to service with the Pope – or, if need be, against him.'

With the Pope – or, if need be, against him? Hawkwood had

spoken with such detachment, thought Boninsegna. This Hawk-wood was a fighting man pure and simple, whose loyalty was routinely bought and paid for and whose allegiance was trans-ferred with the casualness and insouciance others might exhibit in the choice of a new pair of breeches. Boninsegna fought back a sudden surge of anger at the credo by which these itinerant mercenaries lived. They sold themselves with impunity to the highest bidder, supremely confident that the 'battles' they fought were rarely conclusive but more often than not little more than set pieces, in which one company of freebooters squared off against another, taking pains to avoid serious injury, let alone death, only too aware that today's enemy might well be tomorrow's com-rade-in-arms. Prisoners were taken, ransoms claimed, menaces uttered and stipends demanded; but, in the long run, the threat posed by the mercenaries was not so much to one another as to the city states they served.

Boninsegna saw there was little to be gained from pointing out to Hawkwood that the typical mercenary profited less by waging war than by extracting vast sums not to do so. Hawkwood's continuing loyalty to Pisa appeared commendable, but Bonin-segna knew that loyalty to be in part expedient and self-serving. Pisa was a safe haven to which Hawkwood could return time after time, irrespective of his exploits elsewhere. It was a con-venient and secure location to bind his wounds, regroup and re-provision.

'I would gladly persuade you that your better interests may now lie not in Pisa but elsewhere.'

Hawkwood hesitated and Boninsegna pressed the point home. 'When all is said and done, your original *condotta* was concluded with Tommaso Gracchi and the then Council of Guilds rather than with that pompous ass Giovanni Agnello.'

Boninsegna knew Hawkwood secretly despised the self-annointed and self-appointed Doge of Pisa, who had somehow – only God knew how – contrived to cling to his position for so long. But the Englishman had shown few if any scruples when it came to exploiting Agnello's protection, political leverage and so-called friendship. It would be interesting to see how Hawkwood would react now that Agnello had been deposed: the initial signs were that Agnello's successor, Pietro Gambacorta, had little taste for Hawkwood's continued presence in Pisa.

One day, thought Boninsegna, Italy – a united Italy – will be free of them all. We have done ourselves a great disservice by allowing them into our midst and affording them such free rein. But one day – *one day* – we shall rid ourselves of them for good.

'Florence has no pressing need for my services at this time,' said Hawkwood. 'You have a surfeit of Genoese, French and German stipendiaries to do your bidding.'

For that and other reasons, Hawkwood could not understand why Boninsegna consistently courted his Company and his friendship. After all, they had started out as enemies and he had since campaigned both directly and indirectly against the armies of Florence, most recently at the siege of San Miniato – a fortified town which Hawkwood, then in the pay of Milan, had wrested from an inept Florentine commander, Giovanni Malatacca, only for it to be retaken not long after. Yet Boninsegna appeared to bear no grudge.

Boninsegna's reluctant admiration for Hawkwood was rooted exclusively in the fact that, all things considered, the Englishman was the finest mercenary of them all. Politically inept at times, perhaps, but a thoroughgoing professional.

'It is for you to know where your own best interests lie. I command your prudence in that regard and bow to your decision,' said Boninsegna. And thought: you are destined to serve and, sooner or later, you will be conscripted into the permanent service of Florence. 'I would rather you be with us, however, than against us.'

There, thought Boninsegna. I have said it.

Hawkwood was not as naive as Boninsegna believed. For Hawkwood, the prime consideration was that the trade of war should be profitable. The cost of maintaining the Company in the field was considerable, but so too were the stipends and ransoms he collected. Although much of the revenue accrued to Hawkwood's seconds and his fighting men, a large portion went to Hawkwood himself. As a result, he had accumulated a substantial fortune over the years.

This was a subject Boninsegna had long been anxious to broach. He was well placed to know of Hawkwood's finances and felt the time was right to counsel him in that respect.

'It is time to invest, Sir John.'

'I know little of such matters, and care even less.'

'But I venture to assure you that I know all there is to know – and more besides. Much of the splendour you see around you was underwritten by profits generated by Florence's finance houses. We Florentines have long been Europe's bankers. We accept deposits for safekeeping. We deal in coin and bullion. We issue bills of exchange. Our fiorino is the known world's most stable internationally traded currency. We know our business. We make fortunes grow.'

'I have heard tell of the Bardi family, the Peruzzi and others,' said Hawkwood grudgingly.

'Then you must know that their collapse some two decades ago was caused not by their own incompetence but by the dishonourable behaviour of King Edward – your *English* King Edward – who defaulted on his debts and drove the Bardi and Peruzzi into bankruptcy.'

Hawkwood merely nodded. That was in another life now, yet he was still reluctant to speak directly either against or in defence of Edward. An Englishman at heart . . .

'A great banking tradition does not die out with one or two families,' continued Boninsegna smoothly. 'There are many, many others in Florence with experience and expertise. My own bank is among them.'

Hawkwood hesitated. He had already given this some thought, prompted by his obligations to Donnina and, not least, to his daughter, Antiocha.

'What do you propose?' he asked.

'That you consign your assets to us for safekeeping. At your discretion, you may also wish to assign to us an entitlement to make such dispositions on your behalf as we consider appropriate to increase your fortune.'

'I should wish for guarantees.'

'You do well to think thus,' said Boninsegna. 'I warn only that you may gain from such investment but may also lose – that is in the nature of things. As to guarantees, I can suggest two. The first is that you be elected without delay to the governing council of the banking commission of Florence in order that you may help oversee and approve the uses to which your funds are put.'

'And the second?'

'Come, come, Sir John. You have the Company at your disposal. We in Florence would not wish to meet again with your displeasure. What better guarantee could there possibly be?'

'What better guarantee, indeed?' said Hawkwood after a moment's deliberation. 'But there is one further surety I require.'

'Namely?'

'Namely that, in the event of my demise, whether as a friend or foe of Florence, my fortune be disbursed in equal portions to my Company, to my daughter, Antiocha, and to my . . . my good friend, the Lady Donnina Visconti.'

'That you should make such generous provision for your Company is commendable, Sir John,' said Boninsegna with no trace of irony. 'Papers will be drafted to that effect.'

'Then you shall have my authority and my signature tomorrow.'

Giancarlo Boninsegna had come one step closer to binding Hawkwood's destiny to that of the city state of Florence.

Florence, 5 July 1369

Karl Eugen strongly counselled against it and Donnina was incensed, not only at Hawkwood's refusal to listen to reason but also because she regarded his intentions as reckless and, perhaps even worse, as a blatant affront to tradition. She appealed to him to reconsider, but he stubbornly refused, pointing out over and over again that he had given the matter considerable thought. He was in the prime of life and in excellent physical condition. It was an opportunity to do what he had long dreamt of doing.

Karl Eugen pleaded with him in private. This would by all accounts be no leisurely *pas d'armes* conducted for the sheer pleasure of it, but more like a *combat à outrance* fought to the point of disablement or death.

'Nonsense,' said Hawkwood. 'Would you deny me my moment of glory?'

'I seek to deny you nothing,' said Karl Eugen, 'but this is madness. You have no place there, I say. Siena is a hostile city and you, sir, are a marked man.'

'Sienese tradition assures me of safe conduct,' countered Hawkwood. 'Siena is to celebrate the festival of Our Lady of the Assumption and is declared an open city during the festivities. We are at liberty to come and go for such peaceful purpose as we please. None may challenge or hinder us. Nor would they dare, with the Company at our backs.'

Karl Eugen shook his head in disbelief. 'This will end badly,' he said.

'No,' said Hawkwood. 'It will end honourably.'

Donnina wept as the Company made preparations to leave for Siena. Her exhortations had come to nothing. Hawkwood was adamant.

He would ride in the Palio.

XV

Palio

What manner of fellow may you be
So impertinent to contest here?

Siena, 26 July 1369

Karl Eugen was intrigued that, far from being regarded as an enemy and interloper, Hawkwood had been formally welcomed to Siena by a deputation of civic dignitaries. Hawkwood had taken obvious pleasure in the courteous – albeit cautious – manner of his reception. As they walked within the city, Karl Eugen was agreeably surprised at Hawkwood's familiarity with the treasures Siena had to offer. He could only conclude that Sir John had been adequately instructed in this respect by the Lady Donnina.

For his part, Karl Eugen was captivated by the elegant twelfth-century palaces that fringed Siena's shell-shaped Piazza del Campo, dwarfed only by the slender Torre del Mangia belltower. To the right of the Torre – recently completed by the architect brothers Muccio and Francesco di Rinaldo – was the Palazzo Pubblico, whose Sala del Mappamondo boasted not only Pietro and Ambrogio Lorenzetti's celebrated map of the known world but also Pietro and Simone Martini's *Maestà*, portraying the Virgin Mary in all her glory, complete with her entourage of apostles, saints and angels.

Karl Eugen was also nervous: neither he nor Hawkwood carried any weapons. What was to prevent the Sienese from taking them prisoner and holding them to ransom? He had voiced his misgivings more than once, but Hawkwood had repeatedly reassured him that, as was plain for all to see, Siena was indeed – if only for the time being – an open city. No harm would befall them.

They moved from chamber to chamber in the Palazzo Pubblico. They admired Lorenzetti's celebrated allegorical fresco of *Good and Bad Government*, which decorated the Sala della Pace. And Hawkwood paused in the Sala del Mappamondo before Simone Martini's equestrian portrait of Italian *condottiere* Guidoriccio da Fogliano, depicted in full battle dress.

'It seems we are not the first *condottieri* to have made our mark on Siena,' he said.

'No,' replied Karl Eugen. 'And, with certainty, not the last.'

Hawkwood had as yet not made known his intention to ride in the Palio. When he did, the cordial atmosphere altered abruptly.

'I fear that cannot be permitted' was the immediate response from Dario Bruschelli, the senior deputy of the festival.

'Why not, pray?'

'The Palio is our greatest institution,' replied Bruschelli. 'It is the soul of Siena, and only citizens of the Siena *contrade* are admitted to the race. Besides, the ten districts to be represented this year have already been determined and their horses chosen and inspected. The first trials have been run. There remains only the general trial, which will be contested three weeks from today.'

'Then, clearly, an eleventh mount must be selected and put at my disposal for that trial,' said Hawkwood.

Bruschelli shook his head. 'That cannot be. There are forty-two *contrade* in Siena, and only ten are admitted to each Palio – the others must await the outcome of next year's draw. We cannot sanction any departure from this tradition.'

'That is unacceptable,' said Hawkwood with a grim smile. 'How shall I explain to my Company – encamped, as it will soon be, but one hour's march from the gates of Siena – that their captain-general has been rejected by this city? I warrant they will not take kindly to such a grievous insult.'

'We intend no insult,' insisted Bruschelli. 'But be reasonable, Condottiere Hawkwood. Siena cannot countenance infringement of rules honoured these hundred and fifty years and more.'

'Rules,' said Hawkwood gruffly, 'can be broken. I propose you reconsider your decision. I would wish no harm to come to the fair city of Siena.'

He and Karl Eugen waited patiently in the Sala della Pace while the Sienese withdrew to deliberate. Bruschelli was opposed in principle to Hawkwood's participation in the race but was mindful of the implicit threat posed to Siena should the Company take station beyond the city walls. Any disruption to the hallowed tradition of the Palio was unthinkable.

It was Gianluca Pinna, the *sindaco* of the Torre district, who proposed a compromise: that Hawkwood be permitted to ride in the final trial, scheduled to be held on the morning of the Palio itself.

'There can be no great danger in that,' said Mayor Pinna. 'The Englishman may ride well, but he is no match for our own experienced riders. Almost certainly, he will be taken down. It will add to the spectacle to witness his fall from grace. Should he fail to complete the course, he will perforce forfeit his right to enter the Palio.'

There were nods of agreement.

'What if he does not accept those conditions?' asked Bruschelli.

'He is a man of overweening arrogance,' replied Pinna. 'Should he fail in the general trial he will not seek further humiliation. Of that we can be certain.'

'And what if he should acquit himself well?' put in Luca Trecciolini of the Lupa *contrada*. 'What then, I ask you all?'

'Then we shall have a problem of a different order on our hands,' said Bruschelli, 'and we must then seek another solution.'

Pinna's suggestion was grudgingly accepted.

Bruschelli returned alone to the Sala della Pace to inform Hawkwood. He fully expected the compromise solution to be rejected out of hand, and was agreeably taken aback when the captain-general nodded his assent.

'The proposal is good,' said Hawkwood. 'I thank you for the honour you do me.'

'The honour is ours,' said Bruschelli, wondering how this great bear of a man could have come to be known as Giovanni Acuto. *Acuto*? Foolhardy was nearer the mark . . .

Siena, 16 August 1369

The Piazza del Campo was filled to overflowing. Minstrels, fire-eaters and clowns thronged the neighbouring streets, striving to entertain the crowds. Wine-sellers dispensed their wares from goatskin pouches and sweetmeat vendors hawked their *cavatelli*, *ricciarelli* and *panforte*. Pickpockets plied their trade, bumping and jostling this way and that amid the expectant masses, relieving the unsuspecting citizens of Siena of purses and other valuables. Dark-eyed whores rubbed themselves invitingly against city burghers, flitting a hand over a cheek here, clutching a groin there. Above, on the palazzo balconies, Siena's notables gazed out over the square, pointing excitedly as riders and mounts emerged and took up position.

It was the morning of the final trial, the *provaccio* or 'bad trial', thus called because the riders rode more prudently than before, anxious to husband their own strength and that of their mounts for the Palio proper, which would be contested that evening.

John Hawkwood faced his first trial ride with unexpected trepidation. The mounts were without saddle. Each rider carried a vicious whip fashioned from ox tendon. Once the race was under way, no holds were barred, no tactics outlawed. He felt more nervous than before any battle he had ever fought. His mouth was dry and his hands twitched as he sought to control Ambasciatore, the dark chestnut stallion he had been allotted. He ran his hands through the horse's mane and patted it reassuringly on the neck. It was a fine animal, heavily muscled and powerful. He had feared he would be given a mount of inferior quality, but this was manifestly not so.

He looked around at the other riders. They returned his gaze. There was no mistaking the hostility in their eyes. But he saw fear there also – fear of losing, fear of failing to acquit themselves well, fear of shame and disgrace.

It was a fear he now shared.

The course was set out round the circumference of the piazza. Turf had been laid along the outer perimeter to help the horses keep their footing on the polished cobblestones. Padded sections alongside the course afforded a measure of protection to the riders – and to the crowd. The starting order was determined arbitrarily, using coloured balls that were drawn in random sequence to establish who lined up next to whom. Hawkwood had been drawn sixth, squarely in the middle of the starting line-up. He held station as the horses to his left and right buffeted him.

A cannon was fired. There were ten riders in the line. The eleventh started from behind the others and it was his task (and, some believed, advantage) to race forward and pull abreast of the other ten as the hempen rope stretched before them fell away, signalling the off.

The race was under way.

Hawkwood knew what he must do: survive. He cherished no hope whatsoever of winning the race, only of competing well. He settled down midway through the field, moving easily and holding his position without great difficulty as they swept through the initial curve of the course. The horse nearest him swerved abruptly into his path and he checked momentarily. As they completed the first of the three rounds of the Piazza del Campo, he felt the exquisite pleasure that springs from the bonding of man and horse.

He began to ride more aggressively. There were only three riders ahead of him, contesting the lead. The inside horse veered into the path of the other two, crowding them out at the turn. The tactic was as effective as it was ruthless. One horse went down, pitching its rider into the path of those behind. The second shied away, losing ground rapidly.

Hawkwood decided to do nothing rash. He lay a comfortable third as they approached the start line for the last time. To his left, a riderless horse drew level, and he checked his own mount to let it pass: there was no need to take risks.

The noise was deafening as the crowd acclaimed the winning

horse. It was ridden by a lean, wiry man who brandished his whip in triumph and elation as he took a further turn round the piazza.

Hawkwood reined in. He was more than satisfied. He had come through the trial unscathed and had learnt much which would stand him in good stead that evening. The race had been exhilarating, but he knew in his bones it was only a mild foretaste of the main event. He had given a good account of himself, proving he was indeed horseman enough to compete in what was regarded as the most gruelling horse race in all of Europe.

High above the piazza, Bruschelli turned to Pinna. 'There is a problem, is there not?'

'I fear there is,' replied an ashen-faced Pinna. 'And I am honour-bound to resolve it.'

The feast day of Our Lady of August, the Virgin Mary of the Assumption, had been one of incomparable pageantry. Siena was festooned with garlands, tapestries and banners. Flag-throwers had paraded through the streets of the city. Horses and riders had been blessed. A number of prisoners had been ceremonially pardoned and released. And there had been food and drink for all. Thousands of wax candles, many embellished with intricate gold-leaf scrolls, had been placed in the cathedral. And the Pallium, the splendidly ornate strip of precious embroidery that gave its name to the race, had been stuffed with valuable ermine pelts and put on display to the people thronging the Piazza del Campo.

Hawkwood had marvelled at the splendour and sheer opulence of it all, relishing the spectacle as each of the city's forty-two *contrade* paraded its colours, irrespective of whether that year's draw had favoured their inclusion or not. Now, however, as the prescribed hour drew close, he could feel a dryness in his throat. He wiped his hands on his black, tight-fitting breeches. He tried to visualise the course, to gauge in his mind's eye the distances to be covered before each tight turn, assessing in advance when and where best to put on or take off speed, choosing the most opportune and efficient racing line.

The riders sat in silence, each lost in his own thoughts, each steeling himself for the challenge ahead. Three turns of the Piazza del Campo. One thousand paces. One hundred seconds. The shortest of intervals between fame and shame. Goose, Caterpillar, Dragon and She-Wolf. Panther, Snail and Porcupine. Owl, Unicorn and Tortoise. And John Hawkwood on Ambasciatore.

Hawkwood tried to compose himself. He searched the tense faces around him, noting the tell-tale signs. Feet shuffled, fingers drummed, hands twitched. Some prayed, some stared blankly into the distance, others held their eyes closed. They had each looked him over in turn and had made no effort to conceal their animosity. Hawkwood sensed he was a marked man. The evening was warm and still and Hawkwood could feel the sweat pooling under his arms and gathering at the nape of his neck.

He coughed to clear his throat.

Three horses had finished ahead of him in the *prova generale* that morning, but he could identify only two sets of colours with any certainty: the black, red and cobalt blue stripes of the winner, Istrice (Porcupine), and the white, orange and blue stripes of the Leocorno (Unicorn) *contrada*. The riderless horse he had allowed through on the final lap was possibly Oca, from the Goose *contrada*. And the horse that had fallen so heavily during the *provaccia* had, as far as he could recall, carried the red, green and yellow-striped colours of the Drago (Dragon) *contrada*. Its rider now boasted a left arm swathed in bandages. His face was severely bruised. Hawkwood could only admire the man's courage and tenacity.

Bruco (Caterpillar) had finished fifth behind Hawkwood, followed by Lupa (She-Wolf), Pantera (Panther), Civetta (Owl), Chiocciola (Snail) and – appropriately enough – Tartuca (Tortoise). But those placings were irrelevant now. There was no telling what tactics each rider had elected to follow in that morning's trial. Worse, Hawkwood found it impossible to assess the qualities of those who had finished behind him.

Any of us could win, he thought – including myself. But he put all thoughts of winning to one side. It was enough to compete. More than enough.

It was a daunting prospect. Most of the competitors had ridden in the Palio before and knew what to expect. Two horses, Istrice and Bruco, were previous winners, and heavy wagers had been placed on both. Karl Eugen had wagered on Hawkwood, although he secretly believed his captain-general had next to no hope of carrying the day.

At that moment, Hawkwood would have agreed and would have thought twice about placing a wager on himself. He resolved to acquit himself as best he could, but he was already beginning to regret his insistence on taking part.

The draw had been made and Hawkwood found himself consigned to the inside position. This was a serious disadvantage, because the turns would be substantially tighter than on the outside. The horses were escorted to the starting line by their grooms, who, with volunteers from their *contrada*, had spent many sleepless nights watching over their charges and protecting them against interference by rival districts.

The riders were called by their starting order. As each emerged from the enclosure in front of the Palazzo Pubblico, an ear-splitting roar came from the crowd. As a consequence of the draw, Hawkwood was the last to appear. He had not expected a welcoming roar – a ripple of polite applause was probably the most he could have hoped for – but he was wholly unprepared for the hissing and booing that greeted him. A wave of unmitigated hatred swept over a bewildered Hawkwood, and the other riders stared at him with undisguised venom.

Only when he walked forward to take his place beside Karl Eugen, who was holding Ambasciatore at the ready, did he understand why. Hawkwood – the outsider, the interloper – was dressed in black breeches and a plain white *blouson*. Unwittingly, he had chosen the 'colours' of Siena, the hallowed black and white that decorated the city's *balzana* or coat-of-arms, the symbolic black and white of the marble flagstones in Siena Cathedral. The huge crowd screeched their fury at what they took to be a deliberate affront.

As Hawkwood reached his allotted place in the starting line, a man broke from the crowd to his left, a stiletto glinting in his hand. He bore down on Hawkwood and slashed viciously at him. Hawkwood was too stunned to react, but Karl Eugen thrust himself between Hawkwood and his assailant.

The stiletto buried itself to the hilt in Karl Eugen's belly.

He staggered and fell back against Hawkwood. The attacker immediately disappeared into the crowd. It had happened in a matter of seconds and only a handful of people had either seen or grasped what had occurred.

Karl Eugen slumped to the ground. Hawkwood knelt beside him, cradling his head. There was next to no blood, but Hawkwood knew the wound was deep and suspected it was fatal.

The young German lay still, his face contorted in pain. 'Go,' he whispered. 'Ride – ride for me.'

Hawkwood hesitated.

'Go!'

A small group had gathered round them. They gestured to Hawkwood to stand back, and gently lifted Karl Eugen's limp body and carried him to one side. An emaciated but still uncommonly beautiful young woman in a nun's habit stooped and covered him with a simple woollen shawl. Karl Eugen's breathing was shallow, his face a deathly white.

The cannon fired and the lead rider lurched forward. The hempen rope was still in place but the race had effectively started. Hawkwood threw a desperate last glance at Karl Eugen, then turned and mounted. As he did so, the rope dropped.

Hawkwood was last away and trailed the field by several lengths as the leading horses arched into the first turn. He shook his head violently in a bid to concentrate on the task in hand. He felt a fury unlike any he had ever experienced. And he channelled that fury into a race he was more than ever determined to win.

He at once realised there was a considerable advantage to being at the back. He could see how the race was developing ahead of him, while keeping out of harm's way in the early stages. Best of all, his inside draw was no handicap now. He could choose the best line, hold station and reel in those ahead during the second and third laps.

As the field turned towards the finishing line at the end of the first lap, Tartuca was in the lead, closely shadowed by Lupa and Civetta. That morning's winner, Istrice, trailed by a length, while the other horses were in a tight bunch and gradually losing ground.

Hawkwood was deaf to the screams of the crowd as he turned for the second lap. He was closer now, much closer. He closed on and passed Leocorno and Oca on the inside – both riders were clearly surprised by his sudden appearance – and slowly drew level with Drago. Drago's rider swerved against him and lashed out with his ox-tendon whip, catching Hawkwood across the forehead, splitting the skin. Mingled blood and sweat ran down into his eyes and he took a hand from the reins to wipe it away. Drago's rider aimed a second blow, but he had left it too late. The whip caught Ambasciatore on the flank, raising an ugly welt.

Hawkwood wasted no time in retaliation. He was momentarily in the clear as Ambasciatore surged forward. Hawkwood leant low over the horse's neck, shouting encouragement in its ear. Ambasciatore responded, passing Bruco with ease and closing rapidly on Pantera and Chiocciola. Pantera's rider had used the whip on Chiocciola's rider and the latter had reacted by cannoning into Pantera. Pantera's hind quarters slammed into the padded *barriera* with such force that its rider was catapulted from its back. Chiocciola spun away after the impact, leaving a gap between itself and the barrier.

Hawkwood took Chiocciola on the outside.

Ahead, the lead had changed hands: Lupa and Civetta were battling it out up front and Tartuca had slipped back level with Istrice, no more than a couple of lengths in front of Ambasciatore.

They turned for the last time. Lupa, Civetta, Tartuca, Istrice, Ambasciatore.

Istrice was flagging. Its rider flailed mercilessly with the crop but the horse had clearly had enough. Ambasciatore went through on the inside but had to check hard as Tartuca suddenly loomed directly ahead. Hawkwood's reaction was instinctive – and dangerous. He pulled Ambasciatore down inside Tartuca. He felt a moment of sheer panic as his mount scrambled to retain purchase on the churned-up turf that had left the cobblestones underneath partly exposed. Ambasciatore slithered sideways but somehow kept his footing.

The leading duo of Lupa and Civetta were running neck and neck, their riders confident now that one or the other would take the prize. They seemed unaware that Hawkwood and Ambasciatore were narrowing the gap. In a desperate attempt to shake off Lupa once and for all, Civetta's rider swung wide, forcing Lupa towards the barrier. Lupa broke stride. Civetta was ahead – and Hawkwood was a close second.

Ambasciatore seemed to sense what was expected of him. Horse and man were as one. Civetta's rider risked a look over his shoulder, and found Hawkwood bearing down on him. The crowd were on their feet as the two horses neared the final turn. Civetta took it tight, clinging to the inside. Hawkwood saw his opportunity. Ambasciatore had kept his feet once and would perhaps do so again.

Civetta's rider was sure Hawkwood would swing wide and try to take him on the final run-in. Gregorio Camporesi's face twisted into a manic grin as he held his line. Then Ambasciatore appeared.

On the inside.

The two horses collided and Ambasciatore reeled under the impact. Civetta fared worse. His feet slipped from under him and he fell, trapping his rider under the full weight of his body. Hawkwood glanced briefly over his shoulder as man and horse crashed to the ground. Camporesi screamed in agony as his upper thigh bone shattered. The sound was lost in the general uproar.

The finish was only yards away now. Hawkwood knew the only danger might come from a riderless horse. In the Palio, it is the horse, not the rider, that carries the day.

His fears proved groundless. The Sienese watched in incredulous silence as Hawkwood crossed the finishing line, shaking a fist in the air. Less in triumph than in rage and grief.

Bruschelli and the other festival deputies had assembled at the cathedral to present the Palio banner to the victorious *contrada*. Hawkwood dismounted. He laid his head briefly against Ambasciatore's muzzle. The chestnut stallion whinnied in delight.

The deputies waited for Hawkwood to come forward to receive the prize. When he made no move, they seemed uncertain what to do next. There was an awkward pause. Then, after a brief whispered consultation, Bruschelli solemnly extended both arms. One of the deputies took the Pallium and laid it carefully over them. Distress that the precious banner was about to leave Siena showing plainly in his face, Bruschelli walked slowly towards Hawkwood.

The crowd were silent as Hawkwood took the Pallium in his arms. He said nothing, merely bowed his head and stood motionless for what seemed a long time. Then he turned abruptly and, in one swift movement, draped the banner across Ambasciatore's broad back.

In the Palio, it was the horse, not the rider . . .

A few tentative cheers rang out as the significance of his gesture gradually dawned on the crowd. The cheering intensified and built to a crescendo as Hawkwood turned his back on Bruschelli and the others and walked away.

Karl Eugen August Wilhelm von Strachwitz-Wettin was laid to rest the following day in a grave which Hawkwood insisted on digging with his own hands. A white marble slab marked the spot. It bore a simple inscription: *Karl Eugen – A Father's Son.*

It was a measure of Hawkwood's grief that the best efforts of Donnina and Sir Wilfred to console him proved unavailing. Inured though he was to violent death in the field, Hawkwood could not conceal his intense shame at what had happened in Siena. His suffering, as they both knew only too well, was compounded by a deep feeling of guilt. Karl Eugen's death was the result of his arrogance. Competing in the Palio had been an act of shallow *bravura*, and Karl Eugen had paid for it with his life.

As so often, guilt spawned anger, directed not only at himself but at the world at large. Hawkwood vowed that he would one day avenge Karl Eugen's senseless death. How he would do so remained to be seen. But there would be ample opportunity for vengeance in the months and years ahead.

XVI

A Change of Heart

There's nought despicable in all of this,
That one might ever call it cowardice

South of San Gimignano,
14 November 1369

Gennaro Altobardi flinched and ducked instinctively as a stray
quarrel hissed overhead and embedded itself in the ground
twenty paces behind him. He glanced to his right, to where
Hawkwood was conferring with several of his officers. To a
man, they seemed unconcerned.

The day was cloudless and chill. Three leagues to the north,
Altobardi could make out the outlines of the ramparts and the
distinctive towers of San Gimignano, the once-prosperous town
that straddled the traditional pilgrim route from northern Europe
to Rome. The bells on the Torre Grossa and the Torre della
Podestà had chimed incessantly since daybreak. The good citizens
of San Gimignano were only too aware of the menace to the
south.

Hawkwood had at most eight hundred men under his command, and to Altobardi the odds seemed very much against them.
Advance scouts had reconnoitred the papal force and reported
that it numbered in excess of two thousand, mainly Frenchmen,
they thought – judging by the distinctive stirrup crossbows – but
with a sprinkling of Italians and a small detachment of heavily
armoured Germans. The force had by all accounts met only token
resistance during its measured advance north from Viterbo
through Bagno Vignoni, San Quirico d'Orcia and Buonconvento.

The papal army had marched by day and rested by night.
Hawkwood's Company had marched by day *and* marched by

night. The Pope's men were well provisioned and rested, Hawk-wood's weary from their forced march, but none the less in good cheer. They sat patiently on the hilltop. Some drank wine, others munched coarse bread, some attended to their weapons, others still snatched an hour's sleep, oblivious to the occasional cross-bow bolt unleashed in their direction. Most quarrels fell woefully short, and they knew from experience that the enemy fire was speculative, a sporadic gesture of intimidation rather than a genuine threat.

Hawkwood shaded his eyes and pointed north towards San Gimignano, nodding in evident satisfaction. A long column was snaking towards them. As it came nearer, Altobardi saw that among the marchers were children, some no more than eight or ten years old. It was only then that he divined Hawkwood's intentions.

It was a stratagem Hawkwood had favoured on several occa-sions. A lightly armed civilian contingent would be assembled. Its role was to precede the Company into battle, striding purpose-fully towards the enemy lines, then halting at a safe distance and, at a pre-arranged signal, breaking ranks and fleeing back up the slope to safety. The enemy would immediately anticipate a rout and charge after them, at which point Hawkwood's main foot force would ostensibly retreat, luring the enemy up the incline and into the jaws of the Company's defensive position. The longbows then came into their own, firing over the crest of the hill into the advancing enemy and thinning their ranks until Hawkwood's cavalry could charge downhill directly into their midst and mop up the remnants.

Altobardi looked on as three hundred or so men and children dutifully formed into ranks. The men looked nervous but seemed generally to understand and accept what was expected of them. The youngsters were visibly excited by the prospect of playing a part in an exciting game. As in the past, none of the civilians, young or old, raised a voice in protest or gave any indication that they resented having been pressed into service as decoys.

The civilians set off down the slope. A four-hundred-strong

detachment of footsoldiers took station directly behind them. Below, the papal force was already arrayed in battle formation, waiting patiently for the Company to come within crossbow range.

The tactic had worked for Hawkwood in the past.

This time it did not.

From his vantage point on the hill above, Altobardi watched in horror as the civilians drew perilously close to the enemy lines. Hawkwood at last raised his hand and rotated it. Llewellyn dipped a cloth-tipped arrow into a charcoal brazier, took careful aim and sent the burning shaft high over the heads of the Company. It landed squarely between the advancing civilians and the enemy front line. It was the signal to break ranks.

But the civilians hesitated a moment too long. Enemy crossbows were primed and lethal bolts sped through the air like a flock of starlings, scything into the first ranks, shattering breastbones and piercing young limbs. Too late, the civilians broke ranks and turned to flee. A second volley caught them as they turned. A youngster of no more than twelve took not one but three bolts between his shoulder-blades. The impact pitched him forwards a full six paces. One of the older men stooped to gather up a wounded child and hoist him on his shoulder. A quarrel caught him in the back of the neck and exited through his throat. The child slipped from his grasp and was pinioned beneath his would-be rescuer's body as both fell to the ground.

The commander of the papal force had done his homework. Knowing that his men were eager to charge, he rapped out an order to hold the line. His men obeyed. Hawkwood's footsoldiers continued to advance, determined to draw the enemy out as planned and to provoke them into a disorderly charge. The enemy would have none of it. Crossbows sent another volley into the Company ranks. Several men were killed instantly, others seriously wounded.

On the hill, Hawkwood immediately realised his advance force had been compromised. His longbowmen were now too far away to fire on the enemy: the risk of hitting their own comrades was too great. He had no option. He ordered his cavalry to follow him down the hill.

Altobardi's throat constricted as he urged his mount down the slope. Within seconds, or so it seemed, they had drawn level with their own footsoldiers, scattering them left and right, even trampling some underfoot. We are killing our own men, he thought as his horse slammed into a soldier and sent him reeling. He was dimly aware of children screaming in confusion and terror, then he was out in the open again, bearing down on the enemy line. Ahead, he glimpsed Hawkwood plunging into and through the enemy ranks, slashing left and right. Altobardi drove through the gap that Hawkwood had created. He felt a stab of pain as something – a pikestaff? – jabbed into his right side. His horse squealed in protest as a glancing blow opened a gash on its flank.

And then he was through. Behind the enemy's front line.

He hauled on the reins, wheeling his horse to re-engage. On both sides of him he sensed other riders do likewise. He came in fast, swinging his sword in a low, sweeping arc, catching a pikeman full in the face, splintering nose and jawbone. The force of the blow jarred his elbow and numbed his sword-arm. Hands were scrabbling for the reins in a bid to bring his horse down and he kicked out, forcing the attackers away. The noise of battle was all around him and he was surprised to discover he was yelling at the top of his voice. He suddenly found himself shoulder to shoulder with Hawkwood, only for an instant, but long enough to take in the captain-general's manic expression and see blood coursing down his cheek. Then Hawkwood was gone again, hacking his way through the ranks ahead of him.

To Altobardi's astonishment, the Company had not been counter-attacked from the rear or flank. Close-quarter fighting meant that the papal crossbowmen could no longer prove effective. It may be they believed their job was done. Perhaps, perhaps not. At all events, they showed little inclination to join the fray. There was no sign of the German detachment, and Altobardi could only conclude that its captain had, for whatever reason, decided not to engage.

One moment Altobardi was in the thick of the fighting, the next he was out of it, surrounded by footsoldiers in white tunics. The Company had breached the enemy lines and hand-to-hand combat had broken out all around him. He dismounted to fight on foot, but stumbled and collapsed to his knees as searing pain surged through him. He clasped his hand to his side and was surprised to find that his wound was bleeding profusely; he had given no thought to it until now. A gigantic figure appeared behind him and he felt massive hands slide under his armpits and round his chest. Llewellyn gently eased him to his feet and supported him. The first shock of pain had subsided, replaced by a strange lassitude. He was aware of water being poured between his lips.

As he lapsed into unconsciousness, he had the impression that Hawkwood was standing over him. Smiling. Or perhaps he had only imagined it.

A tallow candle flickered and spluttered as Altobardi slowly opened his eyes. The pain in his side was a dull throb now. He had a pressing need to pass water. He looked around to get his bearings, uncertain whether or not he had been taken prisoner. As his eyes began to focus, he saw he was lying on a makeshift litter in Hawkwood's command tent. He put his hand to his side and discovered he had been bandaged with strips of fresh linen. He tried to sit up, but the effort was too much for him. He tried to call out, but no sound passed his lips. He tried again and produced something between a cough and a moan.

The tent flap was immediately thrown open, and Hawkwood entered. He stood for a moment looking down at Altobardi, a slow grin spreading across his face.

'Well, now, at last! We had begun to think the hero of the hour had gone to meet his Maker.'

Altobardi tried to reply but the words would not form. He gestured with one hand. Hawkwood understood at once and brought him a leather water-pouch. He squatted beside Altobardi, poured a few drops into the Italian's mouth, then gently dabbed away the water that trickled down his chin.

Altobardi swallowed, then gestured for more. After a few mouthfuls, he managed to croak the question uppermost in his mind. 'Did we carry the day?'

'That we did, young Gennaro, and no small thanks to you and those like you. The Company acquitted itself well this day.'

'Where were the Germans?'

Hawkwood roared with laughter. 'It seems they had not been paid. A *Söldner* fights for soldi – for pay. Or it may be that they had no stomach for battle when they clapped eyes on you.'

Altobardi's eyelids drooped and he fought to stay awake. He had one more question on his mind. 'The children? What of the children?'

'Some were lost, I fear. Not many. There is always a price to pay for victory in the field.'

'How many?'

'Eleven dead, and twice as many wounded.'

Dio mio, thought Altobardi.

'And the Company?'

'Our losses were acceptable.'

'How many?' insisted Altobardi.

'Forty-one dead; some others gravely wounded.'

Altobardi sighed. He closed his eyes and Hawkwood stood up. 'You must sleep now.'

Altobardi made no reply. Satisfied, Hawkwood extinguished the candle and left.

Altobardi waited a moment or two, then cautiously eased himself to his feet. He pushed back the tent flap and looked outside. Camp fires had been lit and the confused chatter of conversation was punctuated by laughter as the Company re-capitulated the events of the day. Altobardi relieved himself and inched painfully back to bed.

His mind was racing. For some time now, he had wrestled with his conscience. He was a Pisan first and foremost, the eldest son of a respected patrician family. Yet, increasingly, he despaired of the role that circumstances had foisted on him as interpreter, negotiator and apologist for Hawkwood and his Company. By the simple fact of association, Hawkwood's values and priorities had come to be identified with his own. That was untenable. Much as he liked Hawkwood personally and admired his skill as a leader, the blind loyalty the captain-general inspired was something Altobardi could not share. Hawkwood spoke time and again of 'honour', but what honour was there in a day like today, when innocent children had been marched to their deaths?

Some were lost, I fear. Not many. There is always a price to pay for victory in the field.

Hawkwood's words haunted him.

To make matters worse, Altobardi had somehow emerged as a hero of the hour. A hero? By whose standards? He was a Pisan and an Italian, yet today he had fought neither for Pisa nor for Italy. Worse, he had fought against the army of the Holy Father.

May God forgive me, he thought, and may He grant me strength to find honour in true service to a true cause, where life is not meaninglessly squandered in the quest for personal gain and in the pay of the highest bidder. May He also give me strength to do what is right, not what is expedient.

With that, he crossed himself, turned on his good side and slept.

Bordeaux, 22 February 1370

Only a thin line separates the cardinal sin of treason from the lesser transgression of consorting with the enemy. Gennaro Altobardi fervently hoped he was not about to cross that line.

On the pretext of family business, a fully recovered Altobardi had taken leave of Hawkwood and returned briefly to Pisa. He had spent only two nights there in the company of his wife and family before setting off for Bordeaux, confident he could secure an audience with King Edward of England or his son, the Black Prince.

The war between England and France had flared up once again with the arrival in Aquitaine several months earlier of yet another large contingent of English troops. To date, however, hostilities had been confined to sporadic forays as each side sought to probe the other's weaknesses and determine what strategy might work to its longer-term advantage.

Altobardi's progress towards Bordeaux had not been without danger but, as an Italian accompanied only by two valets, he clearly posed no threat to either side. The principal risk to life and limb had come not from French or English forces but from roving bands of cutthroats and highwaymen who scoured the country-side looking for easy pickings. It was with some relief that, four days earlier, Altobardi had at last tracked along the final stretch of the Garonne and seen in the distance the majestic silhouette of Saint Andrew's Cathedral. He had taken lodgings in the shadow of the Gallo-Roman ramparts that corseted the city and had without further delay presented his compliments and credentials – as an ambassador of the sovereign city state of Pisa – to the *quartier général* from which the king and the Black Prince were directing operations.

Altobardi's hopes of being granted an immediate audience were quickly dashed. He had cooled his heels until early that morning, when a herald messenger had been despatched to his chambers to ascertain what specific business brought him to Bordeaux.

'I come at the wish of Pisa and as one who serves Sir John Hawkwood,' he had replied.

Barely an hour later, he found himself in the presence of the English monarch and his son.

'You speak in the name and with the authority of Hawkwood?' asked Edward.

'I do not, your Grace. I speak in the name of Pisa.'

'Then pray state what business lies before us.'

Altobardi had no authority from Hawkwood. Quite the contrary: had the latter suspected Altobardi's presence in Bordeaux he would have considered it an act of disloyalty, even treachery. Altobardi was aware he was guilty of consorting with an 'enemy', yet reminded himself that this was Hawkwood's enemy, not

Pisa's. Besides, Hawkwood himself never showed any qualms about 'consorting' – whenever, wherever and with whomsoever, providing it suited his mood and purpose of the moment and worked ultimately to his advantage.

He weighed his words carefully. 'I am given to understand that *your* business, sire, is to protect and pursue England's interests here in France. To do so, you need men of experience and fortitude. Captain-General Hawkwood is such a man. His Company has proved itself without equal these several years past.'

Edward and his son exchanged glances.

It was the Black Prince who spoke. 'The John Hawkwood of whom you speak is no true servant of England.'

The king gestured for his son to be silent. 'Where is Hawkwood now?' he asked. 'Does he serve Pisa?'

That was precisely the point, thought Altobardi. Did Hawkwood serve Pisa or did Pisa serve Hawkwood?

'He is bound by a contract with Pisa and has honoured that contract to the letter.'

'He fights, then, for Pisa?' put in the Black Prince impatiently.

'He fights in the service of Pisa, but also at the behest of others who retain him from time to time.'

King Edward was confused; or pretended to be. 'Then he does not *always* fight for Pisa?'

'No, sire. He has indeed fought for Pisa, but also, and as circumstances dictate, for Florence and Milan, and against Florence and Milan. Against the Papal States, also.'

'A man of dubious allegiances, it would seem,' grunted the Black Prince.

'A man of great integrity,' said Altobardi, bristling. He could not bring himself to speak ill of Hawkwood. Nor would it serve his present purpose to do so.

'Yet you do not speak for him?'

'I speak in his favour and in that of Pisa. And it would be greatly to his benefit and yours that he now serve England once more.'

'And the benefit to Pisa?'

'The city states of Italy war and intrigue without pause,' answered Altobardi. 'And the *condottieri* who serve us serve themselves at our expense. They are often a greater threat than—'

'The threat they pose,' cut in King Edward, 'is of your own making. I have no use for men whose loyalties shift in the wind.'

'Hawkwood is an Englishman through and through,' countered Altobardi. 'He would again serve England, of that I am certain. And he would serve England well. Of that you, your Grace, can also be certain.'

The Black Prince could scarcely contain his anger. 'He will serve for money, to be sure, but not for love of country,' he rasped.

'As you see, my son has little faith in Hawkwood,' said the king. 'For myself, I am undecided. God knows, we have great need of those with his qualities in the field. But, I ask myself, at what price?'

'That I cannot say, your Grace. For a stipend, certainly, but also for restitution of his rank and reputation. As for myself, I do no more than offer my services as a go-between.'

'And this without his knowledge or consent?'

'Without his knowledge or consent.'

Altobardi had said his piece but was far from certain he had made his case. To him, the re-opening of hostilities between England and France was an opportunity too valuable to be missed: a golden opportunity to free Hawkwood to serve once more the country of his birth. And Pisa and Italy would be – there was no other way to put it – free of him.

In his anxiety to do what seemed best for Hawkwood and for Pisa, Altobardi had given little thought to the imbalances that might ensue in Italy as a whole should his plan succeed. For that matter, he could not even be certain that Hawkwood would consider relinquishing his increasingly lucrative base in Italy and returning to the service of a king and country that had once rejected him.

He felt a twinge of anxiety. Had he reasoned well? Or had he been too naive? If the latter, there was at least one consolation:

should the English king dismiss Altobardi's proposal out of hand, Hawkwood need never know of these negotiations.

Altobardi waited.

'There is much to be considered here,' said King Edward after a long pause. 'I bid you withdraw that we may deliberate. You shall know of our decision this day.'

Altobardi bowed and left the Council Chamber.

Late that same afternoon, a detail of men-at-arms presented itself at his lodgings. His two valets were dismissed and he was escorted to the city dungeon. He was given no explanation why the English king and his irascible son had rejected his overtures out of hand.

'For reasons I cannot fathom,' Edward said to his son later that day, 'that Italian envoy comes at Hawkwood's bidding. Hawkwood seeks to ingratiate himself and restore himself to our favour. I question his motives and I fear his intentions.'

'The Italian weasel had best rot in the jail where he now lies,' the Black Prince replied. 'And a pox be on John Hawkwood and all those who do his bidding.'

XVII

Habemus Papam

Great was the festival they held that day

Avignon, 22 September 1370

To the dismay of the French and their allies, Guillaume de Grimoard – better known as Pope Urban V – had left the opulent Palais des Papes in Avignon some three years previously, fiercely determined to relocate the Avignonese Curia to Rome after six decades of self-imposed papal exile. Only then, he had reasoned, would there be any real prospect of achieving his ultimate goal of reuniting the Western and Eastern branches of the Mother Church.

Urban V had entered Rome in triumph in October 1367, accompanied by an imposing force of several thousand. He left Italy in silent ignominy in early September 1370.

He had been appalled at the physical and moral decay that had devastated Rome. Mendicants and brigands roamed streets strewn with garbage and reeking of urine and human and animal excrement. Public monuments and buildings were little more than ruins, defaced and plundered. The clergy, culled by the Black Death, were as impotent as they were corrupt, their churches crumbling and deserted. In the surrounding countryside, bands of freebooters ravaged outlying towns and villages, foraging for food and plunder and leaving a wasteland in their wake.

The Vicar of Christ had struggled manfully to put the Holy City to rights. For three long years, he had presided over measures conducive to the restoration of Rome. He had ordered streets and buildings repaired and cleaned; he had employed labourers to tend to the city's gardens and public spaces; he had arranged the distribution of papal alms from the treasure trove amassed in Avignon on the strength of the lucrative sale of favours and indulgences; he had attempted to whip into some semblance of order what remained of the clergy; and, above all, he had preached respect for and observance of the Christian sacrament.

The return of the Pope and his court had gone some small way towards a revival of Rome's fortunes, but Urban had soon realised there was too much to be done and so little time in which to do it. It had proved a thankless task. Night after night, he had wept tears of frustration and heartfelt grief at the knowledge that the glorious Rome of antiquity had been consigned to the pages of history.

His other great designs had also been thwarted. He had conducted protracted negotiations with the Patriarch of Constantinople, but no accommodation had been reached: the Greek and Latin branches of the Church remained separate. He had implored the Holy Roman Emperor, Charles IV, to come to his aid. To no avail: the emperor's renowned skills as a diplomat clearly outweighed his military prowess. Charles had ventured once into Italy, only to be met by strong opposition; his supplies running low and his forces depleted, he had promptly turned tail and scurried back to comparative safety beyond the Alps.

Urban had not hesitated to meet the anti-papal forces head-on in the field. He had imposed an economic and spiritual embargo on the renegade city of Perugia, ordering the excommunication of its citizens and all those who aided and abetted them. The Perugians had responded by taking up arms and enlisting mercenaries, among them Hawkwood's Company and freebooters in the pay of Bernabò Visconti. Urban's army had been driven back and forced to seek refuge in Viterbo; the mercenaries duly arrived and laid siege to the city until the Pope beat a hasty retreat to Rome, his tail between his legs.

In the interim, Urban had repeatedly tried to negotiate an agreement of sorts with King Edward of England, the notion being that the latter desist from providing any form of support to the principal Italian thorn in Urban's flesh, the Visconti dynasty of Milan. At one point, Urban had threatened their excommunication *sine die*, but the Viscontis had appeared singularly unimpressed. For his part, Edward appeared to detect little strategic – not to mention monetary – benefit in a *quid pro quo* whereby he would withdraw support from the Pope's enemies in Italy in exchange for the Pope withdrawing support from England's enemies in France. Edward procrastinated, reinforcing Urban's considered opinion that the English monarch was duplicity incarnate.

Urban was forced to acknowledge that he had miscalculated and overplayed his hand. Worse, perhaps, he had erred in other significant ways, not least by maintaining in Rome a papal court which was geographically Italian but, in reality, overwhelmingly French. All Italy – friend and foe alike – was united in its bitter resentment of this. Papal authority was unquestionably at its lowest ebb for centuries. Any hopes he had cherished of uniting Italy were clearly doomed to fail: it would remain a country torn apart by bellicose city states and foreign interlopers.

To his credit, Urban had identified the threat posed to Italy by the proliferation of the mercenary hordes, denouncing them in successive papal bulls. To his intense chagrin, however, his threats of instant excommunication had fallen on deaf ears. The mercenaries ignored him and continued to hold Italy to ransom, and he was powerless to stop them as long as the individual city states had recourse to their services.

It seemed to the Pope that only one course of action was now open to him: if he could not bring the city states to their senses under the unifying banner of the Holy Church, he must allocate a healthy portion of the seemingly endless supply of papal wealth – secreted in the basement of the Palais des Papes – to hire his own *condottieri*.

He had arrived at this conclusion only with the deepest regret. It proved of no consequence, however: Pope Urban V died on the night of 19 December 1370 – of, so rumour had it, old age and a broken heart. It would be for his successor to carry on where he had left off.

Avignon, 5 January 1371

He rose before dawn and walked slowly to and fro on the upper terrace of the papal palace until a limpid winter sun tinged the pink-tiled roofs of Avignon and cast first rays across the silt-brown waters of the Rhône.

The Conclave had emerged from its *cum clavi* seclusion on 30 December 1370 to announce the outcome of its deliberations: thirty-four-year-old Pierre Roger de Beaufort was deemed *papabile* – fit for and worthy of papal office – and was to succeed Urban as the seventh in a line of French-born Avignonese popes dating back to Clement V in 1305.

Beaufort harboured few illusions about his unanimous election and the reasons that underpinned it. There was little doubt in his mind that the cardinals regarded him as altogether too inexperienced. They evidently expected that this new Vicar of Christ – who had taken the name of Gregory XI – would prove preeminent in one respect and in one respect only: his malleability. As well they might, considering that Beaufort had not yet even been ordained into the priesthood.

Gregory was determined to prove the cardinals wrong.

In some respects, at least, he was anything but inexperienced in matters of the church. A nephew and protégé of Pope Clement VI, he had been made a canon deacon at the tender age of eleven, and had been elevated to the rank of cardinal in 1348, when only nineteen. This was even before his admission to the theological faculty at the university in Perugia. There he had immersed himself in, among other things, papal history: not only could he reel off from memory and in sequence the names and terms of office of his predecessors ever since St Peter in AD 32, he could also recite their achievements – or lack thereof.

In that respect, Gregory suspected he would have little to fear by comparison with the majority of the Avignonese popes who had gone before him. Clement V had been little more than the lackey of King Philippe IV of France and would be best remembered for some eclectic contributions to canon law – the so-called

Clementinae – and a preoccupation with amassing and hoarding wealth. John XXII had spent a considerable portion of his eighteen years in office adjudicating what, in Gregory's view, was little more than a petty doctrinal squabble among opposing factions within the Franciscan order, or interceding on a regular basis between Louis IV of Bavaria and Frederick of Austria in their long-running dispute as to which of them should inherit the crown of the Holy Roman Empire. Benedict XII had dabbled in politics, attempting with a conspicuous lack of success to resolve the conflict between England and France (although, to his credit, he had also essayed a series of administrative reforms). Clement VI's career had been 'distinguished' by the purchase of Avignon from Queen Joan of Sicily in 1348 and by his subsequent obsession with the enlargement and embellishment of the Palais des Papes.

In truth, of his papal precursors in Avignon, Gregory privately admitted to genuine admiration for only two, Innocent VI and his own immediate predecessor, Urban V. It was no coincidence that both had worked assiduously to restore the papacy to Rome and to effect reunification of the Roman and Eastern Churches. These were ambitions passionately shared by Gregory XI.

This was not to say that life in Avignon was not to his taste. Far from it. The pontifical and cardinal courts were nothing short of magnificent and the city as a whole had grown in both economic and intellectual stature. Not only was the Palais des Papes a monument to luxury, it was also a heavily fortified haven of papal security.

Today would see Gregory's ritual investiture. In his heart, he profoundly regretted it would take place not at the Holy See in Rome but here, in the surrogate surroundings of Avignon. There was nothing else for it, however, as Gregory was among the first to concede. He had visited Rome during his study years in Perugia and had been shocked to see the wasteland of poverty and squalor the Eternal City had become. He shared Urban's horror at the sight of Rome's proud monuments overrun with vermin, the cattle grazing in what had once been the glorious basilica of St Peter, the soot-darkened shell of St John Lateran, and the terrors of the Roman night.

In a few hours, Pierre Roger de Beaufort would emerge from the sacristy dressed in the traditional white cassock, white stockings and red slippers embroidered with crosses of gold. He would recite the oath of office, vowing to change nothing of the received tradition of the Church, to sustain its stewardship, to cleanse and purge it of all that contravened canonical order, and to guard its holy canons and decrees as the Divine Ordinance of Heaven. On pain of retribution, he would undertake never to act in contradiction of his office. He would also vow to subject 'to the severest excommunication' any and all who acted against evangelical tradition and the purity of the orthodox faith.

De Beaufort would assume the vestments of office and extend his hand to be kissed by the cardinals who approached in order of seniority to kneel before him. The dean of cardinals would place upon Gregory's finger – for the first and only time – the cherished Ring of the Fisherman.

The multitude would gather outside in the Palace Square in awed expectation of his appearance at the balcony window, straining their ears to hear the traditional announcement intoned by the cardinal deacon, 'Annuntio vobis gaudium magnum. Habemus Papam! – I announce to you a great joy. We have a Pope!' At which the crowd would break into a sustained cheer before falling silent again and sinking to their knees as he, Pope Gregory XI, moved out on the balcony and raised his hand in blessing: Urbi et Orbi – to the City and to the World.

He would not celebrate his first papal mass until several days later. As the papal procession moved slowly towards the high altar, it would pause not once, but three times. At each halt, a piece of corded tow would be lit, to the accompaniment of the words 'Pater Sancte, sic transit gloria mundi', a reminder to every pope that he is but mortal and that the glory of this world is transient. At the close of the mass, the crowds would gather once more, this time to witness the triple tiara being solemnly placed on the head of the Supreme Pontiff and Father of the Church before he was whisked away to the papal palace in his portable throne, the Sedia Gestatoria.

It would be a magnificent and moving spectacle. Would that it were to be in Rome . . .

Siena, 19 January 1371

When news of Gregory XI's coronation reached Siena, one young woman sobbed uncontrollably for three whole days, unable to contain her abject dismay at the prospect of yet another absentee Pope skulking in the Babylonian exile that was Avignon.

There were many in Siena who believed Caterina di Iacopo Benincasa to be insane. Others more charitable were inclined to excuse or, if possible, ignore her excesses and 'eccentricities'. Some deplored her obsessive and very public preoccupation with matters they considered best left to the clergy and the state, others viewed as blasphemous her assertion that she was the virgin bride of Christ. Even those closest to her were often at a loss to explain the more bizarre facets of her behaviour. Many had initially doubted her sincerity, whereas others saw in her a woman genuinely and uniquely devoted to God and to a life of renunciation and piety.

Over the years, Caterina's behaviour had perplexed her parents, Giacomo and Lapa. As a young child, she had been as bright and happy as any of her twenty-four elder siblings. They rued the day when it had all changed, when six-year-old Caterina described to them a vision of Christ, arrayed in priestly garments, hovering above the Church of St Dominic. At the age of seven, she took the vow of virginity and devoted herself exclusively to a life of prayer, solitude, penance and self-flagellation. Typically, when her mother insisted she give some thought to her appearance and the prospect of marriage, she promptly shaved her hair, considered by many to have been her crowning glory.

In 1363, Caterina realised her ambition to don the black-and-white habit of the Mantellate, a non-monastic order of Dominican tertiaries, devout women who pledged service to the sick and the poor. Even then, though, she went her own way: despite having been admitted to the Mantellate and committing herself to a life of service to the community at large, she persisted in living the life of a recluse. She never left her rudimentarily furnished room, she spoke to no one but her confessor, she lived on a diet of herbs and water (which she more often than not voluntarily regurgitated), and she made do with only a couple of hours' sleep each night. Her extreme asceticism induced frequent mystical and hallucinatory experiences, some of a distinctly erotic nature, which she pronounced terrifying and uplifting in almost equal measure.

It was three more years, almost to the day, before Caterina at last ventured out of doors to devote herself to a life of ministration punctuated by extraordinary gestures, including licking the open sores and suppurating pustules of the infirm. Her growing reputation for piety and sanctity – not to mention this blatant disregard for her own well-being – reaped its reward in the form of followers and disciples from every walk of Sienese life, the so-called *bella brigata* from Fontebranda, the district where she lived.

Her frequent 'ecstasies' and 'eccentricities' continued to inspire criticism and suspicion, however, and the Fontebranda mystics, as they themselves were content to be known, were widely disparaged as *caterinati*, with Caterina herself routinely derided as the 'Queen of Fontebranda'.

The 'Queen' had learnt to read, but not yet to write. Undaunted, she dictated an extensive correspondence, addressed in the first instance to family and friends but increasingly – and after an allegedly near-death experience, following which she claimed to have received instructions from on high to 'go abroad into the world' – to men of influence both sacred and secular.

For Caterina, Gregory XI's continuing presence in Avignon was yet another running sore she yearned to lick clean. She resolved that, one day soon, she would write to the new Pope and implore him to do what he knew to be right: to return the pontificate to Rome and to be 'not a timorous child, but manly'.

And, also one day soon, she hoped to meet again a certain John Hawkwood, whom she had last seen in the Piazza del Campo in Siena, cradling in his arms the body of a dying friend.

XVIII

Family Ties

Ride where I may, my whole endeavour shall be to thee

Milan, 2 September 1371

'Word of your exploits has reached my ears more than once,' said Bernabò Visconti. 'Permit me to salute you as a man of valour and as an esteemed guest of Milan.'

He extended his hand and Hawkwood clasped it.

'It is I who salute you, Duke Bernabò,' replied Hawkwood, according Visconti a rank to which he was not strictly speaking entitled but which he had long since arrogated.

The two men took stock of each other. Hawkwood saw a man of medium height, broad-shouldered and with a firm, determined jawline. The hand that had grasped his, however, was soft. A schemer, thought Hawkwood, rather than a man given to physical action. Visconti's features were those of some Roman consul or emperor such as Hawkwood had often seen on marble portrait busts, the eyes curiously lifeless, the lips thin and bloodless, the beard sparse but beautifully trimmed.

What Bernabò Visconti saw before him was a potentially valuable pawn in the game of political chess at which he was a past master. This is a straightforward man of simple tastes, thought Visconti, a man said to have little or no political ambition and therefore one who poses no long-term threat. Physically, Hawkwood was as he had imagined: tall, clear-eyed, well muscled and with an animal-like grace tempered in the fires of combat. This, then, was the celebrated John Hawkwood who had conquered the heart of his favourite daughter – of whose taste in men he had seldom approved and, more often than not, despaired.

Donnina looked on as the two men she loved most in the world continued to size each other up. She congratulated herself on her timing: her sodomising pig of a husband had conveniently died – somewhat surprisingly, in his own bed rather in that of one of the male prostitutes with whom he had latterly consorted – and she had conscientiously worn widow's weeds on the few occasions during the last three months when she had shown herself in public. The niceties had now been observed, however, and the mandatory mourning period was over. Best of all, Hawkwood had recently fought alongside the forces of Milan at the siege of Viterbo, when the upstart Pope Urban V had been shamed into submission and forced to withdraw to the sewer that was Rome. No time could have been more propitious for the two men in her life to meet. It was perhaps too much to expect that they would become bosom friends, but one never could be certain.

The three of them sat alone in the vast dining hall. They had feasted on wild boar which, as Visconti diffidently remarked, he had hunted and killed himself. Hawkwood complimented Visconti on the excellence of his table; Visconti complimented Hawkwood on the excellence of his Company.

Sweetmeats were served, and Visconti studiously peeled a fig as he contemplated his next move. The relationship between Donnina and this Englishman was no secret to him. He could scarcely disapprove: that would be crass hypocrisy, bearing in mind the countless children he had sired by a string of mistresses. It might be to his advantage to formalise this liaison: he would lose a daughter (again), but would gain a *condottiere*.

Donnina had not broached the subject of marriage, but she was certain it would be only a matter of time before Hawkwood did so. Time was of the essence. She was carrying Hawkwood's child.

Visconti set down his goblet and looked at each of them in turn. He nodded briefly, as if to confirm he had arrived at a decision and was satisfied with it.

'Am I to understand, Sir John, that you seek my daughter's hand in marriage?'

Hawkwood was taken aback at the suddenness of the question.

He had intended to propose marriage to Donnina ever since her husband's long-awaited demise, but had not disclosed as much to either her or her father, assuming that, like any suitor, he would be permitted to make the first move. Moreover, he had expected that Bernabò would respond with a modicum of tact. Visconti, it seemed, could be every bit as forthright as Hawkwood himself.

'That was indeed my intention,' he said with a distinct edge to his voice. 'But I had hoped to secure a daughter's consent in principle before requesting that of her father.'

Visconti swept some imaginary crumbs from the table. 'Then I propose that you ask her forthwith.'

Hawkwood looked across the table at Donnina. She was smiling.

'It would be an honour to accept Sir John's proposal,' she said calmly, although the colour had risen to her cheeks. 'I do so with all my heart.'

'Then you both have my blessing,' said Visconti. 'There remains only the matter of a dowry.'

Hawkwood made to interrupt, but Visconti raised a hand to claim the floor. 'I intend to settle eighty thousand florins on Donnina – more than on any other of my female offspring.'

Donnina had difficulty suppressing her amusement. No children had been born to her and her late and unlamented husband, and she was in consequence sole inheritor of his substantial estate. In addition, her husband-to-be was a man of considerable means, she knew, and his finances were in the most capable of hands. But she was delighted by her father's gesture and by his willingness to settle on her such a generous sum. By contrast, Hawkwood was shocked by the formality of it all. He was tempted – but only for a moment – to brush the offer aside. He thought better of it.

'The privilege of marrying the Lady Donnina would be enough,' he said.

'Well said, Sir John. Well said. Then we have an understanding, have we not?'

'We have.'

Visconti rose abruptly. 'Come, Sir John. Allow me to show you something of my modest home.'

He led his guest from chamber to chamber, each more ornate than the one before. Hawkwood expressed his admiration for the furnishings and, to Visconti's surprise, identified many of the paintings and sculptures that adorned the palazzo.

'Your knowledge of our artists is admirable, Sir John.'

'For that, as for so much more, I am indebted to your daughter.'

Visconti paused by a sturdy oak door. He opened it to reveal stone steps that curved downwards into the bowels of the building. A blast of fetid air met them as they slowly descended.

Visconti clamped a silk handkerchief to his mouth. 'I trust it is not too soon after dinner to introduce you to one of my pastimes?'

Hawkwood gave a brief nod.

The steps gave on to a flagstone corridor. A brawny guard sprang to his feet as they approached. Visconti said nothing, merely gestured that a further door be opened.

What was left of a human being was suspended by rusting chains against the far wall. One eye had been gouged out. The nose had been neatly excised, as had been one ear, the tongue and several fingers of both hands. The skin of one arm had been peeled away to reveal a bloody pulp of sinew, muscle and bone. A crudely cauterised scab was all that remained of the genitalia.

The figure was still breathing.

'I hasten to say I claim no credit for this,' said Visconti. 'It is my brother Galeazzo's doing. Fascinating, is it not?'

'Fascinating,' replied Hawkwood.

'The punishment – and I stress "punishment" – continues for forty days and forty nights. That, I should explain, is the intention, although some . . . some, shall we say, *candidati* . . . do not endure for that length of time. To help them withstand the pain, Galeazzo grants them respite every other day. There is no need for haste. "*Un poco, un po*", as we say. A little bit every other day. To give them time to lick their wounds, as it were.'

Hawkwood felt utter revulsion at the spectacle, but steeled himself to give no sign. 'Forty days, you say?'

'Yes, forty. The period of the *quaresima* – the Lenten days, as you say in your language, do you not? The period that celebrates the fasting and penitence endured in the wilderness by Our Lord Jesus Christ.'

'I was unaware that, here in Italy, Lent falls in September,' said Hawkwood.

The sarcasm was not lost on Visconti. 'Here in Italy – or should I say, here in Milan? – we celebrate and punish as we please.'

'And this punishment?' asked Hawkwood.

'The man is *un criminale*. He took from me what is rightfully mine. He hunted *my* boar on *my* land.'

'I understand.'

'Yes,' said Bernabò Visconti. 'I am sure that you understand fully.'

Milan, 3 December 1371

A radiant Donnina Visconti (her pregnancy discreetly disguised) was robed in virginal pale blue. On her head was a circlet of ivy interlaced with precious orange-blossom and decorated with white ribbons which trailed down her back, setting off her loose-flowing dark chestnut hair. In her left hand, she held a small posy of herbs – rosemary, thyme, basil and wild garlic – variously believed to confer health, good fortune and fertility. Round her neck was a simple necklace of red and white jasper, connoting love and gentleness. Hawkwood knelt on her right, formally clad in close-fitting black breeches and a tightly laced scarlet doublet over a white silk *blouson*.

They had exchanged vows outside the cathedral of Santa Maria Maggiore, in full view of the huge crowd, before entering the basilica and genuflecting before the altar while the archbishop recited a short prayer and pronounced blessings on their union.

Bernabò Visconti had taken pains to ensure that the marriage of his beautiful daughter to her English *condottiere* would be celebrated by the whole city. Minstrels, jugglers, bear-tamers and fire-eaters displayed their respective talents in the Piazza del Duomo, which had been festooned with banners and carpeted with amaryllis petals. A number of petty thieves and non-political prisoners had been released. Forty-eight oxen had been spit-roasted. And the citizens of Milan had been exhorted to eat their fill, drink copious draughts of cheap but wholesome wine, and dance the night away.

The wedding feast proper was attended by close on three hundred guests, all dressed in their finest. They sat at trestle tables, feasting on whole suckling pig, silvered calves' heads, roast mutton in cherry sauce, knuckles of veal and, as a special treat, *cinghiali*, wild boar culled – with Bernabò's permission – from Visconti woodlands in Lombardy. Others gorged themselves on game birds – capons, pheasants, pigeons, partridges, peacocks and quail – which nestled on beds of sage or stewed cabbage spiced with cloves. Almond and pine-nut-flavoured sugared pastries, cinnamon quinces and a *salviata* mixture of eggs, milk, sage and flour were washed down with mulled wine. Wooden bowls of rosemary-scented water were provided to cleanse hands and palate.

Hawkwood ate sparingly. From time to time, his huge fist would close over Donnina's hand and she would smile and return the pressure. He could not recall ever having been so happy. He had waited patiently for this day and he was determined nothing should taint its memory.

He glanced around at the guests, recognising only a few faces here and there. He was pleased to note how readily Sir Wilfred Perry (who, any day now, planned to retire to his estates in England) and several of his other senior officers had mingled with their Milanese hosts. He was puzzled, not to say even a trifle irritated, that Gennaro Altobardi had not seen fit to return to Milan to attend the celebrations. Gennaro, he could only assume, must have been detained on Pisa's business. His only deep regret was that Karl Eugen had not lived to see this day.

As was the custom, guest after guest came up to the table of honour to pay respects to the bride and groom and to shower them with gifts. Some brought money, others valuable items of jewellery or silver and gold ornaments. At one point, Visconti casually disclosed that he had made over to Hawkwood and Donnina the deeds of the castle of Pessano, together with what he vaguely described as a 'certain number of other small properties'.

Hawkwood had the utmost difficulty keeping track of his wife's siblings. Rumour had it that Visconti had sired as many as thirty children (some claimed many more), a goodly number by his 'real' wife, Regina, but many by a succession of mistresses, one of whom – Donnina de' Porri, by all accounts Bernabò's favourite – was the mother of Hawkwood's own Donnina. As the various Francescas, Biancas, Elisabettas, Ginevras, Enricas and Violantes were paraded before them, Hawkwood gradually discerned a pattern. Most, legitimate or otherwise, appeared to have been expeditiously married off – as Donnina had originally been – in the interests of expanding Visconti's growing network of strategic alliances.

Hawkwood was particularly interested to meet Galeazzo Visconti, Bernabò's elder brother by a couple of years. He had been told that three Visconti brothers had 'inherited' Milan from their father, Matteo, and that the eldest, also a Matteo, had died in his thirty-sixth year in 1355. At that juncture, the two surviving brothers had prudently divided up their inheritance, with Bernabò controlling the area east of Milan and Galeazzo taking the lands to the west. Though it seemed there was no love lost between them, they both recognised that the well-being of the city state of Milan as a whole was best served by observing a cautious truce.

Be that as it might, Hawkwood recalled Donnina having spoken of her uncle Galeazzo in glowing terms as a generous patron of the arts and as a sponsor of the Florentine-born Francesco Petrarch, for whose *Rime in vite di Laura* and *Rime in morte di Laura* she professed unbridled admiration. Hawkwood had dutifully read some of the *Canzioneri*, but found the verses excessively sentimental, not to say self-indulgent – a verdict Donnina dismissed as 'disappointing' in the extreme and excusable only in the light of her husband's vastly improved but still imperfect knowledge of Italian. Not so, Hawkwood had retorted: he admired the rigour and cadences of the *Trionfi* and had greatly enjoyed *De viris illustribus*, an early work which recounted the history of famous men through the ages.

To Hawkwood's mind, the two Visconti brothers could not have been more dissimilar. Whereas Bernabò was thickset and pugnacious, Galeazzo was tall and graceful. Where Bernabò was deliberately outspoken, Galeazzo was a study in restrained elegance. Bernabò was tactless, Galeazzo was tact and diplomacy personified. Hawkwood found it exceedingly hard to believe that this was the Galeazzo Visconti who had devised the gruesome *quaresima* torture.

Bernabò had outstripped his elder brother in one way, however: Galeazzo had only two children. His daughter – yet another Violante – had briefly been married to the late Lionel, Duke of Clarence and son of King Edward of England. Lionel's sudden demise (allegedly by poisoning) in 1368, four months into the marriage and while a guest of Galeazzo, had put paid to any aspirations the latter might have nurtured with regard to an enduring alliance with the English Crown. It had so enraged many English mercenaries serving in Italy at the time that they had made common cause, pooled their resources and turned on Galeazzo, inflicting on him a heavy and, in every sense, costly defeat at Alba later that year. Although Galeazzo had consistently denied allegations that he had been in some way instrumental in Lionel's death – which, indeed, scarcely seemed in Visconti interests – and had formally sworn his innocence before God, suspicion still lingered.

His other child was a son, the twenty-year-old Gian Galeazzo, who had his father's good looks and an air of quiet authority. In Hawkwood's estimation, the young man would bear watching.

Hawkwood understood that, for better or worse, he had now been received into the Visconti family. That it might prove a viper's nest did not trouble him unduly. He had his Donnina now, and that was enough. Not wishing to cast a pall over the festivities, he thought it best not to disclose to her that he and his Company were leaving Milan in less than a month's time to take to the field once more.

With the Viscontis. Or, if need be, against them.

XIX

Volte-Face

And so it is in politics, each for himself

Avignon, 21 April 1372

Gregory XI had good reason to fear the Viscontis of Milan. Bernabò had openly moved against him in 1370, and Gregory had retaliated by excommunicating the Viscontis the following year. To little avail: the Visconti brothers continued to oppose and plot against the Papal States, retaining bands of mercenaries to challenge the papacy at every turn – in Mantua, in Bologna, in Padua, in Pavia, even on the fringes of Rome itself.

Devout man of the cloth he might be, but Gregory was far from unaware of the secular threat posed by Italy's northern city states. What he feared most of all was an unholy alliance between those hitherto implacable enemies, Milan and Florence. Should they set aside their differences and make common cause against his pontificate, the earthly powers of the papacy would be at best greatly diminished and at worst completely extinguished.

Excommunication, traditionally regarded as the ultimate sanction against opponents of the Church, had failed. Gregory had had only one final option open to him: in early 1372, he had formally declared war against the Viscontis, extending the threat of excommunication to all who supported and abetted them. Despite the state of war that now formally existed between the Avignon Pope and Milan, little of note had occurred in the first four months of the year. The papal legate in Bologna, Pierre d'Estaing, had successfully conducted protracted negotiations with Bernabò Visconti and, for the present at least, a fragile truce held. It would prove of short duration, Gregory was sure. Bernabò would plot unceasingly against Avignon. Worse, papal spies reported that clandestine talks were now in progress between Milan and the Signoria of Florence.

Gregory's own position was seriously undermined by the continuing presence of the pontifical court in Avignon. There was a degree of anti-papal sentiment even in the Papal States and in Rome itself, and the Viscontis were intent on exploiting it to the full. In that, they were not without success. To restore papal credibility and authority, Gregory had to make his intentions clear: he must return to Rome.

The letter that lay before him reinforced his determination to do so. It was the most recent in a series from Caterina Benincasa of Siena. Gregory found her epistolary style curiously disjointed and infuriatingly repetitive, but there was no doubting either her sincerity or her intuitive grasp of the political situation, not to mention what she expected of him personally. In substance, Caterina implored him to be 'a good shepherd':

I beg you on behalf of Christ crucified to learn how to rescue that lost sheep, the human race, from the hands of the demons. God sees the evil state and the loss and ruin of these sheep and sees that they cannot be won back to Him by wrath or war. Justice wills that vengeance should be wrought for the wrong that has been done to God. Holy Father, I see no other way for us and no other aid to winning back your sheep which have left the fold and I pray you therefore that you do me this grace to overcome their malice with your benignity. They have no excuse for their crimes but it seemed to them that they could not do differently because of the many sufferings and injustices and iniquitous things they have endured from bad shepherds and governors. For they have breathed the stench of the lives of many rulers whom you know yourself to be demons incarnate. I ask you, Holy Father, to show them mercy. I tell you, sweet Christ on earth on behalf of Christ in Heaven, that they will all come grieving for the wrongs they have done and lay their heads upon your bosom.

Gregory by no means shared Caterina's tortured optimism. He readily endorsed her enthusiastic plea for the sheep to be brought back into the fold and her simplistic conclusion that legitimate injustices and iniquities needed to be addressed, but he saw little immediate prospect of her 'demons incarnate' submitting meekly to his authority and laying their heads upon his bosom. There was undoubtedly legitimate cause for grievances against the Church on account of the shortcomings of its administrators, but the issue was not so much how to correct those wrongs as how to bring to heel those who used such grievances to further their own overtly political ends and their crass aims of territorial gain. On that point Caterina had for once been refreshingly specific:

Come! Come and resist no more the Will of God that calls you. The hungry sheep await your coming to hold and possess the place of your predecessor and champion, the Apostle Peter. For you, as the Vicar of Christ, should abide in your own place. Come, then, and delay no more, and fear not anything that might happen.

Gregory set the letter aside. She was right, of course. As the Vicar of Christ, he should indeed abide 'in his own place'. His absence from Rome and the excessive influence of France in papal administration were tearing his beloved Church apart.

The following day, on the twenty-second day of April in the Year of Our Lord 1372, Pope Gregory XI announced in full consistory – at a meeting of the Papal Council and the cardinals – that he would return to Rome. When?

Soon. When the time was right . . .

Milan, 26 September 1372

Donnina Hawkwood paced the nursery, cradling her four-month-old son in her arms. To the amusement of the ladies of the court, she had elected not to give him into the charge of a wet-nurse but to breastfeed him herself. Their amusement was compounded by her obstinate refusal to leave the daily care of John Hawkwood II to others, as most patrician mothers were more than ready to do, but instead to tend personally to his every need. She paid no heed to these criticisms. This was her first-born and she cherished every hour she could spend with him. Labour had been mercifully short and, while she would scarcely describe it as enjoyable, she had found it strangely satisfying. After all, she had presented John Hawkwood with a son and heir.

Her joy was mitigated by the fact that her husband had not been present at the birth and that, for one reason or another, he had been precluded from returning to Milan in the weeks and months that followed. Donnina had long since despaired of keeping track of him and his movements. She was content to take enormous pride in his achievements and in the respect he enjoyed as a *condottiere*. He had his detractors, true enough, but few dared question his bravery or his prowess. Besides, Donnina loved her husband, whatever his real or imagined shortcomings.

She also loved her father – whatever *his* real or imagined shortcomings – and she was disturbed to see that his notorious bad temper had recently taken a turn for the worse. She attributed this in part to the frenzied comings and goings at the Palazzo Visconti. Much to her surprise, Bernabò and Galeazzo had played host to a delegation from Florence led by one Giancarlo Boninsegna, a man who had also found time to seek her out and congratulate her on her marriage to Hawkwood, for whom he expressed unqualified admiration.

What the Florentines were doing in Milan was not Donnina's concern: she was not one to meddle in affairs of state. From the occasional chance remark, however, she suspected that one reason behind her father's black mood must certainly be that his new son-in-law, John Hawkwood, was now in the pay of Gregory XI.

Near Bologna, 26 September 1372
Dante Alighieri, exiled from his native Florence in 1302 and still disdained by many of his compatriots as an outcast, had banished

traitors and 'sowers of discord' to the lowest circles of his *Inferno*. Was it there, Hawkwood wondered, that he himself belonged?

Mi ritrovai per una selva oscura che la diretta via era smarita.

Had he, like Dante, strayed from the straight and narrow path and found himself in a dark and gloomy wood?

Such doubts had assailed him since the débâcle at Asti in the Piedmont some three months previously, when he had found himself nominally second-in-command to Galeazzo Visconti's son, Gian Galeazzo. Hawkwood had last met Gian Galeazzo at his own wedding the previous year, and had thought then that the young man was someone who would bear watching. He had not expected to have an opportunity to observe Gian Galeazzo at close quarters – and find him wanting.

Asti lay at the confluence of the Borbera and Tanaro rivers south-east of Turin. It was best known for its excellent wines and for its architecture, notably its cathedral, the collegiate church of San Secondo and the imposing Torre Troiana tower. It was also a papal stronghold. Bernabò had ordered it taken, and Galeazzo had, albeit with some reluctance, furnished troops under the command of his son to do so.

Hawkwood had never been a forgiving man in the field. Prudence he could tolerate, but never timidity; caution, but never cowardice. He had ridden forward to assess Asti's defences and had found them poorly marshalled: the town would fall to a direct frontal assault, he concluded. His own officers were of the same opinion, but Gian Galeazzo procrastinated. It was too risky, he maintained; the Visconti forces at his disposal were insufficient.

Although he did not admit it at the time, Hawkwood bitterly resented being placed under the command of a beardless youth whose knowledge of battle was but theoretical.

'I say we attack forthwith,' Hawkwood had argued repeatedly.

'And I say we shall hold station until more men arrive from Milan,' Gian Galeazzo had countered each time.

Eventually, Hawkwood's patience was at an end. 'I will have no truck with this,' he announced. 'We strike now or not at all.'

Gian Galeazzo: 'I have command. And I say we wait.'

'Yes, it is your command and yes, you are at liberty to remain here as long as you wish. I, for one, choose otherwise.'

With that, Hawkwood had called his Company to order and force-marched them towards Bologna.

On hearing of Hawkwood's departure, Bernabò Visconti had been severely disappointed, but had felt that Hawkwood was perhaps justified. His brother had foisted on him – and on Hawkwood – a callow youth with little or no experience in combat and, it would appear, precious little taste for it. On hearing of Hawkwood's subsequent defection to the papal cause, however, Bernabò had been beside himself with rage. '*Bastardo!*' he had screamed time and again, swearing that this vile turncoat would one day pay in full for his craven disloyalty.

As it happened, payment in full had been a major factor in Hawkwood's decision to switch allegiance. Visconti had been generous to a fault when it came to celebrating his daughter's marriage and settling a dowry on her. But Hawkwood had received no payment at all for *condottiere* services rendered, although a substantial stipend had been agreed. The captain-general fought for pay, not promises; he had a Company to feed.

All the same, Hawkwood still had doubts: had he done the right thing? Pope Gregory had made clear his distaste for mercenaries in the services of the Viscontis, but apparently had no such reservations about mercenaries fighting in the papal cause. Gregory had now recruited the most celebrated *condottiere* of them all. Among the inducements offered, Gregory had promised Hawkwood an annuity even greater than that on which Visconti had defaulted. Provided the Pope kept his word, Hawkwood saw no reason to refuse him.

Hawkwood's decision was also opportune inasmuch as the tide of war appeared to be turning. He had been reliably informed that papal troops had penetrated as far as Galeazzo Visconti's own headquarters in Pavia. The Company had already forced Visconti's troops to raise their siege of Bologna, and Hawkwood was at present preparing to leave that city. He intended to drive into the heart of Milanese territory and confront the Viscontis on their own ground.

He could not help wondering how news of his *volte-face* had been received in Milan. And he prayed that no retribution or harm would befall his cherished Donnina and the new-born son he had yet to hold in his arms.

XX

Papal Fallibility

Robed in majesty and power

Palais des Papes, Avignon,
4 March 1373

Gregory XI was bitterly disappointed in John Hawkwood. The Englishman had failed him. The war against Milan was at a virtual standstill and the city had not fallen. The Viscontis were bruised and battered, certainly, but not defeated or deposed. Worse, rumours had reached Gregory's ears that Hawkwood and other mercenary captains in the papal service were once again secretly being wooed by Bernabò Visconti and his equally odious brother. Whether such rumours were true or not, only time would tell.

Gregory was also bewildered. Hadn't he repeatedly communicated to Hawkwood the eternal gratitude of the Holy Church? Hadn't he lifted the ban of excommunication placed on the *condottiere*? Hadn't he assured him of a place in Heaven as his just reward for his valiant services? He had done all this and more besides, including promising Hawkwood estates in the countryside north of Rome and a fine residence in Bologna should he secure a resounding victory over the Viscontis. Surely this was sufficient recompense?

But it seemed this grasping Englishman did not think so. He insisted on being paid his stipend as set out in their agreement, and had suspended military action in northern Italy until his demands were met.

The Papal Council tactfully refrained from pointing out to Gregory that Hawkwood's attitude towards the Pope replicated his attitude to the Viscontis: no pay, no service. Besides, the council had other issues to ponder. The Black Death had stealthily crept back into Avignon. Several hundred had already gone to meet their Maker, among them a number of cardinals. Food supplies were running low and were proving difficult to replenish. Citizens were abandoning Avignon in droves. An air of foreboding hung over the city as the pestilence spread inexorably through its congested streets.

Even more disturbing were reports that Milan and Florence were – as Gregory had long feared – on the point of setting aside their differences and uniting against the Papal States. Papal forces still nominally held Perugia, but the citizens made no secret of their distaste for Avignon's rule. Disaffected Perugians were known to be privy to the negotiations between Milan and Florence, and anti-papal sentiment was growing throughout the north, notably in Urbino, Orvieto, Montefiascone and Sassoferrato, but also in almost every small town and village throughout Lombardy and Tuscany.

Gregory decided to respond by attempting to enforce a grain embargo on Florence. He did so with the utmost discretion and subterfuge, working through the papal legate in Bologna and then officially and publicly reprimanding the latter for having taken such an intemperate and inhumane step. In turn, the legate formally charged Hawkwood with the task of starving Florence out by burning grain crops in Tuscan lands. Hawkwood complied up to a point, but then secretly negotiated with Boninsegna in Florence, offering to cease and desist in exchange for a very handsome payment. Florence paid and was confirmed in its determination to resist the legions of the absentee Pope in Avignon.

The anti-papal confederation was building, as Caterina of Siena did not hesitate to warn Gregory with monotonous regularity. She had even, she said, written to Hawkwood, begging him not to lay waste the lands around Siena, Lucca and Pisa and, above all, not to sell his sword to the highest bidder.

It would be a great thing now if you would withdraw a little into yourself and consider and reflect how great are the pains and anguish you have endured by being in the service and pay of the devil. My soul desires that you and all your followers and companions should change your ways and take again the pay and the cross of Christ Crucified, so that you may, as Christ's Company, march against the infidel dogs who possess our Holy Place. I wonder much at you for wanting to wage war in these parts. I beg you, dearest brother in Christ, to keep in memory the shortness of your time here on Earth and to remain in the Holy and Sweet Grace of God.

The letter, delivered by Caterina's confessor and friend of long standing, Raimondo da Capa, had been brought to Hawkwood wrapped in a simple woollen shawl which he instantly recognised: it was the very shawl that a young Dominican tertiary had gently draped over the body of Karl Eugen von Strachwitz-Wettin.

He kept the shawl and burnt the letter.

The Pope was no fool. He knew things were not going according to plan, that his temporal authority was being eroded. He had consistently reiterated his intention to return to Rome – when the time was right – and there was no time like the present. He would make one final effort to bring Florence back into the fold. If that effort failed, he would detach a large conscript army to pave the way for his triumphant return to the Holy See.

San Martino, near Perugia,
26 December 1375

During the last two years, Hawkwood had kept his head above water only with the greatest of difficulty. His immediate financial resources had been depleted to the point of exhaustion. Once he had defected to the service of the Pope he could hardly expect Bernabò Visconti to pay him, and the monies owed him by Gregory had not been forthcoming. In order to keep his Company intact, Hawkwood had again had to resort to extracting payments not for fighting but for undertaking not to fight. Over time, Siena, Lucca, Arezzo and Pisa (where Hawkwood no longer enjoyed a safe haven) had all agreed terms, reluctantly offering him monetary compensation for his non-belligerence. Florence, too, had paid an extortionate sum and granted him an annual pension under the provisions of yet another *condotta*, this one specifying his commitment not to attack the city for a fixed number of years.

Hawkwood harboured suspicions that the Pope had withheld payment in order to force him to fend for himself and, in the process, destabilise Tuscany to the point where its overtaxed citizens might be driven back into the welcoming arms of a benign pontiff who would then grant them exculpation and absolution. If that had indeed been an element in Gregory's strategy, it had failed conspicuously: Hawkwood had learnt that on 24 July 1375 the wearisome negotiations between Florence and Milan had been brought to a sudden close when the two city states concluded a five-year alliance against the Pope.

Hawkwood was still uncertain where his own best interests lay. With the Pope or against him? This dilemma had promptly been resolved when Gregory XI had shrewdly delivered – in cash, no less – a ninety-thousand-florin retainer to persuade Hawkwood to help ensure the defence of Perugia.

But Perugia had fallen. Its people had risen in revolt early that month, and Hawkwood and the papal representative had been blockaded within the citadel for the past three weeks, desperately seeking cover as rocks propelled from siege engines rained in on them. Eventually, Hawkwood had taken it upon himself to broker a settlement in a bid to extricate himself and his depleted Company from an increasingly precarious situation. It was agreed that he and his men would be afforded safe and unhindered passage from Perugia in exchange for surrender of the city and the simultaneous departure of the papal garrison. The citizens of Perugia had watched silently as they took their leave, then hastened to the citadel and started to tear it down stone by stone.

The Company tramped disconsolately away. The captain-general had rescued his men, but the loss of the city not only dealt a devastating blow to Pope Gregory, but also provided a rallying-cry for the anti-papal league. Worse, Hawkwood had been identified with an ignominious surrender which had blackened even further the already tarnished image of foreign mercenaries in Italy.

There was a new spirit abroad in northern Italy, a sense – premature, perhaps – of a national identity which might one day emerge from a country still ravaged by internal strife and internecine differences; a tenuous belief that Italy might in time resolve itself into a nation that was self-reliant and self-sustaining.

Not for the first time, John Hawkwood asked himself if there would be a place for him and his like in such an Italy.

Avignon, 22 March 1376

Gregory made one last effort to persuade the Florentines of the error of their ways and renounce their pact with Milan. A delegation from Florence was invited to Avignon, ostensibly to review these and other matters. No accommodation could be found, however, particularly since the Pope – to the dismay of his councillors – was determined to lay down the law rather than discuss reconciliation. To the Florentines' utter consternation, he flatly refused to hear their side of the argument. Instead, he accused them of conspiring against him and ordered them to be excommunicated without recourse. He declared Florence and its possessions forfeit, a curiously petulant and pointless gesture in that it could not fail to stiffen Florence's resolve to oppose him.

His own resolve had meanwhile been fortified by a visit from Caterina of Siena, who had begged him once again to return the papacy to Rome. Since he was on the brink of doing precisely that, he felt reinforced and comforted by her arguments. In practical terms, he had already prepared for that eventuality by assembling an army under the thirty-four-year-old Cardinal Robert of Geneva. Robert was a man of integrity, Gregory told himself, a man into whose hands he could safely commit his own destiny and the defence of his temporal dominions.

Yet another Vicar of Christ had demonstrated his fallibility.

Avignon, 23 May 1376

The man to whom Gregory had with such undiluted confidence entrusted the defence of the papal dominions was determined to make his mark and to ride roughshod over any and all who dared oppose him.

Robert de Genève, erstwhile Bishop of Thérouanne and Archbishop of Cambrai, had been elevated to the cardinalate in 1371. Not before time, he thought, believing the promotion to have been thoroughly warranted; indeed, he had already set his sights still higher. His admirers – of whom there were few – saw in him a man of action who did not shy away from difficult decisions. His detractors – of whom there were many – found him cold, arrogant and ruthless.

He rode out of Avignon at the head of an imposing force of close on eleven thousand men-at-arms, principally Bretons who had been lured at great expense from north-western France to prosecute the Pope's war against the anti-papal league. His plan of action was simple. Enter Italy, take Pavia, retake Bologna, strike south-east to headquarter at the papal stronghold of Cesena. Then advance on Florence from the east, where its defences were reportedly at their most vulnerable.

Word had been sent to an English *condottiere* named John Hawkwood to make rendezvous with Cardinal Robert at a township near Bologna. Robert saw no need for reinforcement by this Englishman, whose Company was believed to number a meagre fifteen hundred or at most two thousand men-at-arms. Robert had total faith in himself and in his Bretons, whose reputation preceded them: they were renowned for their savagery in battle and their uncompromising ways in peace. Still, the cardinal reflected, this Hawkwood might have his uses.

Pope Gregory was planning to leave for Rome later in the year, much to the dismay of the French king, the trepidation of the

French cardinals and the shock and despair of the French merchants of Avignon, whose livelihood was seriously jeopardised by the imminent departure of the high-living, high-spending papal court.

Robert was secretly delighted at the prospect of entering Rome in triumph several months before the Pope and his retinue left from Marseilles for the Roman port of Ostia Antica at the mouth of the Tiber. By that time, Robert was certain, the ambassadors of Florence, Milan and the other rebellious communes to the north would have sued for peace. Cardinal Robert of Geneva would emerge as the hero of the hour.

And as the obvious choice to succeed Pope Gregory XI.

XXI

Cesena

And in his heart he wondered if
He should not show his clemency

Cesena, Province of Emilia-Romagna, 1 February 1377

Hawkwood stood on the battlements of Cesena and looked down at the Savio river. It was said that, on a clear day, one could make out the independent *signoria* of Forli some four leagues distant along the straight and narrow ribbon of the ancient Via Aemilia. He had not had an opportunity to put that claim to the test; it had rained incessantly for the past five days and today was no exception.

The Company was cold, wet and dejected. It had been a difficult year, with food and booty in short supply. There had been some defections and the men's mood had at times turned ugly. Brawls had broken out and there had been a number of serious incidents, one of which had resulted in several men being killed. Hawkwood had struggled to maintain morale and preserve the Company's integrity as a fighting unit. The arrival of the Bretons under Robert de Genève had proved advantageous, however. They were a surly lot, but their saving grace was that they came well provisioned. If nothing else, the Company was being fed regularly.

Hawkwood's first impression of Cardinal Robert of Geneva had been anything but favourable. He disliked the man on sight, finding him pompous and overbearing. Dislike had turned to anger at the cardinal's dismissive manner as he surveyed the Company. It was clear that Robert regarded them as little more than a token force and, as fighting men, demonstrably inferior to his Bretons.

We shall see, thought Hawkwood.

He knew that Robert's initial intentions had been frustrated. He might have entered Italy, but he had neither taken Pavia nor retaken Bologna. The former – in the person of Gian Galeazzo Visconti – had simply bought him off for an undisclosed sum. The latter had put up such stiff resistance that Robert had eventually called off his Bretons, anxious not to squander his forces prior to the ultimate push on Florence.

Cesena had thus far remained loyal to the papacy and Hawkwood was puzzled by the cardinal's aggressive attitude towards its citizens. He had put the question directly.

'You know nothing of Cesena's history and reputation,' the cardinal had answered abruptly.

'That is true,' Hawkwood replied, 'but I am willing to learn.'

'They give safe haven to the Antichrist,' the cardinal continued, as if that were explanation enough.

He turned away, but Hawkwood was not prepared to let the matter rest.

'I do not take your meaning.'

Robert shrugged. 'You are an Englishman. I cannot expect you to know of Michael of Cesena and his blasphemies against our Holy Father and the Church.'

Hawkwood was intrigued. 'I am indeed an Englishman and I offer no apology for it. But it rains outside and I have naught else to do this day.'

Robert gave him a condescending look, but could not resist the temptation to enlighten him. He explained at some length that in 1329 Pope John XXII had issued a papal bull excommunicating an 'evil man' – *vir reprobus* – called Michael of Cesena. The latter's crime was that he had insisted on the strict and absolute application of the rule of poverty within the Franciscan order. Inevitably, as an advocate of ecclesiastical poverty, Michael had gone on to rail against the opulence and riches of the 'Whore of Babylon': Avignon. Pope John had, equally inevitably, taken first umbrage, then action, not only against Michael but against his followers, the Fratricelli, the 'Little Brethren' of Grey Friars. They were adamant in their belief that the Pope's convoluted attempts to justify the wealth and property maintained by the Church were in blatant contravention of holy scripture. Accordingly, they asserted to any who cared to listen that the Pope had betrayed his mission and had thus forfeited his authority: he and all those who served the Church were, according to the Fratricelli, guilty of mortal sin.

Hawkwood was tempted to interject that Michael had not been alone in regarding the Avignon papacy as the Whore of Babylon: Petrarch had also referred to the city as '*la puttana*'. But he felt little would be gained by unnecessarily causing offence, so he bit his tongue, content only to make clear to the cardinal that Italy was not alone in despising papal excess.

'I recall a man of that persuasion in England,' he said.

'Ockham,' said the cardinal, almost spitting the name. 'William of Ockham. Another vile blasphemer who dared countermand his Church and Pope.'

'Embracing poverty is no vice,' said Hawkwood.

Robert laughed. 'That is indeed rich, coming from a mercenary such as yourself!'

The exchange had been brief, but Hawkwood had learnt much from it. Whereas he had initially found the cardinal pompous and overbearing, he now regarded him as dangerous and unscrupulous in the extreme. Moreover, Robert's obsessive hatred of Cesena and its citizens still struck him as distinctly odd. One might have expected the cardinal to be more conciliatory, bearing in mind that the Cesenesi had remained loyal to and supportive of the pontiff at a time when many towns and cities were outspoken in their opposition to Avignon and everything it stood for.

Hawkwood shivered and went indoors, shaking the rain from his cloak.

Cesena, 4 February 1377

'Mamma!'

Silvana Vitelleschi was two years, seven months, three weeks and five days old. Her tiny frame was trapped beneath the suffocating weight of her mother's body. Wriggle as she might, Silvana could not wrench herself clear.

'Mamma!'

Mamma could no longer hear her. Still-warm blood from the yawning gash in her mother's throat flowed into Silvana's eyes and hair. She could hear grown-ups screaming. She did not understand why.

From the citadel parapet, Hawkwood watched as his Company and Robert of Geneva's Bretons tried to outdo each other in their indiscriminate massacre of the Cesenesi. The city gates had been barricaded two days previously and, ever since, the defenceless inhabitants had been put to the sword and axe. Many who had snatched a few precious belongings and made a dash for the city walls had been systematically cut down. The few who managed to scale the ramparts had discovered to their horror there was no option but to leap into the fetid moat far below. Those who did not drown among the reeds were mercilessly despatched when they reached the far side.

Breton vied with Englishman, seeking out victim after victim as men, women and children ran frantically this way and that. Bodies sprawled grotesquely in the streets and dogs gnawed contentedly on severed limbs. Fires had been set, and an entire section of the city was ablaze. The conflagration spread quickly as roof timbers crackled and spluttered into flame. A dark cloud spiralled high above Cesena.

Hawkwood was in no doubt: this atrocity was intended as a deliberate and cynical display of papal authority, a planned rather than random massacre; Cesena and its people were deemed expendable. It had been ordained that full expression be given to the long-standing papal grudge against a city which had not only spawned Michael of Cesena but had also tacitly endorsed the latter's fulminations against Avignon and the established Church. The cardinal had doubtless exploited some pretext or other – Hawkwood did not know exactly what, although he was later given to understand that a minor dispute involving some Cesena tradesmen and a group of drunken

Bretons had escalated to the point where two Bretons had been killed and several others seriously hurt. Whether this was true or not, it – or some similar incident – had provided the cardinal with the excuse he sought. He had ordered Cesena torched and its inhabitants slaughtered.

Hawkwood was revolted by the scene below but did not seek to absolve himself from blame or to deny that he and his men had played their part. Cardinal Robert had ordered him to secure the city. He had done so. Robert had ordered him to start a house-to-house search. He had done so. Robert had ordered the Company to kill any and all who breached the city walls. He had done so.

Hawkwood knew he could have refused to obey the cardinal's orders. He had not done so. He should have marshalled his Company and marched them out of Cesena. He had not done so. He should have ordered his men simply to hold station and take no part in the ensuing bloodbath. He had not done so.

Guilt and compassion prompted him belatedly to intervene, to help put an end somehow to this protracted and senseless slaughter for which no pardon might ever be asked or given. He left the citadel and made his way down into the city.

From above, Hawkwood had discerned a logical pattern to the massacre as first one area of the city was subdued, then another. Once on the ground, however, he discerned no such logic: the situation seemed totally out of control. He found it impossible to gauge how many had found death in the streets or in the flames that engulfed their homes. The skeletal remains of several churches dotted the skyline, giving off the unmistakable stench of charred flesh from the smouldering bodies of victims who had been incarcerated there and burnt alive. Rudimentary gallows had been erected on street corners, and bodies hung there, naked and mutilated. In some cases, men had been subjected to ritual crucifixion: horseshoe nails had been driven through their hands and feet into wooden doors and beams and their sides had been gouged with sword and spear in a grotesque parody of Christ's suffering on the Cross.

Mute groups of small children huddled together in doorways,

their eyes rolling in terror. Not far away lay the bodies of their mothers and fathers, the latter stripped of their clothing and belongings, some crudely decapitated, others missing genitals or limbs. For the most part, the women lay half-naked on the cobbles, their skirts yanked high to expose dark patches of pubic hair flecked with blood. An occasional monk stooped to administer the last rites. Hawkwood noted that, to a man, the friars were Dominicans or Augustinians. They, it seemed, had been spared.

The Fratricelli had not. The fountains and wells of Cesena were liberally decorated with corpses clad in the distinctive grey tunics and white waist-cords of the Grey Friars.

On all sides, Bretons and Englishmen were bundling their precious booty into coarse woollen blankets. The occasional quarrel broke out over the division of spoils; but, by common consent, there was more than enough to go around.

The cathedral doors were ajar but guarded by a contingent of Bretons who exchanged glances as Hawkwood approached, recognising him and the determined cast of his face. Reluctantly, they parted ranks. Hawkwood entered.

The cathedral was full of young women, some in their twenties, others barely more than children. They cowered and whimpered as Hawkwood strode among them, taking stock of the situation. There were hundreds of them – a thousand, even – and Hawkwood knew they had been spared for the most obvious reason of all. The matrons and grandmothers who littered the streets and squares of Cesena had been savagely raped and killed in the first surges of rampant male lust, but these young women were chosen vessels, young flesh which would be savoured at leisure and at length once the massacre was at a close.

He left the cathedral and walked the streets, identifying members of his Company and calling them to order. Most obeyed at once, although some resented his intrusion and the fact that their captain-general was spoiling their sport. He formed an *ad hoc* detachment into some semblance of order and returned to the cathedral.

The Breton guards tensed as they approached, uncertain of Hawkwood's intentions, but they made no effort to intervene when he and his men entered the cathedral and rounded up the young women and children. There were mutterings as the women were marched out. The Bretons inched forward, furious that the English were making off with their prisoners. Hands clasped sword-hilts and angry accusations filled the air. Undaunted, Hawkwood and his men escorted the trembling women out of the cathedral, through the blood-soaked streets and towards the city gates. He ordered the gates to be opened, and the women fled through them and dispersed into the countryside beyond.

Hawkwood had no way of knowing if they would survive or how, but he felt he could have done no less. He had assuaged his conscience to some small degree. That said, his guilt could never be fully expiated. Cardinal Robert of Geneva would go down in history as the 'Butcher of Cesena', but Condottiere John Hawkwood would take his guilt with him to the grave.

By late morning on the third day, the infamous massacre of Cesena was effectively over. Even Cardinal Robert had grasped that enough was enough. Ox-carts were commandeered to transport thousands of cadavers to huge pits hastily dug out of the slopes beyond the city walls. No prayers were said over the corpses unceremoniously tipped there.

At around noon that day, a detail of Bretons came across yet another dead woman. *Rigor mortis* had set in and they had difficulty straightening her limbs so that her corpse could be piled neatly into the laden ox-cart.

Underneath the body they found a small child.

Silvana Vitelleschi was two years, seven months, three weeks and six days old. Her face was tear-stained, her hair matted with blood. But she had survived.

'What about this one?' asked one of the Bretons.

'Put her with the others,' came the reply. The speaker grasped Silvana by the ankles and, with a practised movement, swung her limp body on top of the pile of corpses.

Had he been there, John Hawkwood would certainly have

intervened. But he had long since departed. He and his Company were by now several leagues distant, en route for Florence.

Some years before, Giancarlo Boninsegna had promised Hawkwood he was free to return to Florence as and when he wished. 'The gates of Florence are always open,' Boninsegna had added, 'to men of honour and integrity.'

All things considered, Hawkwood wondered if those gates would still be open. Or if his integrity and honour had been fatally compromised by events at Cesena.

XXII

Advise and Consult

Certes, our appetites and fears in war and peace,
In hate or love, are governed by a Providence above

Florence, 11 February 1377
The gates of Florence had indeed been opened wide to Hawkwood and his Company.

Reports of the massacre at Cesena had travelled fast, reaching eager ears in Florence and Milan. The two allies were jubilant, and Hawkwood's defection from papal service was widely welcomed by both. Taken together, these two events would, it was felt, be a potent weapon in the war against the Papal States. Hatred and contempt for the Avignon *puttana* was certain to intensify in the wake of Cesena. There was a genuine prospect that Italy as a whole might make common cause to reject the Whore of Babylon and its representative on Earth, Pope Gregory.

On his arrival in Florence, Hawkwood had been astonished to discover that the events in Cesena had improved rather than undermined his standing. He was equally astonished to learn that the death toll in Cesena had been grossly inflated. It was now accepted almost without question that over fifteen thousand had perished, at least three times what Hawkwood estimated the number to have been. Rumour also had it that Hawkwood and his Company had actually rallied to the Cesenesi's defence and opposed the slaughter perpetrated by Robert of Geneva's bloodthirsty Bretons.

When Hawkwood took issue with such falsehoods, Giancarlo Boninsegna wondered, not for the first time, at Hawkwood's naivety. He was quick to dispel the *condottiere*'s misgivings.

'These rumours serve us well, Sir John.'

'Yet they have no substance.'

'And what, pray, is substance? The cardinal has played into our hands by his ill-considered actions. Others now rally to our cause and we shall soon rid ourselves of the papal upstart from Avignon who dares – *dares* – inflict his malodorous papacy on Rome. *That* is substance, Sir John. And you have played your part in it.'

I have indeed played a part, thought Hawkwood, and an ignominious part it was. His shoulders slumped, and he shook his head slowly. 'I grow weary of all this.'

'As well you might.'

Boninsegna sensed this could prove a turning point in Hawkwood's relationship with Florence. He chose his next words with great care.

'The moment has come, Sir John. You must at last throw in your hand with Florence and its allies. I offer you this: supreme command of all Florentine forces in exchange for a stipend and a lifetime annuity. You know well that Florence can be most generous to those who espouse her cause and serve her in good faith.'

'There is much you do not know,' answered Hawkwood.

'Then tell me, my friend. There have been few secrets between us in the past.'

Hawkwood paused. He had thought long and hard on the march back to Florence. It seemed to him that his life had lost purpose and direction, was little more than a carousel of shifting allegiances. He did not deny that his world was of his own making, but it was a world for which he felt increasing distaste. Cesena had proved the last straw.

It was time.

'I intend to disband my Company,' said Hawkwood. 'The men will return to England, if it so pleases them. My work here will be at an end.'

Boninsegna studied Hawkwood's face, noting the lines that creased the brow, the streaks of grey that flecked the temples, the eyes that no longer glinted at the prospect of long days in the field but were dulled by months and years apart from those he loved. He is not the man he once was, thought Boninsegna. He wearies of it all.

'Your intention is rash and difficult to accept,' replied Boninsegna. 'There is much to consider. You are respected even by those who have cause to oppose you. But . . .' It was his turn to pause.

'But?' prompted Hawkwood.

'But you will stand diminished in all eyes in the absence of your Company.'

Hawkwood bristled. 'Those are harsh words, sir.'

'Harsh but true. Without the Company at his command, Sir John Hawkwood is no longer an asset. More importantly, he is no longer a threat.'

Hawkwood sighed. It was true. By far the major part of his revenue had been in the form of payments received for non-belligerence. Without his Company, he could not enforce such payments from the likes of Siena, Pisa or Lucca. Or even from Florence and Milan.

'Then my value is as naught?'

'Your value is as you choose to make it. I say again: the armies of Florence are there for you to command. Shape them as you will. On that you have my most solemn word.'

The prospect of exchanging his twilight status as a *condottiere* for the substantially more respectable position of commanding general of the armies of Florence was one which Hawkwood could not dismiss lightly. Not only would he have at his disposal a large military force, he would also be in a position to call on the ostensibly limitless resources of Italy's richest city state. He owed loyalty to his men, but these were not the men who had been at his side in the early days. Karl Eugen was dead, Gennaro Altobardi had disappeared without trace, Sir Wilfred Perry had returned to England. Only Llewellyn remained. Hawkwood owed loyalty to his Company, certainly, but their loyalty to him was – like his own – bought and paid for.

'I owe loyalty to my Company,' insisted Hawkwood.

'And that loyalty shall be honoured in full,' replied Boninsegna smoothly. 'Your men shall be returned home at Florence's cost. Let it never be said that those who served with Sir John Hawkwood went empty-handed from the field.'

'The offer is more than generous, Signor Boninsegna. I shall think on it. In all honesty, my finances are at present . . . limited.'

Boninsegna burst out laughing. 'Your finances are in excellent order, Sir John. I have watched over them myself, and I am proud to say I have invested well on your behalf. You are not the richest man in Florence – far from it – but the spectre of bankruptcy does not hover over your head. You need trouble yourself no more in that regard.'

Hawkwood could think of no appropriate reply. This put an entirely different complexion on the matter. There was, however, something else he had repeatedly turned over in his mind.

'I myself have considered returning to England,' he said.

'I understand that a man may yearn for his native soil,' answered Boninsegna. 'But your roots are here now, Giovanni Acuto. You are as much an Italian as any of us. Your destiny is here. I urge you, do not reject it.'

Hawkwood's memories of England had dimmed with the passage of time. What was there for him now? He thought of Donnina and the four-year-old son he had not yet even seen. Boninsegna was right. His destiny *was* here. He hesitated no longer.

'I place myself and my sword at the service of Florence.'

'Your decision is most wise, Sir John, and long overdue.'

Florence, 14 March 1377

Hawkwood despatched Llewellyn and a detail of forty men to Milan to escort Donnina and his son to Florence. He was less than happy with the arrangement, but decided it might be premature to venture into the presence of her father. He was not certain how he would be received, or if Bernabò would ever forgive his erstwhile defection to the papal banner. Besides, now that he had elected to remain in Florence's service, he considered

Donnina's rightful place to be with him there, rather than in Milan.

He was provisionally quartered in Boninsegna's palazzo, but was anxious to find a home for himself and his family. After so many years of a nomadic existence in the field he found the prospect of settling in one place uncommonly appealing. I must be getting old, he chided himself. He had already viewed a number of houses, but decided to await Donnina's arrival. It was only proper that she should have a voice in their choice of home.

Hawkwood was impatient for Donnina to arrive. As the days went by, however, doubts crept into his mind. Had she chosen to remain in Milan after all? Was she slighted by his not having fetched her in person? Had the years apart caused a breach in their relationship? He prayed that was not so, but he could not be certain all was well until she arrived.

To his immense relief, word came one morning that Donnina's party would arrive later that same day. Hawkwood could not contain his excitement. The hours dragged by and still there was no sign. Then, late in the afternoon, her carriage at last drew into the courtyard. Hawkwood raced down the palazzo steps. The sight of Donnina descending from her carriage reminded him sharply of his first glimpse of her those many years ago when she had appeared at his camp near Florence. Her face might have softened into maturity, but she still had the vibrant grace that had originally drawn him to her.

He opened his arms and she came into them without a word. They stood locked together for a full minute before he drew back and held her at arm's length.

Donnina returned his gaze, taking in the greying temples and the lines that etched his cheeks. He has aged, she thought.

She had never loved him more.

Hawkwood was so captivated by the moment that all other thoughts went from his mind. With a hint of a smile on her face, Donnina disentangled herself from his embrace, turned and beckoned to Llewellyn. The Welsh giant shuffled forward, bent almost double to clasp the hand of a tousle-haired little boy dressed in the black breeches and white tunic that Hawkwood himself favoured.

'May I present Master John Hawkwood. Your son,' said Donnina with unmistakable pride.

Hawkwood had prepared himself for this moment, steeled himself for his first encounter with his own flesh and blood. Would the child be afraid of him? Would he be shy? Would he be a son a *condottiere* could be proud of?

The boy strode confidently forward and thrust out a tiny hand in greeting. 'Welcome home, father.'

Hawkwood stooped, picked up young John in his arms and swung him high above his head. He could feel the firmness of the child's body locked securely within his grasp. The youngster giggled his delight as Hawkwood twirled him first one way and then another, tossing him high in the air, then catching him and holding him tightly against his chest. When he set the child down again and turned to Donnina, his eyes were moist.

'I have a son,' he said.

She nodded indulgently. 'Yes, my dearest husband. You have a son.'

He pumped Llewellyn's hand, thanking him over and over again for having escorted and guarded Donnina's party. The hard-bitten Welshman was embarrassed, not least at the sight of his captain-general moved to tears. 'He's a fine lad,' he said gruffly. 'He'll grow up to be like his father.'

'No,' said Hawkwood. 'God forbid. I pray only that he grows to be everything his father should have been.'

As Llewellyn set off back to his quarters, Donnina said, 'There is someone else you should meet. May I present the English envoy to the court of Milan, Sir William Coggeshall?'

A tall, elegantly attired man in his late thirties or early forties came forward from where he had been waiting patiently until the family's greetings were over.

'Forgive me, Sir William,' said Hawkwood. 'I fear I have done you a discourtesy.'

Sir William smiled. 'There can be no discourtesy in the presence of such happiness.' He beckoned to the young woman who had been waiting with him. She was tall, slender, poised: an English rose if ever I saw one, thought Hawkwood.

'May I present my wife, Sir John? I believe it is time you made her acquaintance.'

She stepped forward and extended a hand in greeting.

'Permit me,' said Sir William, 'to introduce you to Lady Antiocha Coggeshall.'

Antiocha? *Antiocha?* The blood drained from Hawkwood's face, and his hands shook as he took Antiocha's in his. In the course of a single afternoon, he had been presented with both a son and a daughter.

That evening with his family was one of the happiest that Hawkwood could remember. He held his son on his lap until the youngster, weary from the long and arduous journey to Florence, nodded off, contentedly sucking his thumb. It was with some difficulty that Donnina persuaded a doting Hawkwood to release the child so that she could put him to bed.

He listened intently as Antiocha spoke of her childhood in Essex, her comfortable but strict upbringing at the hands of her maternal grandmother, and her betrothal and marriage – when barely sixteen – to Sir William, a neighbouring landowner and a man over twice her age. Like any father worth his salt, Hawkwood secretly believed no man could ever be good enough for his daughter, but he pushed the thought away: he had not been there to advise on the choice of husband. Besides, he had taken to her husband without hesitation. His new son-in-law was reserved to the point of diffidence – a trait implicit perhaps in his chosen profession as a diplomat – but his general manner was one of respect tempered by unassuming self-confidence. Coggeshall's affection for Antiocha was plain for all to see.

Hawkwood was pleased to learn that his own interests in England were at present in the capable hands of none other than Sir William, who soon informed him that those affairs were in good order, although he would welcome instructions as to their future conduct and any dispositions to be made.

Thus reassured, Hawkwood was more than eager to hear about England. Coggeshall readily obliged. King Edward was in the poorest of health and was not expected to live many months, let alone years. The Black Prince had died the previous year, of a pernicious stomach ailment, and the heir to the throne of England was his son, Richard of Bordeaux, a young lad of ten.

Until Richard came of age, affairs of state would be in the hands of the nobles who had counselled King Edward during the final years of his reign. The *primus inter pares* was without doubt John of Gaunt, Duke of Lancaster, a man whose motives and self-serving character were, as even the diplomatic Sir William guardedly conceded, 'questionable'. The prospect of Edward's imminent demise had engendered widespread unrest, notably among England's peasant population.

'And how fares the war against France?' asked Hawkwood, anxious to know the truth or otherwise of such rumours as had come to his ears.

'The king is at present in no condition to prosecute the war,' came the bland response.

The answer did not satisfy Hawkwood. 'In no condition?' he persisted.

'Not only does his health preclude it,' replied Sir William after a short pause, 'but so, too, does the state of England's finances.'

It was for good reason that Hawkwood had a reputation for plain speaking. 'And that, Sir William, is your mission here in Italy?'

An unruffled Coggeshall held Hawkwood's gaze. 'That is part of my mission here, yes—'

'To raise fresh funds for the continuance of the war?'

'That is so.'

'And?'

'And that mission has proved difficult. It would appear that the conflict between the papacy and the anti-papal league has depleted this country's resources also.'

Hawkwood pressed the point home. 'You have failed to raise monies in Milan?'

'Until now, yes. The negotiations continue.'

'And here in Florence?'

'I am conducting negotiations here, too.'

Satisfied, Hawkwood settled back in his chair.

Donnina adroitly turned the conversation to other matters. From the casual manner in which they conversed, Hawkwood was certain that she and Antiocha had become close friends during his daughter's stay in Milan. Donnina had taken the young Englishwoman under her wing, it seemed, doubtless because she had discovered who Antiocha was.

It was not until after Hawkwood and Donnina had retired to their bedchamber and made love – twice – that he raised the thorny subject of Bernabò Visconti.

Donnina's brow furrowed. 'My father is advanced in years. He no longer has the energy or ambition of his younger days.'

'And what of his brother?'

'They have never been close, as you well know. But Galeazzo is also old and frail. It is his son, Gian Galeazzo, who is the greatest threat to my father.'

Hawkwood was silent for a moment. Gian Galeazzo? The Gian Galeazzo who had been a guest at their wedding? The gutless Gian Galeazzo who had so arrogantly rejected his military counsel in Bologna in 1372, prompting his defection to the Pope? The Gian Galeazzo whom he had twice since bested in the field?

'Gian Galeazzo is of little consequence,' said Hawkwood.

'Gian Galeazzo is of *great* consequence,' retorted Donnina. 'You do wrong to underestimate him and his ambition.'

Hawkwood grunted. Worn out by the emotional and physical demands of the day, he was already asleep in Donnina's arms. Cautiously, so as not to wake him, she leant across him to extinguish the flickering candle. She found it impossible to describe how happy she felt to have her husband back at her side.

Pavia, 16 April 1377

Gian Galeazzo Visconti had long-term plans. He had a clear vision of a single and united Visconti dynasty in Milan as the vehicle for the creation of a still greater political unity, that of northern Italy as a whole. Under his leadership – that went without saying. These lofty ambitions were precocious, to say the least, given that he was only twenty-six years old, but Gian Galeazzo felt in his bones that he was destined to achieve great things.

Sadly, there were some obstacles in his path, not the least of which was the continued lordship of his uncle, Bernabò Visconti, over Milan's territories to the east. Bernabò and his brother had spent a lifetime bickering over Milan's destiny, yet they had cooperated in the administration of the city's affairs and contrived to keep their respective grievances in check and avoid open hostilities.

The most immediate stumbling block, however, was Gian Galeazzo's own father, or, to be more precise, his father's irritating refusal to die. Granted, he was old now and largely incapacitated by gout and other ailments, but he still held sway over the western territories of Milan from his stronghold in Pavia. At one point, Gian Galeazzo had considered poisoning his father, but had dismissed the notion as unworthy. He hoped only that Galeazzo would die.

Soon.

And then, vowed Gian Galeazzo, I shall wrest dominion of the eastern territories from Bernabò and his legion of bastard children. I shall transform Milan into the unified city state it once was under the stewardship of my great-uncle Giovanni. And then – *then* – I shall subdue Florence.

For the time being, however, he prudently kept these ambitions to himself.

Council Hall of the Signoria, Florence, 7 May 1377

Voluminous dossiers bound with ribbons lay at each of the sixteen places set round the waxed oak conference table in the council hall of the Signoria. The serving members of the Banking Guild of the City State of Florence took their seats in almost total silence, conscious that the decision at hand was of major import to the city's future financial well-being.

Hawkwood sat at the lower end of the table, flanked by the most senior representatives of the Florentine banks, who served in rotation under the current presidency of Giancarlo Boninsegna. Hawkwood had attended several such meetings, but had contributed next to nothing to the discussions. The plain truth was that, without exception, he had found himself out of his depth and, as a result, seriously bored by it all.

Today was different. Hawkwood listened attentively as Boninsegna went through the formalities of welcoming the participants by name and calling the meeting to order. There was, he said, only one item on that day's agenda. He tapped the dossier before him.

'You have been invited to render an opinion on documents submitted by the English Crown, which now solicits a further major investment underwritten by the banks of Florence in furtherance of a protracted state of war between the kingdoms of England and France. You have had an opportunity to study that evidence in detail, and I now call upon you to vote in favour or against.'

There was a nodding of heads.

'My role here today is limited to ensuring that the ballot is conducted under the conditions enshrined in our articles. I shall not participate in the ballot, nor shall I seek in any way to influence its outcome. As president, however, I am required by statute to remind you that the petition relates to a very large sum – twenty-five million florins, to be at the unfettered disposal of the client petitioner over a period of five years – and that collateral is offered only in the form of certain lands and territories which England currently holds in France. The value of those territories is conditional upon an outcome of the war in England's favour. In the event of default, you must take account of their real value to Florence. Finally, I recall for the collective benefit of this assembly the lesson of history: England has in the past been granted large loans and has not made full restitution, much to the detriment of some of the banks represented here today. On the other hand, the terms appended to the proposed loan are onerous and, in the event of non-default, the annual interests accruing to the member institutions of this Guild are so substantial as to be without precedent.'

Heads nodded again.

Hawkwood was in a quandary. Boninsegna had set out the case succinctly. There was a suggestion in his instructions to the Guild that the English Crown might default on the loan and there was indeed a distinct likelihood that England would find it impossible to repay, as had notoriously been the case in the past. Meanwhile, on a personal level, Hawkwood realised this was his chance to exact retribution, however indirectly, and repay Edward for the injustice he had done to Hawkwood almost two decades previously.

The voting procedure was simple. The Guild members present would be balloted on behalf of the full membership, who would then be duty-bound to honour the decision and participate in the loan agreement on a pre-established *pro rata* basis.

Boninsegna rang a small silver bell, and a senior clerk entered the room. He carried a purple velvet pouch. Each participant had been issued with a white ball and a black ball. A white ball connoted approval of the motion before the assembly, a black ball opposed it. The guildsmen would be called forward in order of seniority and invited to deposit in full anonymity one ball each into the pouch. Boninsegna would then reveal its contents. A unanimous vote was required: a single black ball would defeat the motion.

When his name was called, Hawkwood stood up and walked the length of the table. He placed a ball in the pouch. Boninsegna smiled and thanked him. Hawkwood resumed his seat.

Boninsegna announced that the vote was in. He took up the pouch and removed the balls one by one, calling out – somewhat superfluously, Hawkwood thought – the colour of each ball as it was displayed. 'White . . . white . . . white.'

Three whites. Then another. Hawkwood's mouth was dry. He glanced around at the other participants. They sat impassively, but there was no denying the tension round the table.

'White . . . White.' Then, 'Black.'

Hawkwood's heart skipped a beat. The vote was divided. The motion had been denied.

Procedure required, however, that the remaining balls be exposed. Another white, followed by two more. Then a second black, followed by the remaining four whites.

'The motion is hereby defeated,' declared Boninsegna. 'Accordingly, I declare this vote duly cast and counted.'

Hawkwood rose to leave, but his neighbour to the left laid a restraining hand on his arm. An important item of business had yet to be concluded.

The English delegation was called into the Council Chamber. Besides Sir William de Coggeshall, Hawkwood recognised one or two others who had given testimony before the Guild at an earlier meeting, among them a singularly outgoing young man called Geoffrey Chaucer.

'It is with the deepest regret,' said Boninsegna, 'that I must convey to you the decision of this assembly not to proceed with the loan as requested.'

Sir William bowed. 'In the name of King Edward and England, I regret this also,' he said. 'Permit me to ask the outcome of the ballot.'

Hawkwood regarded this, on the face of it, as a not unreasonable request. He was suddenly aware that Sir William was looking directly at him. He felt the colour rise to his cheeks, but did not look away.

'The voting procedure takes place under conditions of the strictest secrecy, Sir William. The results are not disclosed beyond the walls of this room,' said Boninsegna, following Coggeshall's gaze. 'In a matter of such import, however, I shall admit an exceptional departure from procedure and inform you that the motion was defeated by two dissenting votes out of fifteen.'

Coggeshall gave a wry smile, thanked Boninsegna and ushered the English delegation from the chamber.

Hawkwood was greatly relieved that his son-in-law would now have no reason to ask him whether he had voted in England's favour or against.

XXIII

A Farewell to Arms

Who grieves now that he may no more resume the fight?

Via Emilia, 4 May 1385
Sleep would not come.

John Hawkwood, Supreme Commander of the Armies of the City State of Florence, squatted on his haunches under a stand of cork oaks and pondered the futility of it all.

Bolts of lightning punctured the night sky and peals of thunder resonated in the distance, making the tethered horses whinny in alarm. The rain drove into Hawkwood's face and he pulled the sodden blanket more tightly round his shoulders. His men lay scattered in small groups under the trees. Some slept, but most tossed and turned and, every now and then, one would curse loudly.

Hawkwood's boots were caked with mud. Streaks of grime ran down his cheeks and into his greying beard. His eyes were bloodshot from lack of sleep. His bones ached and old wounds shot stabs of pain through his body.

Futile.

Over the years, he had often had occasion to reflect on his life and his chosen profession. Never more so than now, drenched to the skin on a hillside no more than a day's march from Florence. What was the point to all this? Supreme Commander? Call me what you will, I am still little more than a hireling. In the pay of Florence but at the beck and call of all and sundry.

Another flash of lightning lit up the sky, throwing into sharp silhouette the figures of his men huddled under the trees. They are my consolation, he thought. A third of the Company had returned to England, their passage paid by Florence and their money belts bulging with florins. Others – a couple of hundred or so – had left for France, where rich and easy pickings were reported. For Hawkwood and for those who remained with him, life carried on much as before.

Futile.

Hawkwood had been in the field almost continuously since 1378. In the main, he had harried Cardinal Robert's Bretons the length and breadth of northern Italy and as far south as the gates of Rome. A skirmish here, a pitched battle there; some victories token, some engagements indecisive, some defeats unavoidable. There had been casualties, of course, but his Company had always suffered substantially fewer losses than it had inflicted.

Futile.

This 'war' was pointless, thought Hawkwood. He had predicted as much ever since Pope Gregory's arrival in Rome in January 1377 to witness at first hand the annihilation of his sworn enemies to the north. The war had raged on, and the services of Hawkwood and his Company had rarely been in such demand. But, for years now, both sides had been exhausted, both physically and financially. The legendary bottomless coffers of Florence, already severely hit by embargos and confiscations visited by Gregory XI on the anti-papal league, were perilously close to empty. The citizens of Florence laboured under the burden of escalating taxes; revolt was in the air. In Rome, too, conditions had deteriorated to the point where rioting was the rule rather than the exception. Milan and Florence routinely sent infiltrators there to stir up hatred against the Pope. Rome returned the compliment by sending its agents to Milan and Florence to incite rebellion.

Futile.

Admittedly, the warring factions came together from time to time to explore the terms of a durable peace. Hawkwood had himself been involved in some of these negotiations and had always known they were doomed to end inconclusively. Mutual antipathy was too deeply entrenched. The well-intentioned but increasingly hysterical interventions of Caterina Benincasa, who had repeatedly implored both sides to cease hostilities, had done little to help. She was dead now and, to Hawkwood's mind, that was no great loss: he had always thought her an interfering busybody at best, and, at worst, an attention-seeking spy and informant who meddled in affairs not of her concern.

Futile.

Yes, Caterina was dead – she died in 1380, Hawkwood seemed to recall – and so, too, were King Edward of England and Pope Gregory XI. Since the latter's death in late 1377, the western arm of the Christian Church was a house divided. The cry had at once gone up for 'an Italian Pope, if not a Roman'. In 1378, Bartolomeo Prignano, the former Archbishop of Bari, had been rushed into office as Pope Urban VI. Someone, somewhere had gravely miscalculated. Urban's erratic behaviour and sporadic outbursts of abuse and even physical violence had soon made him run foul of his French cardinals. They had responded by convening secretly to elect their own Pope, none other than Cardinal Robert of Geneva, the 'Butcher of Cesena', a man reviled throughout Italy.

It was an absurd situation. At times, Hawkwood had found it hard to tell which Pope it was that he was fighting, as one or the other of these two Vicars of Christ, one in Avignon, one in Rome, and each with his own Curia, repeatedly denounced his counterpart as an apostate and 'odious despoiler of Christianity'. At one point in 1382, 'anti-papal' Florence had even despatched its own *condottiere* and commanding general, a bewildered John Hawkwood, to the service of Pope Urban.

Futile.

Futile. Futile. *Futile*.

'Supreme Commander of the Armies of the City State of Florence?' he muttered to himself as he pulled the rain-soaked blanket up round his ears and made one final effort to catch at least a few hours' sleep.

Supreme Commander, my knightly arse!

Varese, 5 May 1385

Bernabò Visconti ruled over his allotted portion of Milan with a fist of iron. He had never been a popular ruler, and his subjects deeply resented the swingeing taxes to which he subjected them. Open revolt was out of the question, however: Bernabò's subjects trembled at the prospect of the swift and merciless retribution that would inevitably follow. At the same time, they looked with unconcealed envy at those of their fellow Lombards who prospered under the seemingly benevolent rule of Bernabò's nephew, Gian Galeazzo. The latter's own carefully nurtured public *persona* was that of a pious and contemplative *savant* who treated his vassals with respect and leniency.

The uneasy truce that had existed between Bernabò and his brother Galeazzo did not sit at all well with Gian Galeazzo, who rightly saw in his uncle the principal obstacle in his own path to supreme lordship over the territories of Lombardy. Bernabò was in his seventies now, but had lost little of the arrogant ruthlessness that had sustained him over the years. That arrogance would, in Gian Galeazzo's estimation, prove to be Bernabò's Achilles' heel.

On the pretext of settling ongoing differences with his uncle, Gian Galeazzo had proposed that he and Bernabò should meet at a neutral venue near Varese to agree upon the future governance of Milan. Gian Galeazzo was relieved to discover that Bernabò, arrogant and dismissive as ever, had appeared that noon with only a modest retinue.

Gian Galeazzo was already there in force.

A bemused Bernabò Visconti was taken prisoner, then marched under armed guard to one of Gian Galeazzo's strongholds near Pavia. Gian Galeazzo's plan was to incarcerate Bernabò indefinitely at Trezzo Castle, together with Donnina de' Porri, his erstwhile mistress, whom he had since married. Bernabò's possessions would be declared forfeit and his children disinherited. There was every indication that the citizens of Milan would rejoice at Bernabò's downfall and unhesitatingly acclaim Gian Galeazzo as the saviour of Lombardy.

Gian Galeazzo was persuaded that his plan had worked. He had accomplished at a stroke what papal armies had for years failed to achieve: the irrevocable eclipse of Bernabò Visconti.

Florence, 5 May 1385

Hawkwood's first action on his return from the field was to pay his respects to his employer.

Giancarlo Boninsegna came out from behind his cedarwood desk and walked forward to meet him, both hands extended in greeting. 'Welcome, Sir John. It is good to have you back safe with us once more.'

'It is good to be back, Giancarlo. Many are the times I have longed for civilised company and a warm bed.'

Surveying Hawkwood's haggard face, Boninsegna realised that Florence's supreme commander was at the end of his tether. His eyes had dulled and his movements were perceptibly slower. How old was he now? Sixty-three? Sixty-five, more like. And looking his age.

'You look well, Sir John.'

Hawkwood smiled. 'As do you, Giancarlo.'

'In faith, neither of us is in the first flush of youth.'

'My creaking bones remind me constantly.'

Hawkwood drew up a chair and settled down to report in detail on his movements over the previous several months.

'Inconclusive, then?' asked Boninsegna when he had finished.

'Inconclusive,' replied Hawkwood. 'The word is well chosen.'

The two men sat in silence, neither wishing to voice the unspoken thought that lay between them.

It was Hawkwood who eventually spoke first. 'My men must rest, Giancarlo. They have spent too many years in the field. As for myself—'

'As for yourself, you also deserve rest. You have served us well, Sir John, and Florence owes you and your Company a great debt.'

'It is time, I fear, to collect on that debt,' said Hawkwood.

Boninsegna nodded. 'Then pray make your wishes known.'

'I fear my value to you and Florence is no longer at the head of my Company but, instead, here in the city. I can command and direct, but my fighting days are at an end.'

Boninsegna had long since come to the same conclusion. 'Your value to Florence – and to myself – remains beyond measure, Sir John. That your name is spoken in the same breath as that of Florence is more than value enough. You have kept faith with your Company and with us. And you are right: we must now seek to use you more wisely. You are an asset we cherish and can ill afford to lose.'

Hawkwood was surprised that Boninsegna had so readily accepted the situation. 'Then I shall without delay assume full responsibility for the disposition and deployment of the armies of Florence.'

'Agreed, Sir John. You have commanded from the front long enough. The moment has come for you to command from the rear.'

'An unaccustomed privilege,' said an unsmiling Hawkwood.

'The privilege of rank, Sir John – and a privilege you have undoubtedly earned.'

The two men shook hands again as Hawkwood stood to take his leave. There was a new lightness in his step as he mounted his palfrey and urged it towards San Donato, where Donnina would be waiting.

Waiting with their son, John, and their new-born daughter.

San Donato, 8 May 1385

'John!'

Hawkwood took her in his arms and stroked her hair, reassuring her, as he had so often done in the past, that he had indeed returned safely.

Donnina's delight at his homecoming was doubled by the news that he had reached an accommodation with Boninsegna. She had waited so many years for the moment when her husband would be relieved of day-to-day field command and removed from harm's way. Like the wives of soldiers everywhere, she had lived in a state of almost permanent anxiety and insecurity, uncertain whether her husband would return unscathed from the wars. Each home-coming had been bliss, each departure a cruel torture.

Hawkwood revelled in their property in San Donato. It was modest by comparison with some of the lands he had been gifted elsewhere over the years, for the most part as payment in lieu of services rendered. Those that lay to the south – and closer to Rome – were veritable strongholds in their own right, and the monies he disbursed on their upkeep were considerable. He could only hope that one day, when these futile papal wars were over, he could divest himself of them at a profit. Until then, they were little more than a drain on his purse.

No matter. He would always have San Donato, a beautiful domain set amid the verdant hills of Tuscany. This was home; and he was never happier than when he was able to spend a week or so here, riding to the hunt, playing childhood games with his son and spending quiet evenings with Donnina.

His second daughter – Catherine – had been born a few weeks previously. Hawkwood felt a twinge of shame that he had not even known Donnina was once again with child. He vowed he would never again spend months in the field away from her side. Catherine's eyes were those of her mother, her wisps of chestnut hair a foretaste of Donnina's proud mane. He held the infant in his arms and mouthed the absurd terms of endearment that a doting father reserves for his offspring.

These peaceful pursuits were interrupted by the arrival of a messenger from Florence, bringing news of Bernabò Visconti's fate at the hands of his nephew. Donnina was beside herself with worry, convinced it would be only a matter of days before Gian Galeazzo conveniently and clandestinely arranged for her father's death. Hawkwood did his best to console her – 'We shall negotiate for his return,' he said repeatedly – but Donnina was not convinced.

She also had some difficulty concealing her disappointment that her husband, the celebrated *condottiere* John Hawkwood, had not immediately volunteered to ride to her father's rescue.

'I have never meddled in your affairs,' she said, 'but I ask this of you: that you do whatever lies in your power to secure my father's release.'

'We shall negotiate, have no fear. Your father is in no immediate danger. Gian Galeazzo will not put his reputation at risk by sanctioning the murder of his own uncle. Be patient. We shall negotiate. All will be well.'

Donnina feared otherwise. On seizing her father, Gian Galeazzo had promptly declared her father's belated marriage null and void, thus making her a bastard again. She had little doubt that Gian Galeazzo's next move would be to confiscate her mother's property, effectively disinheriting Donnina and, in the process, seizing that which would have one day devolved to her and her husband. To Donnina's mind, Hawkwood should act at once.

'You must do something,' she said over and over again.

Hawkwood continued to reassure her as best he could, but he knew there was precious little he could do. He could not place so personal a matter before his professional obligations to Florence. What was more, he did not have the men at his own immediate disposal to contemplate a full-scale campaign against Gian Galeazzo. Besides, Florence and Milan were still parties to an alliance. To Donnina's dismay, he felt his hands were tied, for the moment at least.

'Gian Galeazzo will be brought to heel, on that you have my word,' he told Donnina.

But how and when remained an open question.

XXIV

Parthian Shots

There comes at last an end to every deed

Near Verona, 10 March 1386
A disconsolate Dino Scarlatti perched on a grassy knoll in the hills overlooking the graceful arc of the Adige river that fringed Verona.

His goats were gone. All nine of them. He had tried to stop the soldiers, but they had carelessly shrugged aside the twelve-year-old's frantic efforts to protect his tiny herd. A burly sergeant-at-arms had laughed and given him a playful slap. Dino's ears were still ringing from the blow. The soldiers had roped his goats together and led them off down the hill. Dino put his head in his hands and wept bitter tears of frustration.

On the plain below, the armies of Padua and Florence were encamped before Verona. They had been there for many weeks and Dino had tended his goats and watched as sporadic attempts were made to breach the city walls and batter down the Arco dei Gravi portal. Each assault had been beaten back. There had been no attacks for several days now.

Dino wiped his reddened eyes, blew his nose on his sleeve and gathered up his few possessions. There was nothing for it: he would have to go home and face his father's wrath.

Just then there was a flurry of movement below on the plain. Tents were struck and the besieging army seemed to be preparing to move. Dino's first thought was that a further assault was in the offing. He settled down again to watch. But when the troops began to move, they marched not towards Verona but away from it. The city had survived.

Dino's only wish was that his precious goats had done likewise.

Verona, 10 March 1386

John Hawkwood was in his element once more. He was in the field again. One last time, perhaps?

Siege warfare had never been to his taste. He had always thrived on the quick and decisive thrust of pitched battle rather than the protracted and wearisome process of attrition. It was clear to him that the Veronesi might contrive to hold out indefinitely behind their towering ramparts; if not indefinitely, certainly until such time as a relieving force could arrive from Venice. Hawkwood's supplies were running dangerously low, and the seven-thousand-strong force of Paduans and Florentines under his command had been forced to forage daily through a surrounding countryside already stripped bare of crops and victuals.

Francesco de Carrara, Lord of Padua, had petitioned his Florentine allies to release Hawkwood temporarily into his service in order to prosecute Padua's drawn-out conflict against Verona and its powerful ally to the east, the city state of Venice. Florence had been more than willing to oblige, not least since the papal wars were at a stalemate. Besides, Florence had demanded and received generous payment for Hawkwood's secondment and the deployment of the remnants of Hawkwood's Company together with a large contingent of battle-hardened Florentine troops. Francesco de Carrara had duly appointed Hawkwood to sole command of his armies, issuing unequivocal orders that a first priority was to engage and defeat the Veronese. At whatever cost.

Hawkwood decided it was time to make his move. He ordered his men to strike camp and to withdraw in ragged formation as far as their supply train to the rear. He was certain that, once the siege had been lifted, the Veronese would rush out to pursue him, eager to inflict such losses as they could on an enemy in evident disarray. He would feign retreat, then attack from a defensive posture: like the Parthians of old, who had dispersed on horse-back, then turned in the saddle to empty their quivers into the ranks of their pursuers. The ruse had served Hawkwood well in similar – albeit lesser – confrontations and it would serve him well again, of that he was convinced. It was only a question of scale.

The retreating Paduan army had barely crested the hill when the gates of Verona creaked open and the Veronese flooded out. Hawkwood's stratagem had worked.

He force-marched his men back as far as their supply lines, then ordered them to eat and rest. Hawkwood had scouted the terrain and found himself on familiar ground – in every sense. To his front lay a narrow irrigation ditch, to his right a broad river, to his left a large swathe of marshland. He decided he would deploy his army into two contingents of dismounted men-at-arms, with himself at the head of two detachments of mounted cavalry held in reserve at the rear.

They would wait.

Castagnaro, 11 March 1386

Try as they might, the Veronese forces could not match the pace set by Hawkwood's Englishmen, Paduans and Florentines. The Veronese captain-general, Giovanni dei Ordelaffi, urged his men on and they responded as best they could. Anxious not to exhaust them, however, he ordered them to make camp for the night. He suspected that Hawkwood would retreat only as far as his supply lines and then, and only then, make a stand.

It was not until late the next morning that Ordelaffi and his Veronese finally breasted the rise and looked down on the small village of Castagnaro. By noon, Ordelaffi had formed his troops into provisional battle order. He had noted that the majority of Hawkwood's forces were deployed to protect the area beyond what appeared to be a long irrigation ditch. Ordelaffi at once recognised this as a crucial position which, if taken, would leave Hawkwood with no line of retreat. The Paduans would be forced to submit.

There was a problem, however. The ditch was not wide, but it was wide enough to prevent the Veronese leaping it on foot and in full armour. Ordelaffi ordered his men to collect faggots and reeds and bind them into bundles – fascines – which could be thrown into the ditch to provide his men-at-arms with some semblance of a foothold.

By late afternoon, the fascines were ready. A driving rain now swept over the two armies and the earth underfoot rapidly churned into a muddy quagmire. Ordelaffi ordered his cavalry to dismount. They would fight on foot.

Hawkwood's pikemen held station on the Paduan side of the ditch, their long spears at the ready as the Veronese advanced and hurled fascine after fascine into the ditch at regular intervals. A first wave of Veronese swept forward, struggling to keep their balance on the improvised bridges. Three paces on, they came within range of the pikemen, who jabbed their lances into the faces and breastplates of the attackers. The first wave checked momentarily, but those behind pressed forward, stepping on and over the bodies of their dead and wounded comrades.

Hawkwood's defensive line was not penetrated, but it inched back as more and more Veronese crossed the ditch. An impatient Ordelaffi concluded that his men were gaining the upper hand and at once committed additional troops to reinforce the attack.

Hawkwood waited.

The Paduans were gradually forced back as more and more Veronese triumphantly crossed the ditch and pressed home their dearly bought advantage.

Hawkwood waited.

A section of the Paduan line gave way and a number of Veronese broke through, swinging round to attack from the rear. They were quickly despatched by Hawkwood's second line of defenders, but the first line was now yielding ground rapidly.

And still Hawkwood waited.

Giovanni dei Ordelaffi's pulse raced. The scent of victory was in his nostrils. He decided to delay no longer and ordered the full force of his reserves into the fray.

This was the moment Hawkwood had been waiting for. At his signal, the first detachment of cavalry veered right towards the river and plunged in where it was at its shallowest. Within seconds, they were on the far bank, wheeling left to attack the enemy from the flank and rear. A second detachment galloped straight downhill. The pikemen opened ranks to allow them through and they ploughed into the Veronese footsoldiers who had crossed the ditch.

The cavalrymen were also skilled with short bows. They loosed shaft after shaft into the Veronese ranks. Ordelaffi saw too late that he had been caught in a pincer movement. Hawkwood's bowmen, anxious not to hit their own men, dismounted, cast their bows aside, drew their swords and charged. The Veronese were trapped. They fought back in desperation, but their position was hopeless. They fell in droves.

Ordelaffi attempted to respond by ordering his immediate bodyguard to essay a counter-attack. It came to nothing. The battle was already lost. Ordelaffi and his men were soon surrounded and compelled to lay down their arms.

Victory was total.

The loyal remnants of Hawkwood's Company had, with the Paduans and Florentines, defeated a Veronese army which far outnumbered them. An initial count established that over four thousand Veronese had perished. A further five thousand had been taken prisoner; together with an invaluable cache of weapons and equipment.

John Hawkwood was elated. He had not felt like this since the battle of Poitiers those many, many years ago.

XXV

Nemesis

A short conclusion, yet it shall stand

Florence, 17 March 1394

In Florence and throughout Italy, John Hawkwood's crushing victory at Castagnaro was widely regarded as the crowning achievement in a military career which now stretched back over five decades. There were those who disagreed, arguing that his command of the Florentine army during the campaign against Gian Galeazzo's Milan in 1390 and 1391 was even more re-remarkable – not least by virtue of the skill Hawkwood had shown in coordinating the safe retreat of Florentine forces from the Adige in 1391.

Hawkwood himself did not share the latter view. In his eyes, the struggle against Milan had been at best inconclusive. Neither side could justifiably claim to have won outright victory although, admittedly, it had been Gian Galeazzo who eventually sued for peace and paid an exorbitant sum in restitution.

It grieved Hawkwood that there had been no such settlement for Donnina. Her grievance against Gian Galeazzo had not been resolved and, to this day, she was convinced that Gian Galeazzo had not only usurped her father's rule but had been directly responsible for his death in December 1385, allegedly of poisoning. In truth, Hawkwood now harboured a measure of respect for Gian Galeazzo, who had emerged on the whole as a capable and forward-thinking ruler of Milan. He never dared confide as much to Donnina.

The most recent peace concluded between Florence and Milan had effectively marked the end of Hawkwood's stewardship of the former's armies. His standing in the Florentine community had changed beyond all measure. He was no longer a hireling but a statesman and diplomat in his own right. Hawkwood particularly relished the fact that none other than King Richard II of England had prevailed upon him to act as his *ad hoc* plenipotentiary in negotiations with Italy's city states.

Times had indeed changed.

Now, in his seventy-fourth year, John Hawkwood was at last a man of leisure. He and Donnina spent most of their time at San Donato, where he delighted in the company of his son and three daughters. He devoted his leisure time to the arts, reading and rereading Dante, belatedly developing a taste for Petrarch, marvelling at the timeless frescoes of Giotto di Bondone in the Guigni Chapel in Santa Croce, and walking in the architectural splendour of his adoptive Florence.

There was much in his life that he regretted, but many memories remained to be cherished. He was at peace now, with the world and with himself. At one point, his financial problems had weighed heavily but, through the good offices of his friend Giancarlo Boninsegna, he had weathered the storm: unwanted properties had been disposed of and annuities arranged. He was emotionally and financially secure.

Hawkwood sat across the desk from Boninsegna in the latter's palazzo in Florence. Giancarlo was well into his eighties now, but still retained much of the vigour of his younger days. The Florentine handed over a final document for Hawkwood's signature, then leant back in his chair and contemplated the Englishman who had been his adversary and friend for over thirty years.

He said, 'I wish you God's speed on your journey to England. I trust you will find much to your liking there, but not *too* much, for I pray we shall soon meet again here in Florence.'

'Never fear,' said Hawkwood, gathering together the documents on the table before him. 'I have matters to settle in England, but my future is secure here in Florence.'

The two men stood and embraced.

When Hawkwood left the palazzo, the crisp light of an early spring day made him blink against the glare. The street was teeming with elegant Florentines going about their daily business. Out of the corner of his eye, he caught sight of a slight, shabbily dressed figure limping towards him – a beggar, no doubt. Hawkwood reached into his purse for a coin as the figure drew abreast of him. He saw an angular face and piercing eyes.

He had seen this man before.

Somewhere.

Not recently.

'*For Siena and for me!*'

As the words hissed out, Hawkwood felt a sharp blow to his chest.

Gregorio Camporesi scuttled off as best he could, his deformed left leg dragging behind him on the cobblestones. Camporesi had not ridden in the Palio since that day in 1369 when he had been bested and crippled by a vile Englishman called John Hawkwood.

Hawkwood looked down at the tiny speck of blood that had formed on his tunic. He had felt a short stab of pain, no more. He took a pace forward, stumbled and sank on one knee. Startled passers-by saw Giovanni Acuto fall forward on his face.

Giancarlo Boninsegna was summoned. He promptly ordered Hawkwood to be carried back into the palazzo and laid on a stone bench in the courtyard. A doctor was called, but it was too late. At three minutes to the fourth hour on 17 March 1394, John Hawkwood opened his eyes one final time.

He whispered something – 'Donnina'?

And died.

Boninsegna was beside himself with grief, but his efficiency did not desert him. It would be to Florence's eternal shame if the sordid truth about Hawkwood's death became public knowledge. The doctor and those who had attended Hawkwood in the final moments of his life were sworn to secrecy.

The following day it was announced that Sir John de Hawkwood, *condottiere* and erstwhile Supreme Commander of the Armies of the City State of Florence, had died of a stroke in the early hours of 18 March 1394.

The whole city mourned his passing. To a man, the Signoria assembled to pay their last respects, filing past the bier where Hawkwood's body lay in state, his favourite sword resting upon his chest and the baton of command clasped in his right hand.

Donnina Hawkwood and her children fought back the tears as Hawkwood was laid to rest. At the last moment, Donnina moved forward and carefully placed atop the bier the small carved ivory box that Hawkwood had given her years before as a charm to ward off evil and ensure good fortune and good health.

She turned quickly away as the coffin was lowered into the ground.

Epilogue

He lived his life – what more is there to say?

On his death in 1394, the Republic of Florence accorded John Hawkwood – Giovanni Acuto – a public funeral of almost unprecedented magnificence. This was an honour that was not extended to arguably Florence's most famous son, Dante Alighieri, whose political leanings were not to the taste of the powers-that-were in Florence. The Signoria also announced plans for a marble monument to Hawkwood to be erected in the Duomo (reconsecrated in 1436 as the Cathedral of Santa Maria del Fiore) in celebration of the life and exploits of one who was beyond question the most prominent and most respected foreign mercenary in Italy. The statue was never executed, but Paolo Uccello was subsequently commissioned to paint an equestrian portrait in *terre verte* for the inner façade of the building.

Donnina Hawkwood eventually reached an accommodation with Gian Galeazzo Visconti which included the restitution to her of an estate near Lodi, where she spent her final years. She never remarried. The date of her death is not on record.

Of Hawkwood's four children by Donnina Visconti – John, Janet, Catherine and Anna – the eldest daughter, Janet, married Count Brezaglia di Porciglia, and his second daughter, Catherine, wed a young German *condottiere* named Conrad Prospergh. Anna Hawkwood married into the prominent Milanese family of della Torre. Hawkwood's son, John, took English citizenship in or around 1406 and went on to live in Sible Hedingham, where he assumed responsibility for the management of Hawkwood Manor and the estate.

Sir William de Coggeshall, together with his wife, Hawkwood's daughter Antiocha, returned to Sible Hedingham after a protracted period of diplomatic service abroad.

The body of Karl Eugen August Wilhelm von Strachwitz-Wettin was exhumed in 1402 and interred in the family crypt in Meissen.

Gennaro Altobardi languished in a Bordeaux prison until 1376 and died there of malnutrition. He was buried in an unmarked pauper's grave.

Sir Wilfred Perry retired to his estates in England. He died in 1388 following a hunting accident.

Geraint Llewellyn returned to Wales after Hawkwood's death and bought a small farm in the Vale of Glamorgan. He married for a second time in 1396 and went on to sire eleven children.

Giancarlo Boninsegna died in 1398 at the age of ninety-six. Detailed records of Hawkwood's service to Florence were not found among his private papers.

Pope Urban VI, whose election to the papal throne in 1378 sparked the division of the papacy – the Great Schism – died in 1389. His counterpart, the antipope Clement VII (formerly Robert of Geneva, the 'Butcher of Cesena') died in Avignon in September 1394.

Gregorio Camporesi died in a poorhouse in Siena in 1397.

Caterina Benincasa was canonised in 1461 as St Catherine of Siena. She was declared a doctor of the Church over five hundred years later, in 1970. She is the patron saint of Italy.

Gian Galeazzo Visconti is credited with bringing the dynasty of that name to the height of its power by unifying the Visconti dominions. Historians applaud him as an able administrator and a shrewd political tactician. After his annexation of Verona, Treviso, Pisa, Siena, Bologna, Perugia and other towns in Umbria, only Florence stood between him and absolute lordship of all northern Italy. He was assembling his forces to attack Florence in 1402 when he fell victim to the Black Death.

The intermittent war between England and France continued into the fifteenth century. Known as the Hundred Years War, it extended in fact from 1337 to 1453. The war put paid to

England's taste for colonial expansion in Europe. By 1453, France had retaken all of Aquitaine, and only Calais remained in English hands. Calais itself was finally relinquished in 1558. French historians understandably take issue with any suggestion that the Hundred Years War concluded with the much-vaunted English victory at Agincourt on 25 October 1415.

At the written request of King Richard II of England, the Signoria of Florence agreed in 1395 to return John Hawkwood's remains to England. It is not certain that his body was conveyed there, but traces of a monument to Hawkwood can be seen in the parish church of St Peter in Sible Hedingham.

Apologia and Acknowledgements

To the extent that history is *a priori* immutable, the author foolhardy enough to try his hand at historical fiction finds himself time and again between the proverbial rock and hard place, between the dictates of academic accuracy and the temptations of narrative licence.

Condottiere is no exception.

The novel has its origins in a first visit to Florence many years ago, at which time the author admired Paolo Uccello's celebrated equestrian portrait of John Hawkwood in the cathedral of Santa Maria del Fiore. It was second nature to ask what sequence of events could conceivably explain why a comparatively obscure fourteenth-century English freebooter had been so honoured in – and by – another country.

Condottiere is written partly in a bid to answer that question, but primarily out of a desire to entertain. Many of the *dramatis personae* are inevitably drawn from history, whereas others are constructs or 'composites' designed to underpin and advance the narrative. By the same token, some events have a demonstrable basis in fact, whereas many others are figments of the author's imagination. Most timelines have been respected, but some have been marginally distorted. For this, only token apology is offered.

On the fundamental question of what made John Hawkwood tick, the jury is still out. It has recently been speculated that he may have been a model for Chaucer's 'perfect gentle knight' (in which case, Chaucer's irony must have been significantly more subtle than even he is given credit for). On the other hand, writing only a matter of decades after Hawkwood's death, the chronicler Froissart described him as a 'poor knight who saw no advantage in returning home', a view evidently shared by later commentators, among them the venerable Sir Arthur Bryant, who dismissed Hawkwood as 'the son of an Essex tanner who, after ravaging southern France, led his gang of desperados to Avignon to "see" [sic] the pope and cardinals'. Earlier, Niccolò Machiavelli had made passing reference to Hawkwood in *Il principe* (The Prince), pointing to the Englishman's apparent lack of political ambition. Not least, Sir Arthur Conan Doyle later profiled the White Company in an eminently forgettable (and surprisingly unreadable) work by that title.

A first commendable effort to piece the 'real' Hawkwood story together came in 1889, with *Sir John Hawkwood: Story of a Condottiere*, by John Temple-Leader and Giuseppe Marcotti. But it was not until 2004, with the publication of *Hawkwood: Diabolical Englishman* by Frances Stonor Saunders, that the Hawkwood story came under closer academic scrutiny. Saunders's study is a beautifully crafted and impeccably researched evocation of the fourteenth century. Yet, despite the wealth of ancillary evidence she adduces, even Saunders freely concedes that John Hawkwood was – and remains – an enigma.

For the record, the present account of Hawkwood and his times deviates from the historical evidence in a number of ways. Hawkwood was by no means a comparatively wealthy man when he embarked on his career as a mercenary, nor was he the original captain-general of the White Company (that honour belonged to Albert Sterz). Hawkwood and Donnina Visconti met much later in Hawkwood's life than described here, and they married not before but after the massacre at Cesena. And, of course, Hawkwood did not ride in the Palio, let alone win it.

Condottiere stands or falls on its own merits as a work of fiction. After all, as Napoleon Bonaparte once remarked, 'What is history if not a fable agreed upon?'

A short list of sources is presented in a separate annex. Chapter-heading quotes are adapted from the 'Prologue' and 'The Knight's Tale' in Nevill Coghill's excellent transposition into modern English of Geoffrey Chaucer's *The Canterbury Tales*.

The author owes a debt of gratitude to all those who helped nurture *Condottiere*, particularly Harald Hotze, Tony Glover, Graham Booth, Maire O'Reilly, Nick Robinson and Michael Wightman, all of whose criticisms were forthright, freely given and invariably germane. Thanks also go to my publisher Hugh Andrew, to the dedicated professionalism of his team at Birlinn/Polygon, and to text editor Helen Simpson, an iron fist in a velvet glove.

Credit must also go to Sheila Taylor, whose loyalty and patience were once again tried, but – as in the past – never found wanting.

La Roche-Bernard, Brittany
September 2005

Sources

The following primary and secondary source materials are often flawed and all too frequently contradictory. They proved useful, however, and are gratefully acknowledged:

Allmand, C. T. (ed.), *Society at War. The Experience of England and France during the Hundred Years War*, Edinburgh, 1973

Allmand, C. T., 'War and Profit in the Late Middle Ages', *History Today*, vol. 15, 1965

Ayton, A., *Knights and Warhorses: Military Service and the English Aristocracy under Edward III*, Woodbridge, 1994

Ayton, A., 'War and the English Gentry under Edward III', *History Today*, vol. 42, 1992

Barber, R., *The Knight and Chivalry*, London, 1970

Barnie, J., *War in Medieval English Society: Social Values and the Hundred Years War 1337–1399*, Ithaca and London, 1974

Barraclough, G., *The Medieval Papacy*, London, 1992

Bayley, C. C., *War and Society in Renaissance Florence: The 'De militia' of Leonardo Bruni*, Toronto, 1961

Block, W., *Die Condottieri: Studien über die sogennanten 'unblutigen Schlachten'*, Berlin, 1913

Bryant, A., *The Age of Chivalry*, London, 1963

Bueno de Mesquita, D. M., 'Some Condottieri of the Trecento', *Proceedings of the British Academy*, vol. 32, 1946

Burckhardt, J., *Die Kultur der Renaissance in Italien*, Basel, 1860

Canestrini, G., *Arte militare meccanica medievale*, Milan, 1946

Cannon, J. (ed.), *The Oxford Companion to British History*, Oxford, 1997

Carr, A. D., 'Welshmen and the Hundred Years War', *Welsh History Review*, vol. 4, 1968

Catherine of Siena, 'Letters of Saint Catherine', ed. and trans. by S. Noffke, *Medieval and Renaissance Texts and Studies*, New York, 1988 *et seq.*

Chamberlin, E. R., *The Bad Popes*, London, 1970

Chatelain, A., *Architecture militaire médiévale: Principes élémentaires*, Paris, 1970

Chaucer, G., 'Prologue' and 'The Knight's Tale', *The Canterbury Tales*, London, 1386; transposed into modern English by Nevill Coghill, London, 1951

Conan Doyle, A., *The White Company*, London, 1891; reprinted 1975

Coss, P. R., *The Knight in Medieval England, 1000–1400*, London, 1993

Covini, N., 'Condottieri ed eserciti permanenti negli stati italiani', *Nuova rivista storica*, vol. 69, 1985

Croce, B., *Un condottiere italiano del quattrocento: Cola di Monforte, conte di Campobasso*, Bari, 1936

Dahmus, J., *Seven Decisive Battles of the Middle Ages*, Chicago, 1983

Delbrück, H., 'Geschichte der Kriegskunst im Rahmen der politischen Geschichte', in *Mittelalter*, Berlin, 1923

Fowler, K. A., 'Sir John Hawkwood and the English Condottieri in Trecento Italy', *Renaissance Studies*, vol. 12, 1998

Fowler, K. A., *Investment in Urban Defence: The Frontier Regions of France and England during the Fourteenth Century*, Prato, 1977

Frauenholz, E. von, *Entwicklungsgeschichte des deutschen Heerwesens*, Munich, 1935–7

Fry, P. S., *British Medieval Castles*, London, 1974

Gaupp, F., 'The Condottiere John Hawkwood', *History*, vol. 23, 1938–9

Hale, J. R., 'The Development of the Bastion, 1440–1534', in *Europe in the Late Middle Ages*, London, 1965

Hale, J. R., 'War and Public Opinion in Renaissance Italy', in *Italian Renaissance Studies*, London, 1960

Hanawalt, B., *The Middle Ages: An Illustrated History*, Oxford, 1998

Hardy, R., *Le Grand Arc: Histoire militaire et sociale des archers*, Lausanne, 1978

Hay, D., 'The Division of the Spoils of War in Fourteenth-Century England', *Transactions of the Royal Historical Society*, 1954

Hewitt, H. J., *The Organisation of War under Edward III*, Manchester, 1966

Hewitt, H. J., 'The Organisation of War', in K. A. Fowler, ed., *The Hundred Years War*, London, 1971

Heywood, W., *A Study of Medieval Siena*, Siena, 1901

Huizinga, J., 'La Valeur politique et militaire des idées de chevalerie à la fin du Moyen Age', *Revue d'histoire diplomatique*, vol. 35, 1921

Jäger, G., *Aspekte des Krieges und der Chevalerie im XIV. Jahrhundert in Frankreich: Untersuchungen zur Jean Froisarts Chroniques*, Berne, 1981

Jones, T., *Chaucer's Knight: The Portrait of a Medieval Mercenary*, London, 1980

Jorgensen, J., *Saint Catherine of Siena*, London, 1938

Keegan, J., *A Brief History of Warfare: Past, Present, Future*, Southampton, 1994

Keen, M. (ed.), *Medieval Warfare: A History*, Oxford, 1999

Kramer, H., 'Condottieri und Feldhauptleute (14.-16. J)', in *Geschichte und ihre Quelle*, Festschrift Friedrich Hausmann, Graz, 1987

Lea, H. C., *History of the Inquisition of the Middle Ages*, London, 1988

Lewis, N. B., 'The Recruitment and Organisation of a Contract Army', *Bulletin of the Institute of Historical Research*, vol. 37, 1964

Macfarlane, L., 'An English Account of the Election of Urban VI', *Bulletin of the Institute of Historical Research*, vol. 26, 1953

Machiavelli, N., *Il principe*, Florence, 1513; trans. by G. Bull, rev. edn, London, 1995

Mallett, M., 'The Art of War', in *Handbook of European History, 1400–1600: Late Middle Ages, Renaissance and Reformation*, Leyden, New York and Cologne, 1994

Mallett, M., *Mercenaries and Their Masters: Warfare in Renaissance Italy*, London, Sydney and Toronto, 1974

Mallett, M., 'Venice and its Condottieri, 1404–54', in *Renaissance Venice*, London, 1973

Müller, H., *Historische Waffen. Kurze Entwicklungsgeschichte der Waffen von Frühfeudalismus bis zum 17. Jahrhundert*, Berlin, 1957

Niese, H., 'Zur Geschichte des deutschen Soldrittertums in Italien', in *Quellen und Forschungen aus italienischen Archiven und Bibliotheken*, Berlin, 1905

Pieri, P., 'Milizie e capitani di ventura in Italia nel Medio Evo', *Atti della Reale Accademia Peloritana de Messina*, vol. 40, Messina, 1937–8

Pope, S. T., *Bows and Arrows*, Los Angeles, 1962

Prestwich, M., *Armies and Warfare in the Middle Ages*, New Haven, CT, 1996

Prestwich, M., *The Three Edwards: War and the State in England 1272–1377*, London, 1980

Ricotti, E., *Storia delle compagnie di ventura in Italia*, Turin, 1893

Roger, C. J., 'Edward III and the Dialectic of Strategy, 1327–1360', *Transactions of the Royal Historical Society*, 6th series, no. 4, London, 1994

Saac, A. K., 'Condottieri, stati e territori nell'Italia centrale', in *Federico di Montefeltro, lo stato*, Rome, 1989

Sandberger, D., *Studien über das Rittertum in England, vornehmlich während des 14. Jahrhunderts*, Berlin, 1937

Saunders, F. S., *Hawkwood: Diabolical Englishman*, London, 2004

Schama, S., *A History of Britain*, vol. I, London, 2000

Simeoni, L., 'Note sulle cause e i danni del mercenarismo militare italiano del 1300', in *Atti e memorie*, Modena, 1937

Tabanelli, M., *Giovanni Acuto, capitano di ventura*, Milan, 1975

Taylor, A. J., 'Military Architecture', in *Medieval England*, Oxford, 1958

Temple-Leader, J. and Marcotti, G., *Sir John Hawkwood: Story of a Condottiere*, London, 1889

Trease, G., *The Condottieri: Soldiers of Fortune*, London, 1970

Tuchman, B., *A Distant Mirror: The Calamitous Fourteenth Century*, London, 1987

Varanini, G. M., *Mercenari tedeschi in Italia nel trecento: Problemi e linee di recerca*, Sigmaringen, 1995

Vries, K. de, *Medieval Military Technology*, New York, 1992

Warner, P., *The Medieval Castle: Life in a Fortress in Peace and War*, London, 1971

Wright, N., 'Ransoms of Non-Combatants during the Hundred Years War', *Journal of Medieval History*, vol. 17, 1991

Ziegler, P., *The Black Death*, New York, 1971